What wa... the deser... ...s becoming clear.

It was a man.

Valerie could see him clearly now. He was examining his hands, the way a man might if he suddenly found himself alive instead of dead, she thought distractedly.

She stopped and stood perfectly still. She knew now, with absolute certainty, who this man was. She was certain she would forever see this lone figure in her dreams, feel his presence in her heart.

She ached to touch him, to ensure his reality, but feared to do so every bit as much as she longed to. Her fingertips tingled, and her breath tangled in her chest.

Tears welled in her eyes and blurred him, softened him, turning him from man to mirage. She blinked furiously, terrified he would dissappear like so many mirages, so many dreams. But he was still there, a man out of time, out of place, a traveler from the vast unknown.

He was Major Perry Deveroux—last seen on earth on July 16, 1945.

Dear Reader,

The hits just keep on coming here at Intimate Moments, so why not curl up on a chilly winter's night with any one of the terrific novels we're publishing this month? American Hero Duke Winters, for example, will walk right off the pages of Doreen Roberts's *In a Stranger's Eyes* and into your heart. This is a man with secrets, with a dark past and a dangerous future. In short—this is a man to love.

The rest of the month is just as wonderful. In *Diamond Willow* one of your favorite authors, Kathleen Eagle, brings back one of your favorite characters. John Tiger first appeared in *To Each His Own* as a troubled teenager. Now he's back, a man this time, and still fighting the inner demons that only Teri Nordstrom, his first love, can tame. Terese Ramin's *Winter Beach* is also a sequel, in this case to her first book, *Water From the Moon*. Readers were moved by the power of that earlier novel, and I predict equal success for this one. Two more of your favorites, Sibylle Garrett and Marilyn Tracy, check in with, respectively, *Desperate Choices* and *The Fundamental Things Apply*. Sibylle's book is a compelling look at an all-too-common situation: a woman on the run from her abusive ex-husband seeks only safety. In this case, though, she is also lucky enough to find love. Marilyn's book is something altogether different. A merger of past and present when a scientific experiment goes wrong introduces two people who never should have met, then cruelly limits the time they will have together, unless . . . You'll have to read the book to see how this one turns out. Finally, welcome new author Elley Crain, whose *Deep in the Heart* is a roller-coaster ride of a story featuring a divorced couple who still have an emotional tie they would like to deny, but can't.

In coming months look for more great reading here at Silhouette Intimate Moments, with books by Paula Detmer Riggs, Rachel Lee (the next of her Conard County series), Marilyn Pappano and Ann Williams coming up in the next two months alone. When it comes to romance, it just doesn't get any better than this!

Leslie Wainger
Senior Editor and Editorial Coordinator

THE FUNDAMENTAL THINGS APPLY

Marilyn Tracy

Published by Silhouette Books New York

America's Publisher of Contemporary Romance

SILHOUETTE BOOKS
300 East 42nd St., New York, N.Y. 10017

THE FUNDAMENTAL THINGS APPLY

ISBN: 0-373-07479-4

First Silhouette Books printing February 1993

Printed in the U.S.A.

Books by Marilyn Tracy

Silhouette Intimate Moments

Magic in the Air #311
Blue Ice #362
Echoes of the Garden #387
Too Good To Forget #399
No Place To Run #427
The Fundamental Things Apply #479

MARILYN TRACY

lives in Portales, New Mexico, in a ramshackle turn-of-the-century house with her son, two dogs, three cats and a poltergeist. Between remodeling the house to its original Victorian-cum-deco state, writing full-time and finishing a 40-foot cement dragon in the backyard, Marilyn composes full soundtracks to go with each of her novels.

After having lived in both Tel Aviv and Moscow in conjunction with the U.S. State Department, Marilyn enjoys writing about the cultures she's explored and the people she's grown to love. She likes to hear from people who enjoy her books and always has a pot of coffee on or a glass of wine ready for anyone dropping by, especially if they don't mind chaos and know how to wield a paintbrush.

This is for my sister, Holly, who has given me an unfinished dragon, a half-finished house and a whole time traveler named Perry Deveroux.

Prologue

July 16, 1945

"T-Minus forty seconds and counting..."

Perry heard the scientist's voice boom out from the megaphone across the empty desert, the echo hanging in the early morning crisp air before scattering to the winds. He drew a deep breath, holding it, savoring the flavor of anticipation, the dry, slightly sour taste of curiosity.

"Hey, Major Deveroux, smile for the birdie!"

Perry ignored the group photographer calling his name. There would be time enough for photographs later, if there was a later. He wanted only to catch the last of New Mexico's delicate dawn, the roseate, almost feminine stretch of soft, pastel colors. What would it look like tomorrow? After the atomic explosion, after much of this stretch of grassland was blown into clouds of dust?

"Major! Perry Deveroux! Look this way."

Perry sighed and turned to see the young photographer wrestling with his heavy camera. He frowned slightly, not at the young man, but because the glare of the sun was reflecting off something just beyond the photographer's right shoulder.

Whatever lay in the tall, yellowed grass that was still damp with morning dew, it had produced a rainbow haze in the air, a shimmering vertical rainbow in the middle of the White Sands Missile Range.

Had one of the scientists dropped a lens of some kind? One of their smoked glass shields? Suddenly a full spectrum of color shot up and outward, spraying ribbons of color.

Perry started to tell the photographer to turn around, to catch a glimpse of this early portend of peace on the morning of a test of the biggest, most dramatic bomb in mankind's history, when the rainbow shifted, moving as though alive.

It writhed, twisting and ribboning in the purest, most radiant of colors—blues, reds, greens—all somehow separate, intertwining but not mingling. The sight stole Perry's breath away, and made his heart ache with the wonder of it and start to pound in sudden, irrational fear.

The rainbow neither faded nor expanded, but suddenly, inside the swirling bands, visible not ten yards away from him, where there had been nothing only split seconds before, he saw a man.

A man who shouldn't be there. *Couldn't be there.*

His mouth was suddenly dry, and his fingertips spasmed in warning, in mute protest. He couldn't have moved then, couldn't have spoken if he'd tried, because he had met the man's eyes. He felt his soul shrivel in instinctive denial, in vital, desperate protest.

"T-Minus twenty-nine seconds and counting..."

"Smile, Perry."

Dimly he heard the photographer, was almost shocked that the man acted as though nothing untoward was happening. He couldn't possibly have obeyed the simple command. He couldn't even think. All he could do was stare at the apparition in the rainbow, feeling a slow wonder creep up in him, followed by a terrible fear, which gripped his body, shaking it.

The flashbulb on the camera exploded and Perry was blinded, his ears ringing with the pop, the muted sounds of Oppenheimer's team, the dull roar of the grassy plain. He raised his hand, trying to see, blinking furiously to clear the spots from his eyes.

The photographer turned away, never once looking behind him, and Perry wanted to cry out for him to stop and look, to have someone else share this amazing sight.

"Wait . . ." he murmured, unable to force his voice any louder than that single note.

But the photographer didn't hear him. No one heard him.

The ribbons surrounding the figure stretched, unfurled and seemingly danced on the air, teasingly, enticingly. Unable to drag his eyes from the apparition in the rainbow's core, but needing to see if the snaking ribbons of light had substance, he lifted a hand, reaching toward them, afraid, excited, filled with wonder.

Not one of the men standing at the Trinity test site on that hot July day ever saw Major Perry Deveroux again.

Chapter 1

"T-Minus twenty minutes and counting..."

Valerie had remained tense throughout the preparation phase of the final test. Now, with less than twenty minutes to go, her fingers were intertwined, and her heart beat too rapidly for comfort. Her mind was a jumble of conflicting images, flickering like streaks of lightning across a night sky.

But this was dawn and a roseate glow stretched across the eastern horizon of the New Mexico desert, and, in less than a half hour from this precise moment, the entire course of her life would be different, changed forever. Everything— her career, her future in quantum physics, her dreams— hung on the balance of this one test. This final test.

Her stomach ached from the lack of the breakfast she couldn't possibly have eaten and her soul cried for something, some proof of rational explanation for the universe's mysteries, those indefinable intangibles only vaguely imagined, never realized. Her entire body trembled with the need to reach out and touch the unknown, and shook with a craving that forever remained unfulfilled, unspoken. And she longed to be doing anything else but standing in command of a desolate New Mexican test site waiting—*praying*—for a miracle, knowing all the while that the odds were desperately against it.

She, Dr. Valerie Daniels, was in charge of this federally funded opportunity to see what might be hidden beyond that proverbial mysterious veil. Why was she so terrified today? Wasn't she the so-called "golden-girl," the prima-scientist? Those were the labels so often accorded her—by supporters and detractors alike—but they were tags she'd laughed away, confident that she'd achieved her status in the quantum physics world by sheer hard work and a colossal amount of luck.

So where was that sense of luck hiding this predawn morning?

On one level, her eyes took in the rough, jagged terrain—flat and compressed, dry and thirsting for moisture, miles and miles of desolate terrain stretching into the distance—but on another plane, her thoughts imagined alternate scenes. Like a video recorder in need of repair, her mind reeled jerky, sepia-toned sequences, film clips and photographs she'd seen all too many times in the last two months. A pair of eyes gazing too thoughtfully into an undisclosed distance flashed through, bits and pieces of documents she'd read so many times they were indelibly printed on her very soul made their appearance, too. These revealed accounts of inexplicable disappearances, mysteries that hadn't been solved, solutions that her team of eager physicists hadn't been able to discover.

Yet.

Rays from the still-hidden sun created a halo on the horizon, a golden promise of the day to come. *Please,* she begged silently, *let it be promise.* She could smell the morning's quickly evaporating moisture stealing the scent from the stunted and musky mesquite brush, from the malodorous skunk bush, and could hear the subtle sigh of the dried, yellowed grasses as they whispered the news of dawn's coming to the desert creatures still hiding in burrows and crevices.

Were the many disappearances and anomalies in such a relatively small area akin to these desert creatures, hidden from view but really there all along?

Valerie sighed. The White Sands Missile Range didn't look like the sort of place that invited mystery. It was more the epitome of the desert Southwest. It had too vast and weighted a sky, too little water and entirely too much uninviting land.

This stretch of ground, roughly the size of New Jersey, nurtured no homes, no families, only a few hundred head of wild and misshapen horses, an occasional jackrabbit or coyote, the stray and scrawny bobcat or two and the ever-present rattlesnakes. And interspersed among the random brush and the dying grass, were the bleached skeletons of creatures who had learned all too well that this was a land hard to live on, harder to die on.

A male voice interrupted her confused reverie.

"Last chance to find your Bermuda Triangle in the middle of the desert, Dr. Daniels. And when it goes bust, you and your crew of clowns will have to pack up your little road show and start looking for some other grant to con out of the government."

Valerie didn't bother to turn and face the man at her side. His eyes would be veiled by sunglasses and his soul camouflaged by thirty-odd years of whatever rigid doctrine he prescribed to, whatever beliefs he held to be absolute.

She tried not to fault him; he wasn't a quantum physicist, he didn't follow the mysterious trail of trying to explain energy in terms of light, radiation, and, perhaps most important, the unknown.

Captain Don Pelligrew had been working with her four-member team as air force liaison for two months and still scoffed at the electromagnetic laser experiment. As he had little more to do with the experiment than serve as group pilot or chauffeur, and coordinator of their mobile quarters and supplies, it remained another of the many mysteries surrounding Valerie these days why he seemed so disdainful of the experiments.

The tests, all laser conducted, and, unfortunately, less than totally successful to date, seemed to threaten Pelligrew somehow. And, to be fair, Valerie thought she could understand why. She and her coscientists weren't simply recording possible electromagnetic pulses for data's sake, for use, perhaps, by meteorologists or some other band of *hard* science followers. They were actively seeking a conceivable wrinkle in the very fabric of the universe, a tear in the most mysterious of all inconstants: time.

She sighed inwardly, wishing for the millionth time that she could encounter someone who neither ridiculed her chosen profession nor stared at her with slack-jawed awe upon discovering her to be a quantum physicist. But that someone didn't seem to exist.

Consequently, she explained—for what seemed like the equally millionth time in the last two months—that she wasn't looking for a Bermuda Triangle, but that she and her team of physicists were studying this parched stretch of New Mexico because, in one unique aspect, it was remarkably similar to those mysterious Triangle waters: people, animals and equipment simply disappeared from this location, never to show up again. Anywhere.

Valerie and her three-member team contended that the disappearances were electromagnetically engineered, and that shifts in the earth's magnetic fields, sudden pulses or surges, could possibly explain the disappearances. After voluminous amounts of paperwork, her small team had secured a nine-week fully funded grant to conduct electromagnetic laser testing at the White Sands Missile Range, home of Trinity Site, home of the first atomic explosion and, incidentally, location of a host of inexplicable disappearances.

What they hoped to find was some sort of anomaly in the area that would be triggered by the lasers, actually register on their ultrasensitive equipment, giving the world new proof of Max Planck's quantum theory, the theory of radiation thus far successful in explaining the energy aspects of light. Her team had postulated that the best way to locate such new proof would be through the use of the laser technologies perfected in the last four years. They were, in essence, hoping to use quantum theory to discover another magnetic field, but one that governed time, not space.

This was what bothered Pelligrew and so many like him. The notion of finding evidence of the so-called time continuum, of actually discovering a portal into the fourth dimension, flew in the face of all those who dearly held to linear, conceptual time. It would tear apart the bedrock of limited vision.

As the test area in question, the site of the most disappearances, White Sands Missile Range, was much the same general triangular shape as that of the Bermuda Triangle but much easier to work around, the scientists wouldn't have to contend with both anomalies *and* the roiling ocean—and because each of the team members held top honors in their field, Valerie's team had been granted the money, equipment and time to conduct their study.

Discovery of something, some small glimmer of proof, was their mission. Finding a mystery that posed even greater questions, required even more research, was their dream. Or, at the very least, it was Valerie's lifelong ambition.

"Can't answer that, can you, Doctor?" Pelligrew asked.

All too conscious of the few minutes left before the first strong rays of sunlight stretched across the rose-colored sky, the few remaining seconds before either success or failure marked her future with indelible ink, Valerie nonetheless felt compelled to try once again to explain the magnitude of their endeavor to the captain.

She said, "In 1927, a wagon that only moments before had been hitched to a team of mules simply vanished. The mules were still standing where the driver had tethered them.

The driver reported an odd sequence of lights, and a smell he didn't recognize."

Pelligrew snorted. "The driver sold the wagon and handed out a bunch of baloney to some gullible cowboys."

Much as it irritated Valerie to admit it, even if it was only to herself, she and her crew had postulated almost the same all-too-plausible scenario.

"There have been numerous disappearances in this area," she said firmly.

"Come on, *Doctor,*" he said. "In this stretch of moisture-starved, federally-seized slice of New Mexico, is it all that unlikely that someone could disappear and never be found?"

If she had answered this, she would have had to grant him the negative. Indeed, it was all too likely; White Sands didn't reveal its secrets.

As if he hadn't spoken, she continued, "No trace was ever found of Judge Albert Fountain, who disappeared with his son in 1886. A medicine man claimed a rainbow god stole his medicine bundle right from his hands. A dozen witnesses accompanied him to the base to back him up. No one ever found the remains of a shiny new P-40N Warhawk, either. It took off one morning in 1943 on a regular practice flight and vanished from the radar screen less than an hour later. The pilot, however, walked in on his own two feet, but couldn't remember anything after witnessing a 'blinding splash of color.'"

Valerie started to add more, then trailed off, her mind sifting through the dates, the times, the many disappearances. The Warhawk, minus its pilot, had vanished two years before the Manhattan Project test was conducted at Trinity, just two short years before the equally curious disappearance of one Major Perry Deveroux. Deveroux's vanishing was all the more disconcerting because he had been standing in full sight of at least twenty people the morning of July 16, 1945, hands in his pockets, felt hat pulled low over his brow to cut the hard, early morning rays of the New Mexico sun.

One second he'd been there, and then, like Judge Fountain, the plane and that long-ago wagon, Perry Deveroux simply wasn't. He wasn't *anywhere*. Except hidden away in a few carefully sealed top secret files, in a worn and cracked photograph—no longer in any file—and in the minds of a handful of people still alive to tell the tale.

Because of the historical significance of that particular morning, and because the men standing about holding smoked glass in front of their eyes and crossing their fingers had been watching the sun come up at the Trinity Site—exactly as she was doing some fifty years later—waiting for the first official test of the Manhattan Project—Oppenheimer's experimental atomic bomb—no immediate investigation of Deveroux's disappearance was ordered. And when it finally was, at the insistence of Deveroux's personal friend, Colonel Dwayne Roberts, all involved simply said that their minds had understandably been on other things besides the possible whereabouts of a man who had only been invited as a courtesy and wasn't even officially on the team of working scientists.

A routine search party was eventually organized, but as the grounds surrounding the command post at Trinity were blockaded due to possible effects of radiation, not much could be accomplished.

The case had been closed, the files locked away and the few personal effects still remaining of one Major Perry Deveroux had been long ago handed to Dwayne Roberts. Until she'd started working on the project nearly two years ago, Valerie herself had never heard of this Deveroux, and up until the first laser test, all she'd known of the man was that he'd disappeared on that desert plain on July 16, 1945.

Apparently—except for his close friend—Perry Deveroux's curious disappearance had never caused too many ripples, especially since the test he'd been there to observe was labeled a success. The U.S. government had grappled with much mightier concerns, such as dropping the first atomic bombs on Hiroshima and Nagasaki less than one month later.

The only information the files gave was that some of the team speculated Deveroux had wandered too near the blasting site and had been literally blown off the face of the earth. In any case, the only thing left of Perry Deveroux was a satchel containing his leather jacket, a couple of personal letters—long since remanded to Dwayne Roberts—and an empty thermos minus the lid. All personal items, things that left no clue as to his whereabouts, but nonetheless had clearly painted the picture of a man who hadn't intended to leave the site, who had planned on some kind of future after the Trinity test.

Dwayne Roberts had never given up hope of seeing Perry Deveroux again. It was Dwayne, now in his mid-to-late eighties, who had brought Major Perry Deveroux to life for Valerie. In a voice as dried as the man looked, weathered with age and sheer will, he'd told Valerie that Perry had been sent stateside to a desk job as supply administrator following a German bullet that had nearly torn most of his shoulder from his body.

Perry had apparently proved helpful to the Oppenheimer project and was kept on in Los Alamos. According to Dwayne, Perry Deveroux had been curious to know if the atomic explosion would—if it didn't cause a chain reaction that would implode the entire earth—harm the plants and wildlife in the area.

Perry Deveroux was, Dwayne claimed, a man ahead of his time. Valerie agreed.

In many ways, she thought now, so was his friend Dwayne. She'd met him the first day of the tests. He claimed to have read about them in an article in the Albuquerque paper. Since Valerie knew the article had been buried on page twenty-two, she had immediately fallen for the man. Anyone who would drive seventy miles from his ranch to watch what the article had described as "weather phenomena tests" was the kind of man who should command respect.

Though Project Anomaly was federally funded, armed with enough sensitive equipment to monitor the home life of a burrowing prairie dog on another planet and the hoped-for results were supposedly to be top secret, no roadblocks or other security devices had been considered necessary for the project. The rationale was simple and twofold. First, the entire White Sands Missile Range was essentially off-limits to the general public; so few people ever wandered into the Range that tight security wasn't an urgent priority. And second, Project Anomaly was operating on a relatively low-budget grant, and hardly rated rigid security measures.

Dwayne Roberts had found his way to this spot, telling them that since he didn't have anything better to do with his time, he thought he'd check it out.

Somewhere between the first shared cup of coffee and the conclusion of the first negative test run, the eighty-six-year-old Dwayne had captured Valerie's heart. He wasn't a reporter, he wasn't any danger to the project and he did have a vested interest in that his friend had vanished from that exact location some fifty years earlier. He could tell her about the missing Perry Deveroux, and unlike most civilians, he seemed fairly conversant with many of their experimental techniques.

She'd had to argue with Captain Pelligrew about his presence on-site, but—as Valerie was in charge of the project—in the end even Don Pelligrew didn't seem to have the heart to send the older man away. And while the captain drew the line at Roberts's staying overnight in one of the mobile units—Pelligrew's only territorial prerogative—he had ceased his objections to Dwayne's presence during daylight hours. Dwayne was always the first one out of his car at sunrise on the mornings they tested and was always the last to leave at dusk.

Soon, his age notwithstanding, Dwayne had Valerie wrapped around his proverbial finger. And she suspected this was largely mutual. She often caught him studying her with a probing expression, as though trying to come up with answers as to why she was in this strange business of quantum physics, why this project was so important to her.

There was no answer to this, there was never a reason for curiosity, it simply was. Like Dwayne's faith that his friend hadn't simply disappeared forever but was merely missing, her faith in science sustained her, nurtured her.

For her, having Dwayne Roberts on the site was rather like having her grandfather around again. She suspected that her other team members felt the same way. Dwayne was rather like a living reminder of linear time, knowing things that happened from the days of horse and buggy to the days of men walking on the moon—or women trying to discover magnetic fields in the atmosphere at White Sands.

And he was a constant reminder of a mysterious disappearance, an elderly, dry-witted addendum to Perry Deveroux's forty-eight-year absence. He was a friend who had been left behind to always wonder, worry and speculate about the young man who had become just another statistic of the secretive White Sands.

From the way the older man acted and talked, Valerie might well have assumed that upon learning of his friend's disappearance, Dwayne had never left New Mexico, but in fact remained on a ranch outside Socorro, always keeping a weather eye out for any clue to Perry Deveroux's whereabouts. But the older man had told her just last week that he'd actually purchased the ranch six months before his friend had vanished. In fact, the last time he'd seen Perry had been from the doorway of his ranch. Nearly fifty years ago.

She had frequently wondered during the last two months if Dwayne was not seeing Project Anomaly as she and her team were viewing it—as a hope for some proof of the fourth dimension—but as a viable hope for some clue to where his friend might be now.

She couldn't blame him. If the project did uncover some proof of the long-dreamed-of time continuum, then it was altogether possible that some day, some *when,* someone might discover the key to Perry Deveroux's whereabouts.

"T-Minus ten minutes and counting," a voice boomed over the megaphone.

Pelligrew snorted and stomped off. Valerie had almost forgotten he'd been standing beside her. She smiled, relieved at his departure, amused at the reason for it; sometime during the last two months the calling of time had become his job.

Valerie's tension escalated another notch. Ten minutes and counting. Counting on what? On a dream to come true? On the promise seen in a golden aureole on the eastern horizon, a portend of the beauty of the day? Childishly, she crossed her fingers and, as though the rays of the sun were the brilliant light of a falling star, made a wish.

She suddenly thought of the photograph she had taken from the files, a sepia-toned and time-crinkled photograph of Major Perry Deveroux. Had he felt this way waiting for the Manhattan Project test? Or was it different to be watching as a spectator, an adjunct to a project and not the ringleader of a team of tinkerers in things unknown?

She glanced around to make sure Dwayne Roberts was not only on hand for the test but had an excellent view of what was to transpire. He deserved it. Eighty-six years old, grizzled by time and weather, he was a sentinel of sorts, the unofficial watchdog of their project.

He was the last person on earth who truly remembered the missing Perry Deveroux. She remembered that Pelligrew had argued with the group of scientists just yesterday. "A man doesn't suddenly disappear into thin air. No sir. No way. It had to be something else. Maybe the guy just wandered off and couldn't find his way back. This desert ain't any picnic, you know."

None of them had bothered to answer, though Valerie was certain that each of the others had equally strong desires to vent their frustration, their uncertainty and their considerable persuasive capabilities on yet another non-believer.

Annoyingly, Pelligrew had continued, "Or he just didn't want to be found. You know, to gum up the Manhattan Project. The guy was against the bomb from the beginning. Or maybe he had wife trouble—"

Valerie had objected to that last argument, and hadn't realized how vehemently until her entire crew had turned to look at her in some surprise when she exclaimed, "He *wasn't* married!"

She wondered now, eyes on the sun's newborn rays, if all the talks with Dwayne Roberts hadn't made Perry Deveroux just a little too real for her.

"Where did you go?" she whispered, knowing there was no answer, wishing she could hear one nonetheless. He had been standing there one minute, was gone the next. Seconds before he disappeared—or, at least, before anyone had known he was missing—the team photographer had snapped his picture. There'd been a certain look on Major Deveroux's face in that snapshot, a wondering, stunned look, as if something wondrous, confusing, mysterious or just out of reach, something too beautiful or frightening to be missed had been right in front of him. What had caused that look?

A gust of wind grabbed at her hair, tumbling the curls. Out of habit, she raised her hand to curtail the blond mass. Her first smile of the day curved her lips. She'd forgotten that she'd cut it shortly after coming to the desert. She pressed her hand against the curls; they felt somehow foreign, as though they belonged to someone else.

She shifted her hand to her face and smiled wryly. She'd only been in what Pelligrew called 'this godforsaken part of New Mexico' for two months, and yet she knew she looked as though she'd spent a lifetime there—cropped hair, chafed skin, dry lips and squint wrinkles showing at her eyes.

She had flown directly from lush, verdant Norfolk, Virginia, into this seeming wasteland, and had suffered the most severe of culture shocks. From a beautiful oceanside city with lawns that stretched to country lanes, with flowers in abundance, and large high-rises glistening in the moist air, she had come to what looked like the edge of the universe, the last rest stop before infinity.

The first few days she had desperately missed her light and airy condo with the soothing colors, comfortable elegance and dramatic view of the Chesapeake. She'd thought of it longingly every day that she awoke to find herself living in a low-ceilinged, efficient mobile unit with tacky furniture, a continual barrage of green-winged flies and a single-window view of a pockmarked and lunar-appearing terrain.

But soon Valerie had discovered a whole new side to the desert. It didn't happen overnight, not even during the course of the passing months, but one day, standing alone, she'd discovered that she had truly come to appreciate the wild and stark beauty of the desert Southwest. No verdant plains, only shades of gold, brown and red. No lush vegetation, only hints that life clung ferociously despite wind, scorching dry heat and freezing nights.

Standing here now, trying not to listen to the hurried preparations only ten yards behind her, trying to think of anything but the test too-shortly to get underway, she found herself already homesick for the peace of the desert, the silence that had frightened her at first before it slowly, subtly had shifted to a gentle whisper of all things. This desert was nature at its most elemental. A place in which dreams could sweep in and take over, a corner of time and space where anything was possible.

She closed her eyes and thought of night. It was the night that had made her fall in love with the desert, for then, as if some magic cloth had been waved by a kind genie, the harsh, dry lands metamorphosed. That same sky that pressed so heavily in the daytime, that bore down from some point of infinity, carrying the rough, cruel rays of an indifferent sun, in that instant of following the desert's swift mauve and orange twilight, transformed to inky black.

And mysteries upon mysteries unfolded.

The desert night sky stretched endlessly outward, pricked with a thousand million stars that shone so brilliantly, so mischievously that the tomblike blackness of the desert seemed unimportant, that the seemingly infinite stretch of parched ground turned to softest velvet and, still warm from the day's heat, became welcoming. The night became the very stuff that invited dreaming, the material on which to weave a million fantasies.

She shivered, responding to the early morning desert coolness, the chill temperature making her wish she'd worn a jacket, despite the weatherman's prediction of one hundred five degrees of blistering heat before midday. Now she felt a little silly wearing a dress. But the very solemnity of the occasion had suggested she grace it with a touch of decorum. The truth was, she'd wanted anything that would make her feel happy about the ending of a remarkable undertaking.

The last test, she thought, and felt the duality of emotion that always accompanied a final run: excitement—*could this be the one?*—and a mixed bag of fears. The fears—loss of the grant, inconclusive results, starting over again—were all normal, everyday scientific reaction to an ailing experiment. But there was another emotion this morning, a greater sensation this time, one that felt curiously like dread.

Again Valerie felt a chill, but this frisson couldn't be attributed to the desert-morning temperature. Goose bumps raised on her arms, at the base of her neck. *Today was July 16.* The very significance of the date awed her.

July 16, 1945. Trinity. The first atomic explosion.

The fact that the date was no mere coincidence, that she herself had slated the calendar for this final test, filled her with a vague sense of playing with toys that didn't belong to her. Or worse, that she had chosen Door Number Two and there might be a black hole behind it.

Today, almost fifty years ago, Major Perry Deveroux had disappeared and had never been seen again.

But it *was* only coincidence. The two dates had absolutely nothing to do with one another. The tests were entirely dissimilar. Except that both dealt with electromagnetic fields and radiation, didn't they? Was this the reason for the dread?

The atomic explosion at Trinity hadn't produced anything untoward, if one took a very narrow view of the long-term effects of that particular test. Nothing untoward, that was, except Major Perry Deveroux had disappeared while standing within twenty yards of everyone present at Trinity.

Valerie had that image of Door Number Two again and shuddered. Her team would be standing behind their Plexiglas enclosure, protective glasses on. Six people: Pelligrew, her team and Dwayne Roberts. Would one of them disappear? Should they tie ropes around each other, linking them together?

The thought of being roped to Pelligrew snapped the image from view.

Nothing was likely to happen, anyway. Wasn't that the general consensus? And yet, while the tests conducted thus far might seem inconclusive and certainly not what one could call an unqualified success, during the last two, the lasers *had* detected an anomalous factor in the atmosphere, a refractory phenomena or, for want of a better word, a wrinkle in the sky, a bend in the light rays.

The infrared photographs had backed up this discovery and the results were stunningly beautiful colors, an aurora of sorts, a rainbow but with none of the traditional unilateral curvature. It appeared the colors splashed outward in seemingly random sprays of light from that unseen wrinkle that they now suspected might be an actual magnetic field in the sky.

Natural or man-made? Was this a leftover of the atomic explosion, or something that scientists might detect in several other locations around the world, locations where disappearances were frequent? Her heart constricted just thinking of the possibilities, the inherent promise such evidence might provide.

Thinking about the multitude of opportunities today's test might reveal, and clinging to the hope of what this one final test might uncover for physics, for the world at large, Valerie turned a deaf ear to her inner cries of fear and longing, and gave one final glance at the golden light on the horizon—the universe's most compelling proof of quantum theory.

"T-Minus five minutes and counting..."

Please, oh please let this be the one, she begged of whatever powers that commanded the outcome of dreams.

Chapter 2

"Gonna make it, Valkyrie?"

Valerie turned and gave Phil Newsom, her chief aide, a small smile. He was the resident nicknamer. Every team seemed to have one, and this unusual project was no exception. No one on the small field staff had escaped his flair for the outrageous name tag. The nicknames themselves weren't so spectacular, it was the stunning aptness of the designations.

The label he'd given her, for instance, not only played on her name, but alluded to her height, blond hair and Viking-like features, but most of all, it captured perfectly her strong independence and questing spirit. Jack Chew he called Chow-down, which fit the large Oriental to the proverbial T; George Franklin was Franklinstein, a comment on the man's nearly seven-foot frame and his habitual but comic way of acknowledging orders with a "yes, mawster"; and Pelligrew was, behind his back, Pettyshrew. Only Dwayne Roberts escaped a nickname, and was always accorded a sir.

Jack Chew stepped out from behind the Plexiglas barrier, the last of a candy bar disappearing into his mouth, his almond eyes hidden by a pair of prescription sunglasses. "All set?"

Directly behind him, Pelligrew's voice boomed over a megaphone, causing Jack to jump. "T-Minus three minutes, twenty-eight seconds and counting. Okay, people, get to your stations. This show is on."

Phil gave him a disgusted look and muttered, "I'll bet he uses that damned megaphone at home in bed with his wife. T-Minus three minutes and counting. Okay, woman, lights out!"

Valerie couldn't even picture Pelligrew having a wife. She shook her head to hide her smile. "This is it," she said and felt her stomach knot at her words.

She flicked a glance at the site just beyond the crew's large mobile homes off to her left. Dwayne Roberts was leaning against her mobile unit's step railing, eyes on her, a little smile playing on his wrinkled lips. She gave him a slight smile back. He slowly cocked a single thumb and mouthed, "Give 'em hell, girl." She waved him forward, motioning to the barrier.

He'd driven over from Socorro to watch every test, having to rise long before dawn in order to make the hour's drive across the empty desert. He deserved to stand with the team on this last day of tests.

Valerie took mental stock. Everything seemed normal. Jack eating; Pelligrew booming the countdown over the megaphone; George Franklin pushing his glasses up his narrow nose; Phil lifting a hand to her shoulder; Dwayne Roberts watching everything with a fatherly, if tense, air.

Her smile felt wan as Phil squeezed her shoulder in gentle affection. "Not to worry, Valkyrie. If this one doesn't fly, we'll find another lonely grant floating out there somewhere."

"It's not that, Phil. For some reason, today I'm sort of afraid it *will* work," Val said. Her eyes again strayed to the tall, slightly bent figure of Dwayne Roberts. His friend had disappeared on this day some fifty years ago. Would one of them vanish today? She thought of the photograph of Perry Deveroux and hoped that if one of them did disappear it would be her.

Phil tapped her shoulder gently, making her look at him. He studied her with a half worried, half perplexed expression, and opened his mouth as if to comment, but Pelligrew's harsh voice reminded the crew it was T-Minus two and counting.

"It sure won't work if we don't get with the program. But literally," Phil said, turning to the large, semicircular barrier and stepping behind the controls of the electromagnetic lasers.

Valerie wondered what Oppenheimer and crew had been thinking of that fateful morning. Had they been as filled with mixed emotions as she was experiencing now? Had fear and awe been so intertwined as to make the two concepts inseparable? Had excitement and anticipation gnawed at their innards as if those feelings were alive and eating their way to freedom?

"T-Minus one and counting!"

Valerie moved to her post behind the barrier with a curious sense of reluctance. From the corner of her eye, she saw Phil wave Dwayne Roberts to protection behind the Plexiglas. With almost numb fingers, she raised the lightweight ultraviolet ray blocking glasses to her eyes at the same time everyone else donned a pair. Her lips were dry, and this time she didn't think it had to do with the air's lack of moisture or the already heating desert beneath her feet.

"T-Minus twenty-nine seconds and counting..."

She held her fingers over the triggers that would start the lasers on their tracking of the peculiar "wrinkle" that had shown up during the last two tests. Then the strafing had captured the shockingly beautiful rainbow light show. What would it discover this time?

"T-Minus seven seconds...six...five...four..."

Valerie felt, more than saw, Phil's quick glance in her direction, but she heard his prayer for success. Her fingers pulsed with the need to depress that button.

Then, on the heartbeat before Pelligrew shouted "Fire!" she heard Phil activate the camera, she triggered the lasers, Jack fired up the computer program and George discharged the recorders.

Pelligrew's megaphone chopped the air with a decisive swipe, and the sun caught the silver and reflected brightly, sharply, creating a flash of light that startled them all.

This was it, the final test, the last hope.

As one, all eyes raised to the pale blue, utterly clear sky. For that split second of time before the lasers' beams appeared in striking reds, razor-sharp pulsating streaks strafing the rarefied air, Valerie wondered again if what they were doing was wrong. Project Anomaly was a scientific inquiry, but did that make it right? And if they did discover a magnetic field in the sky, what would it mean? And in what ways might it connect to the team's more private and hopeful theory that such fields were doorways in the time continuum? What would they do with such a tremendous find?

She actually opened her mouth to ask the question, or perhaps to voice a sudden inner conviction that something was amiss. But at that precise moment, like a fireworks display from fate itself, the lasers locked on a seeming ripple in the sky, and it looked as if the light were bouncing back from the gates of heaven.

Yellow, green, violet and blue strips of color shot out of nowhere, pouring forth from the sky as though desperate for freedom. Orange, indigo and red ribbons, seemingly endless and utterly fluid, radiated outward from an invisible point. The Apache medicine man had called whatever stole his precious medicine a moving rainbow. This had to be what he'd seen.

A strong wind, neither hot nor cold and smelling oddly of the ocean, seemed to accompany the rainbows of light and slammed down on the empty desert like a smith's sledgehammer on an anvil. Valerie suddenly knew what that long-ago driver of the mule team had smelled—the ocean. How? Why?

Reeling from the combined impact of light, wind and smell, Valerie grabbed for something to cling to. If the team hadn't been safely tucked behind the barrier, she was sure they would all have been knocked flat by the force of the gale, if not picked up and blown westward. But the ribbons of color were unhampered, they shot straight through the protective barrier, through *them* and continued onward, stretching west, reaching for something, curling over themselves like living Mobius wheels, bending at some invisible wall, then turning back and exploring the desert, all the while carrying that velvet soft air with the beams of pure light.

"Holy mother of..." Phil shouted, and several heads, including Val's, turned toward him. It wasn't until that moment that Valerie realized there was no need to shout. There was no sound to the wind that rushed past them. There was only the scent of water and the amazing color display.

As one, they all shifted gazes back to the colors in the sky. The display wasn't unlike the aurora borealis, and equally mysterious and awe-inspiring. And it totally underscored Valerie's conviction that the phenomenon could be explained by quantum theory. They had been right—time continuum portal or not, they had uncovered another of the few magnetic fields on their earth.

Unbridled awe coiled in her, making her hands tremble, her heart pound with wonder and trepidation. An aurora...here, gloriously curling, rippling around them.

They had done it! Their faith had been rewarded.

For a long time auroras were believed to be caused by a refraction of light against minute ice particles in the sky, but a couple of decades earlier, a theory had blossomed that auroras were actually visible atomic particles expelled from the sun and trapped in the Van Allen belts, the earth's magnetic fields. Apply quantum theory to that, and the result was the display they were now watching in utter silence.

Supposedly, the encounter of these clouds of solar wind with the earth's magnetic field weakened the field so that previously trapped particles were allowed to impact with the upper atmosphere. The collisions between solar and terrestrial atoms resulted in the glow in the upper atmosphere called the aurora.

This was like that, but somehow different. In the case of the two most noted auroras, Borealis and Australis, the glow was most vivid where the lines of magnetic force converged near the magnetic poles. Strangely that convergence was often accompanied by magnetic storms whose forces disrupted electrical communication. And coincided with reports of missing people, both in the Bermuda and Dragon's triangles and, more important, right here at White Sands.

It was notably different because all six of them were still right behind the barrier.

And it was different in the most dramatically obvious aspect of all. This was man-made, man-discovered and man-induced. Valerie's aurora. The dream come true, the culmination of a lifetime of work, effort and hope.

This, then, was what her team had so diligently worked to discover. This was it.

History, Valerie thought. That's what we're seeing now. Here, on this desert plain, or more perfectly, trapped in a ripple in the atmosphere, a tuck in the sky, was another magnetic field. And, opened by the lasers, another mystery, hinting at even greater magic inside. Not merely an aurora, but the essence of all auroras, magnificent, awe-inspiring in all its glorious splendor.

Unlike the northern lights, however, this spectacle wasn't limited to reds, yellows and violets. Nor did the streams of color seem to move between earth and sky. This was more as if color itself were condensed into spiraling bands of light, ribboning out of a single spool and spilling down toward the land, the few people behind the barrier and points far beyond. They, the incredible ribbons, made her wonder what the other side of that invisible hole would look like.

"It's so beautiful," Pelligrew murmured. He was standing close enough to her that she could feel his body heat and, for a wonder, she was grateful for his proximity. As though the bizarre phenomenon in the sky held some kind of bonding agent, she flicked Pelligrew a glance that was warm with sincere appreciation. They were sharing something that few, if any, had seen before. How many people had ever witnessed such a miracle? Had Perry Deveroux? Was that why Deveroux had that odd expression on his face in the sepia-toned photograph she had of him? She would never know.

She stole a glance at Dwayne Roberts, who was standing just to her right. His eyes, hidden by the glasses, revealed nothing, but his mouth was open and slack, his wrinkled features awash with the mingled hues of the strange phenomenon in the sky.

"You were right," he murmured, but Valerie had the impression he wasn't talking to her. "You were telling the truth..."

Valerie turned back to the display, compelled and drawn to the ribbons of color as she had been drawn to nothing before. She couldn't think of anything to add to the murmurs of awe from those around her. There were no superlatives big or sweeping enough to verbalize the concrete reality of the amazing array of light and color. Perhaps birth, to a newcoming infant, would look like this. Or death, for a frail, and long bedridden terminal patient.

Apocalyptic was the only word she could think of, the only concept that seemed to coalesce in the jelly that had become her mind.

Triggered by the timing program within the computer, one by one the lasers ceased to send their red arrows of light at the ripple in the sky's fabric. And slowly, as though reeled in by unseen hands, the colors slipped back onto their invisible bobbins. And with whirs and a few clicks, sounding like the rewind mode on a video tape machine following the conclusion of a movie, the equipment shut down.

Valerie felt a stab of disappointment so intense, so pervasive, that a sob of dismay wrenched from her, almost as if those ribbons of light had taken her heart with them as they went home.

As suddenly as it had begun, the incredible light show was over.

And yet, it wasn't over at all. In the sky, where the ribbons of light had unreeled, then been called away, a swirling mass of bubbling, boiling color remained visible. Nothing spilled outward, but Valerie knew that just beyond that writhing incorporeal mass of color was the source of the light ribbons. Or was this the source itself?

The odd hole—or whatever it was—took up no more space than the sun appeared to in the sky, and yet given the knowledge of the actual dimensions of the sun, it seemed enormous. Valerie thought it looked like an exploding cloud or perhaps a pot of boiling paint, oil-based so that none of the colors blended and melded with the heat. A darker image occurred to her: a collection of live, writhing snakes, each a vibrant color, each deadly.

Valerie wondered in sudden terror what they had done. Then, in a surge of pure joy, wondered if perhaps this wasn't a portal, a doorway to the unknown.

The natural disquiet of the desert returned, sagebrush whispering the spectacle to stunted cactus, which, in turn, spread the tale to the whining wind, which carried the news to the small burrowing creatures, who chittered and spread the word along through their many underground tunnels and crevices.

The display had actually lasted only five minutes, yet it felt like lifetimes. Valerie had a disorienting notion that while the colors had passed through their very bodies, she and the others might have been invisible to other eyes. As though not in this dimensional plane. She shook her head and saw that the others were doing the same. She counted heads. They were all there.

Captain Pelligrew cleared his throat. "Well, Dr. Daniels. I...I don't know..." He pulled off his protective glasses with hands that shook, with fingers that were dead white.

"Thank you, Captain," Val said softly, taking the uncompleted sentence and the trembling hands as acknowledgment of the project, as tacit apology for the two months of harassment he'd tendered, though she was relatively certain that he hadn't meant them as such.

"V-Valkyrie...?"

She turned gratefully away from Pelligrew; it was difficult to reconcile her previous experience of the man and this humble person with whom she'd shared a glimpse of the vast unknown forces that comprised their universe.

"I...I think...*look over there!*" Phil said.

Thinking he meant the whirling mass of color still visible in the sky, she nonetheless crossed the short distance to his side, asking, "What is it?"

He pointed a wildly shaking hand, not at at the anomaly in the sky, but straight ahead, out at the flat plain of overbaked desert.

"Tell me you see what I see," he croaked.

Valerie saw it. Everyone behind the barrier saw it. She felt Dwayne Roberts's clawlike, brittle hand circle her upper arm and grip fiercely.

Some four hundred yards from the Plexiglas barrier, a plane rested on the desert floor. Certainly no plane had rested there only moments before. It shimmered in the early morning sun, its grinning mouth open, shark teeth appearing to leer at the astonished team of scientists, one very rattled young army captain and a suddenly shaking old man. Its reality was incontrovertible.

"It's a god-damned Warhawk...a P-40N Warhawk," Pelligrew whispered. "That's what it is, isn't it?"

Glancing at him, Valerie saw the confirmation of that on his face, and saw something else, as well. The big man was as close to coming unhinged as a man could do and remain standing. He suddenly looked his age, young and vulnerable. His nostrils were pinched and his lips an unearthly blue. The trembling had extended to his entire body now.

"I'm going to look," Phil said in a choked tone, but he didn't move.

"I'll go with you," Jack said. He didn't take a step, either.

"It won't have any candy bars worth eating, Chowdown," Phil said without looking at Jack. His voice was scarcely above a thread and yet had still cracked. "Unless you like fifty-year-old chocolate."

"Let's all—" George Franklin began, but was cut off by a sudden near-scream from Pelligrew.

"There's something *moving* out there!"

Several voices overlaid in harmony asking "Where?" and then Valerie felt the awed silence that descended when each of them saw the moving figure for themselves. Animal or human, it seemed to hover in the air.

"Mirage," Valerie said.

"That's no mirage, Valkyrie. There *is* something, and it is *but definitely* moving," Phil said.

Valerie hadn't meant that the *figure* was a mirage, but that the cold-heat phenomenon common in the desert made it appear to walk on a ribbon of water. But she didn't bother correcting Phil. She wasn't sure she could speak.

"I don't think it's a candy bar," Jack quipped, but his voice quavered.

"Dear God in heaven," Dwayne whispered.

Valerie couldn't have said later what made her move. It wasn't bravery, or any deranged notion of reaching whatever the desert had in store for them first. If she could have made sense of the force that impelled her legs to motion, her limbs to direction, she would have said it was instinct. Pure and simple curiosity to see what their man-made magic had wrought.

"Valkyrie!"

"Dr. Daniels, come back here! That's an order!"

"Let her go," she heard Dwayne say softly, firmly. "This is her baby. This is the way it's supposed to be. Valerie has to be the one to see it first."

"He's right," George said. "This is Val's show."

"Cut the crap, Franklinstein, aren't you really saying let's have Valkyrie check it out first so we won't have to be the ones to discover some kind of hoodoo is going on here?"

Dwayne's voice, when he answered, no longer sounded old or weathered, and it certainly didn't sound dry with age. "'There are more things in heaven and earth, Horatio, Than are dreamt of in your philosophy.'"

"Not mine, sir," George mumbled. "Not anymore. Not with that hole in the sky and those things on the ground."

"We're with you, Val," she heard Jack call, and though she didn't turn to look, she didn't think any of her crew had moved from behind the barrier. Though the opposite should have been true, their reluctance somehow made her feel braver.

She picked up her pace, not running, but walking at a brisk, focused stride. Now she could feel the dry heat of the sun pressing down on her shoulders and she was grateful for it, for she felt dreadfully cold inside.

The nearer she drew to the plane, the less the rarefied air distorted the image before her. What was moving out there became clear and her steps faltered.

It was a man. He stopped, facing her, and she stumbled slightly, more in surprise than because she had tripped over anything in her way.

He was some fifty yards away and she could see him clearly now, no desert-induced waver blurring her vision. He was wearing a slouching felt hat with a wide brim in the front that was curled up in the back. His pants were loose and full, light in color, and despite the already increasing July morning heat, he was wearing a brown leather jacket. An odd, narrow, short tie hung around his neck, but had been loosened at the collar of his white shirt, making him appear relaxed and somehow more masculine. She couldn't see more of his face than his squared jawline, but his long fingers were held out, well away from his body, as if he were studying them. The sun glinted from a ring on his right hand.

He was examining his hands the way a man might do if he suddenly found himself alive instead of dead, she thought abstractedly. The way a man might study his own familiar features upon waking up in a strange location, not a familiar thing in sight. Or like a man would do upon discovering he was a ghost.

When she was in hailing distance, her determined steps faltered, a tingle running down her spine. She stopped and stood perfectly still, fighting an urge to turn tail and run, forcing her knees to remain locked no matter how boneless they felt. She knew now what was wrong with his clothing, about his appearance. And in realizing it, knew with absolute certainty that he wasn't the pilot of this curious plane that had suddenly appeared in the middle of their test site. Nor was he someone who had somehow wandered onto their project site—at least not in any traditional manner.

He was a man who was suddenly on a desert in another time.

Her heart pounded painfully and her ears roared with the atavistic scream of denial she was holding inside. She glanced upward at the roiling, churning hole in the sky. It seemed a portend, a bright-dark forecast of things to come. It was both an answer to a thousand questions and a single, shocking question with no answers.

All but choking on her withheld scream, she returned her gaze to the man standing before her. She was sure she would faint and yet afraid she wouldn't, certain she would forever see this lone figure in her dreams, feel his presence in her heart.

He nodded slightly, acknowledging her. His wide, rather thin lips were unsmiling. She felt the blood drain from her face. She ached to touch him, ensure his solidity, his reality, but feared to do so every bit as much as she longed to. Her fingertips tingled, and her breath tangled in her chest, warring with the unvoiced whimper.

Tears welled in her eyes and blurred him, softened him, turning him from man to mirage. She blinked furiously, terrified he would disappear like so many mirages, so many dreams. But he was still there, a man out of time, out of place, a traveler from the vast unknown.

He was Major Perry Deveroux, last seen on earth on July 16, 1945.

Chapter 3

For a split second Valerie was a child again, standing in front of the Christmas tree, more fearful than glad at the sight of the lights, the presents, the full stockings on the mantel. Magic had happened overnight, the evidence lay strewn all around her. How had it happened?

It couldn't be. The man had disappeared *in 1945*.

Adult now, she felt the same shock and fear, that identical sense of magic stretching sinuous arms around her. And she knew a moment's unrestrained awe. *How had it happened?*

This is impossible! her mind raged even as her heart exulted. It couldn't be real. The child in her, the part that had been amazed that right jolly old elf could slip into her house, decorate it and leave presents behind while everyone slept peacefully upstairs, seemed to clap with glee even as the rational side of her could only repeat over and over again that such things didn't really happen, *couldn't* happen.

She closed her eyes and opened them slowly, and felt a stab of dismay—and a jolt of delight—when her mysterious figure didn't fade away.

Major Perry Deveroux *was* there. He was right in front of her. And he looked very much alive and well not ten yards away, almost half a century after his mysterious disappearance. He looked exactly as he did in the sepia-toned, worn photographs with his name scrawled across the back of them. And yet this was real, this was now. And *then* was such a long, long time ago.

She'd studied those photos often enough to recognize him easily. Almost too easily. There was one in particular. She'd often wondered what he was thinking as he gazed out of the photograph, eyes obviously seeing something beyond the range of the camera, the expression on his face more than merely thoughtful, almost as if he was seeing some amazing thing no one else saw.

And she'd wondered if he'd realized that something was happening to him when he disappeared, if, wherever he'd gone, he had missed his friend Dwayne Roberts as much as Dwayne had obviously missed him. A friend who still questioned what had happened to Deveroux, who steadfastly refused to believe, even after all this time, that he was dead, despite the fact that he himself was now a great-grandfather and hadn't seen Perry in almost fifty years.

Dear lord, how happy Dwayne Roberts would be that his friend was back safely. He had always believed Perry wasn't dead. He would be ecstatic. Or would he be? The man before her looked exactly the same as he had all that time ago. What would a nearly fifty-year absence do to a friendship?

And then her disjointed thoughts came to a standstill, reality striking her full force. She said nothing. Couldn't have spoken. What did one say to a dream, to the living, breathing proof of another dimension, to the wish of a lifetime?

His lips compressed, and instinctively Valerie knew it wasn't in anger or even irritation, it was more as if he was sealing a host of questions inside.

She flushed now, remembering how she'd once wondered if Perry's thin lips had been firm or soft, if his eyes were really as brown as his friend claimed they were. The Perry Deveroux of the photograph, of his friend's memories, had been a safe fantasy, something to drive the all-pervasive loneliness of a dedicated scientist's solitary nights away.

Now he was real. He was here. Perry Deveroux, born in 1906, stood mere yards from her, looking the same thirty-nine years of age he'd been the day he'd disappeared. Same squared jaw, same shaded eyes, same earth-tone colored clothing. Same lips that had intrigued her so.

It simply wasn't possible. He should be eighty-six years old. The age of his friend Dwayne. An old, old man. A man who had lived nearly a century.

Everyone else in those photographs was dead. The thought chilled her.

The two of them remained facing each other, both perfectly still, for all the world, Valerie thought, as if they were ready to have a shoot-out.

For a moment she had the disquieting sensation that they were the only two people on earth. Adam and Eve ejected from the garden, warily eyeing each other while trying to make some sense of this new and terrifying terrain.

But she could hear her team cautiously crossing the crunching sand behind her, and looking over Deveroux's shoulder she could see the bright silver of what should have been—but wasn't—a dusty hulk of a war relic. And around it, bits and pieces of other should-have-been artifacts: a Rube Goldberg jumble of what looked like a brand-new car engine, a harness from a wagon, a bundle of rags and other things she couldn't identify, all as equally out of place on this plain as the man before her.

"Wait…" he said, and in spite of herself, Valerie jumped. Had her desire to run been so obvious? She would have to study the recorder later to see, assuming one of her team had turned it back on. She faked a semblance of calm she was

far from feeling. She tried to speak, found she couldn't and
nodded instead.

Was he real? Was he some figment of her imagination?
Pelligrew had seen a P-40N Warhawk; she had seen a snub-
nosed, shark-toothed plane wavering in the desert heat. The
others had seen something moving; she was looking at a
man.

The man—*Perry Deveroux,* her mind insisted—didn't
advance toward her. He raised the brim of his hat, lifting the
shadows from his face. He met her eyes. Just as the ribbons of color that had shot from the invisible hole in the sky
had mesmerized her so, too, did the bronzed hues of mahogany that made up his eyes. They seemed to draw her toward the man, an implosion of allure. She had to physically
lean back to resist the urge to step closer.

"Who are you?" he asked and though his tone was af-
fable enough, Valerie knew with absolute certainty that the
man was rigidly controlling his voice. It was evident in the
muscle working in his jaw, the tension fairly radiating from
him. Controlling fear, anger...or something else?

She wondered suddenly how she would cope with such a
monumentous transition in her life. One minute here, the
next fifty years in the future. Did he know where he was?
Where had he been all this time? His first question had been
to ask who *she* was. What did that matter in the face of such
an amazing feat as he had apparently accomplished?

She felt incipient tendrils of hysteria working through her
system. She wanted to touch him to see if he was as real as
he looked. She wanted to turn and run, run as fast and as far
as she possibly could. She did neither, merely stood there,
her heart racing too furiously for comfort, her hands icy, her
head spinning with vertigo.

Valerie realized he was waiting for her to say something
and frantically cast back to his statement. Of course. He'd
asked who she was. She had to clear her throat before she
could get enough moisture to answer, but she couldn't. Too
many questions, too many hours spent in the quest of a

dream prevented her. She'd wanted to find a magnetic field, and instead had found a portal.

And someone had come through it. The very magnitude of this stole all rational thought.

Around and about the notion that this simply couldn't be happening was the gleeful thought that at last she'd finally found the one thing for which her heart had yearned: a living, breathing mystery.

She heard the rest of her project team gathering behind her and was grateful when the man turned his mahogany-brown eyes away and looked over her shoulder. And then she was chilled, as well, for it reminded her all too much of the way he'd looked in the photograph that had been snapped just moments before his inexplicable disappearance.

"I don't seem to know any of you," he said. And while his words implied simple puzzlement, his tone clearly leveled an accusation of sorts.

Valerie, certain Dwayne Roberts stood among the collection of stunned people behind her, knew a moment's sharp pain for her older friend. The man he'd spent half a lifetime searching for hadn't recognized him, didn't know him. Could any fate be more cruel than that?

Then, a new and wholly disturbing thought occurred to her. Would Perry Deveroux have disappeared from 1945 had they *not* performed the laser test this morning? Had *they* brought him forward in time? Dear God, was it their doing, not some curious portal, some mysterious anomaly in an unknown and sketchily theorized time dimension?

Were she and her crew the anomaly, the catalyst ... the cause? Thoughts of having created a paradox rattled around in her mind, hammering at her heart.

Having heard about a disappearance, had they been the unwitting cause?

A glance upward at the colorful, writhing blotch in the sky gave her at least half an answer. It was definitely something she and her team had done. But what? How did they stop it, and what would happen to this man if they managed to succeed?

She looked at Perry at the same time he shifted his gaze to her. Her heart jolted with uncomfortable acknowledgment. He didn't smile, didn't so much as move a muscle, but Valerie had the oddest notion that they joined in some fashion, as though they were communicating their innermost thoughts via this tenuous contact.

Lost in his gaze, she experienced a fleeting certainty that his reappearance had nothing to do with lasers, anomalies or even electromagnetic fields. For one blinding second it seemed that it was will that had brought him to this juncture in time, to this time... *her* will.

"It's Deveroux," Phil said. His voice clung to the last syllable of Perry's name like a plea. Or a repudiation. His words, his tone, shook free Valerie's notion that it was her dreams that were the instrument of Perry Deveroux's delivery into the present.

"It can't be him," Pelligrew snapped. Valerie could hear the residue of panic whittling his voice to raggedness.

"If it's not him, he's got a double," George said. His voice was also pitched higher than usual.

Slowly, as though reluctant, Perry Deveroux's eyes shifted away from Valerie's. She fought the sensation of abandonment, of being a marionette dropped by the puppeteer. She had to shift her legs to regain her balance, to avoid dropping to the dry, hard-packed sandy ground.

"I'm Major Deveroux," he said. His voice was deep, like the lowest notes of an oboe, and rich. Valerie found herself awed by the thought that no one had heard that voice in almost fifty years.

Something, perhaps the group of people at her back, lent Valerie the courage to step closer, to walk within touching distance of the man standing so close to them but so alone in the center of the desert. Or maybe it was another kind of need altogether, a desire to protect him, an urge to stand at his side, guarding him from the curiosity that was sure to be unleashed at any moment. Or perhaps it was much more basic than even that, a primal instinct—pure and simple desire.

"Don't touch him, Doctor. He might have radiation." It was Pelligrew talking, and Valerie wanted to snap at him that a person didn't "have" radiation.

She remained silent, however, and perhaps because of Pelligrew's return to buffle-headed caution, she allowed the wary gaze of the man before her to draw her forward. But the angry captain's words played and replayed in her mind. He couldn't be right, could he? No, she told herself firmly, stretching a noticeably shaking hand toward Perry Deveroux. This stranger who was no stranger wouldn't have radiation poisoning.

Valerie felt a little silly while she stood there, inches away from him, waiting for him to move. She was close enough to him now to see the fine spray of laugh wrinkles emanating from his eyes, and the scent that clung to him was the same waft of the ocean that had accomplished the amazing light show. It reminded her of home. *Home.*

He looked at her hand for a long moment, as if distrusting his own eyes. Achingly slow, as though each minute motion of his hand were a freeze-frame, he reached for her. The gesture, by its very hesitancy, by its slowness, garnered weight, became symbolic.

Valerie's heart raced and her hand no longer shook from any kind of fear, but from an anticipation so strong, so pervasive that she had to bite her lips to keep from moaning aloud.

In the slowest of motions, the symbolism took concrete form. In the action of hand stretching for hand, one large, the other made small by comparison, it was a reach across time, contact with the past, a bonding for the present.

For a very real second, Valerie was afraid his hand would pass right through hers, that he would prove no more corporeal than the air they were breathing, than the ribbons of light she had witnessed and experienced only minutes earlier, than the writhing swirl of color still present in the gaping hole the size of the sun just over and to the left of Perry's broad shoulder.

Then their palms met, warm flesh against flesh, man against woman. Long fingers wrapped around hers and grasped firmly, as though he, too, had feared a lack of solidity, as though he'd thought *she* wasn't real. She looked up from his hand, more shaken by this simple meeting than she had ever been by anything in her life.

It was a bridge across the most mysterious of dimensions—time. Her mind spiraled and swooped with the implications, and she could feel her whole body shaking in reaction. She was conscious of a great joy, an almost overwhelming excitement. And relief. The man was real. She wasn't crazy; she wasn't imagining things.

Somehow, in some inexplicable fashion, this man had traveled nearly fifty years. And she was holding his hand. And never wanted to let go. The elemental rightness of it rocked her very soul.

As if he were reading her thoughts, or perhaps thinking along the same lines as she, he smiled, a wondrous, bemused smile that somehow lit his eyes and turned them liquid.

Simple, stark relief washed over his face. "I thought you were a ghost," he said. "Or a dream."

She chuckled uneasily. She felt the ragged edges of hysteria feathering her laugh and tried swallowing it, but it caught in her throat and clung there. A line from a song in a famous children's movie played across her mind: "I know you, I danced with you once upon a dream..." It was too close to the truth, too painfully, ecstatically close.

As much to reassure herself as him, she returned the pressure of his hand. He didn't let go. Like her, he didn't seem to want to.

"Who are you?" he asked again, but this time, Valerie knew it wasn't her name he wanted. He wanted her to tell him everything, who she was, who they all were, why they were there, why *he* was there. His voice was so soft, Valerie doubted if anyone else heard his question, though she was certain everyone was straining to catch every word. She knew he wasn't asking lightly; he didn't want a mere tag, a polite response. The "who" in his query was threaded with a desperate need for answers, an absolute demand for reason in this insane event.

But she had none. She could only answer the obvious part of his question. "Valerie Daniels," she said. "A physicist with Project Anomaly."

"Valerie," he repeated, as if testing her name on his lips to see how it felt, how it tasted, as if her name held answers for him in a far deeper sense.

He cocked his head slightly. "A physicist? Do you mean you're a scientist?"

"A quantum physicist," she elaborated, nodding, but still too stunned to feel anything other than that strange combination of wild excitement and tingling fear.

While his smile didn't lessen, a slight furrow appeared between his eyebrows. He raised his free hand and rubbed at the frown as if trying to erase it.

"What—" he began, then broke off, looking away from her, at the crowd behind her, then over his shoulder at the squat, impossibly new P-40N Warhawk. Still, he held her hand. It was more as if he cleaved to it, like a drowning man to a life buoy. But there was something else in that clasp, accusation, maybe, or blame. *What have your people done?* She could almost hear the words through the pulsing in his strong fingers. Or maybe she was simply projecting her own guilt.

"Project Anomaly?" he asked, not looking at her, gripping her hand so tightly that she might have felt pain had she not been grateful for the intense pressure.

"We were looking for..." What? What could she possibly tell him? They were looking for a magnetic field and had instead discovered a window in time? A tear in the fabric of the universe? For him? That in their heart of hearts they'd been searching for Perry Deveroux after almost fifty years? Could she say that she'd spent all her life in search of such a mystery as he represented? Or that she'd been searching for him, specifically, for absolutely no scientific reason at all?

She could say anything, but nothing would explain how he came to be here, his hand wrapped around hers, that incredible fresh scent clinging to him, his mind and body obviously intact after almost half a century of absence.

And nothing could explain that unsealed hole, like a bubbling puncture, still present in the sky, a baleful, unseeing eye that dominated the pale blue curvature above them. Had they not merely opened a portal, but ripped the door from it? *What had they done?*

Where had he been? she wondered suddenly. What answers to the mysteries of the universe could he reveal to them?

"What happened?" he asked, turning back to look at her. There was no anger in his gaze, nor did there appear to be any other emotion, except that carefully banked interest. And if his hand hadn't been holding hers so firmly, yet still shaking slightly, she would have thought him almost casual, dispassionate. He was anything but.

"You don't know?" she asked, a sharp, almost glassy disappointment edging her words.

"No," he said simply, but his eyes were far away. Fifty years away?

Valerie's disappointment faded abruptly. He didn't need to spill all the answers to universal mysteries. He *was* one.

"So what is going on?" he asked.

"I don't know what happened," Valerie said seriously, refusing to be other than starkly honest. "I don't even know..."

He frowned slightly then, but eventually nodded, as if her inability to complete her sentence didn't surprise him.

"Valkyrie?" Phil called.

Perry's frown deepened, and though he didn't look away from her as anyone else might have done, he had obviously heard Phil. "Valkyrie? I thought you said Valerie. But it suits you." He looked as though he might have said more, but then closed his lips instead. He raised his free hand and gestured vaguely to their surroundings. The hand clasping hers ground her fingers together.

"Where is this?" His eyes shut briefly, then opened again, meeting hers with fierce command.

For the first time since she'd glimpsed him, rising from the desert like a mirage, he was a man, not an anomaly, not a phenomenon, or a mystery, or a photograph to fantasize about on long lonely nights. No ghost, nor wraith from the past. He was a living, breathing man who was holding her hand and gazing into her eyes with a furious uncertainty, a host of wishes and dreams left back in the year 1945.

And she understood by his question, by the pain she glimpsed in his eyes, by the harsh grip of his hand, that he not only didn't realize where he was, he didn't know *when*. Her throat constricted again, but this time for an entirely different reason. In sympathy—and *empathy*—so strong it was as if she could feel his every emotion, his every soul-deep question.

What have we done?

A gust of wind swirled around them, tossing dust and sand in its wake, causing him to drop her hand and cover his eyes. She wanted to cry out against that simple abandonment, half afraid he would disappear if she wasn't physically connected with him. But the sand stung her eyes, as well, and she turned away, shading them against the onslaught, wishing she could cover her legs, as well.

Their stepping apart also seemed to serve as a catalyst for the project team to finally move forward and surround the two of them. Valerie noticed that while several hands touched her, as though needing to reassure themselves that she had suffered no harm, none reached for Perry Deveroux.

She was again reminded of the photographs taken on the day of the atomic testing. There had been one of a group of anxious, excited scientists with Perry in it. He had been off to one side, his hands in his pockets... alone. An outsider at an in-crowd party. What strange destiny commanded this man to forever appear an outsider in the world of camaraderie?

But he wasn't an outsider. He was wholly American, he was the chief anomaly in a project designed to find them, and his best friend—of fifty years ago—stood just behind her. Valerie could almost feel the depth of Dwayne's emotions. Why didn't he say something? But she knew why: he couldn't. He was too choked up to speak, too stunned to do more than drink in the sight of his long-lost Army buddy.

"Who are you, sir, and how do you explain your presence on a restricted testing site?"

Valerie turned an exasperated gaze toward Pelligrew. "Come on, Captain—"

"I'll handle this, *Doctor*," Pelligrew said, his eyes never wavering from Perry Deveroux.

Perry's eyes flicked from Valerie to Pelligrew, his face devoid of expression. Was it her imagination or did his eyes seem sharper now, as though the anger he'd controlled earlier was much closer to the surface? From the blistering potential of it, she fervently hoped he never turned such a gaze on her.

"As I said earlier..." His eyes dropped to Pelligrew's bars and stripes. He frowned, as though baffled for a second, then continued. "Captain? My name is *Major* Perry Deveroux. As for clearance..." He turned slightly, his eyes locking on something behind Valerie. She turned to look at what had caused the quick blaze of anger to fade from Perry's face, to be replaced with something akin to genuine terror.

"It's me, Perry," Dwayne Roberts said. He cleared his throat, but made no move forward. His eyes, still a sharp blue despite his age, met Perry's squarely, unflinchingly. "It's really me."

The contrast between the two men, these two *contemporaries,* was unmistakable and unthinkable. Dwayne was in good shape for eighty-six years of age, but with his thinning white hair and his heavily lined face, the soft folds of skin disappearing into his loose collar, there was no way on earth anyone would believe him to be the same age as Perry Deveroux.

"Dwayne?" Perry asked. A thousand questions flitted across his suddenly pale face, then, as he obviously found answers amid the chaos that must have comprised his mind at the moment, his features hardened. "What did they do to you?" He turned cold, accusing eyes toward Pelligrew.

For a breathless moment, no one answered, least of all Dwayne. He seemed to age another few years before their eyes as his gaze took in his friend of so long ago.

Captain Pelligrew broke the silence. "Do you know this man?" he barked at Dwayne, though it was obvious to one and all that his words were no more than sheer bravado. Valerie was reminded of how close to unhinged the man had been right after the lasers had cut off. He wasn't much better now.

Without looking at the man, Dwayne nodded. "Very well, Captain."

Perry's eyes flicked to Dwayne and clung there.

Again, Dwayne nodded, but this time the affirmation was for Perry alone. "It's Perry Deveroux."

Tears distorted the older man's eyes then, and he raised a knotty, noticeably trembling hand to his brow. "Forgive me," he murmured. There wasn't anything on earth Valerie wouldn't have forgiven him at that moment.

Dwayne dropped his hand, the tears still very much in evidence. One spilled free and slid down his weathered cheek. "Welcome home, Perry."

The tears in Dwayne's eyes and the terribly real combination of joy and anguish in his voice made the entire mys-

tery all too vivid for Valerie and her team. Her heart bled for
Dwayne, for the displaced friend of his youth, and for herself and her team, as well. In an odd way, she ached for the
whole human race now. What wonderful mystery of the
universe had they unwittingly stumbled across? Would there
be other reunions? Would others find their way home
through this portal of her team's making?

But she realized all too swiftly that it was one thing to
look at an anomaly dispassionately, objectively, and an entirely different matter to hear the stark truth in one old
man's voice, see it in a single tear coursing down a much-
lined face.

As much to give Dwayne Roberts time to compose himself as to defuse the explosive tension of the encounter,
Valerie repeated Dwayne's words, changing them slightly.

"Yes, Major Deveroux. W-welcome home."

Perry's eyes shifted again, resting upon hers blankly, no
clue to his inner turmoil showing in the brown gaze. But
slowly, as though coming up for air, he focused on her. As
if he'd reached deep inside her and taken hold with all his
might, he seemed to wrench at the very core of her being,
clinging to her with all the need and desperation of what
he'd now become, a man cast adrift in a strange, alternate
world.

And as he looked at her, she saw him begin to assess the
truth, try to make sense of the tremendous distance he'd
traveled. She saw notions formed and rejected, questions
raised only to be tossed aside.

She said nothing, knowing that nothing any of them
could say would drive home the hard, flat fact that Perry
was a man out of time, out of his element.

The muscle in Perry's jaw worked again, and his eyes
shifted from Valerie to Dwayne and back again. Valerie
could read a terrible sorrow there, and felt it herself. The
comparison between the two men was invidious, but it underscored the reality of what apparently had transpired out
here in the desert on this unbelievable morning.

Perry didn't move. It was as if his entire body was poised, on hold, waiting to see if he should run or fight, to step forward and embrace the old friend he scarcely recognized or turn and slip back into whatever warp had brought him here. If that was even possible.

Valerie told herself it wasn't selfishness that made her touch Perry's arm. It was simple human contact, honest reassurance that he wasn't alone, that the world, while different, wasn't crazy. That *he* wasn't crazy.

His brown eyes, almost lost in the perplexity of the situation, seized hers with the fierceness of a parachutist pulling a rip cord. He didn't have to ask her what was happening; she could read the question all too clearly. *What in the hell is going on?*

Valerie felt an urge to tell him everything in a single rush of absolute truth, but nothing she could say or do would explain away what had happened, because she didn't know herself. For his sake, for her own, she tried, anyway.

"You—we were conducting an experiment. You disappeared in 1945 . . . the lasers . . ."

At his frown and the sharp look of disbelief that crossed his features, Valerie broke her string of incoherent and exceedingly lame explanations. She dragged her gaze from his and looked directly at the boiling hole in the sky. She felt, rather than saw, him imitate her action.

"What's that?" he asked softly.

"We don't know," she answered, turning to look at him.

He remained still, his gaze on the odd, colorful spectacle in the sky. He said, remarkably mildly given the circumstances, "You don't seem to know a whole hell of a lot."

George Franklin giggled. There was no other term for the high-pitched, nearly hysterical release. "You said that right, bro," he said.

Perry's eyes shifted to George, then beyond. Following again, Valerie saw his gaze sharpen on the Plexiglas barrier as he inhaled deeply. "What is that? Where are the others?"

Everyone turned to look in the direction of Perry's gaze. George started to respond, "A test barrier. It—"

"Don't answer any of his questions," Pelligrew interrupted, his voice harsh with suppressed violence. "Not until we've asked a few ourselves!"

"The hell with your questions, Captain," Perry snapped, and Valerie had the distinct impression of a volcano about to erupt. "I've got more than plenty to go around. You people seem to know what's going on, and I want some answers. *Now!*"

All of them, including Pelligrew, jumped like guilty children caught at some misdeed. Playing with fire, maybe? Valerie wondered if that wasn't exactly what they were, children playing with the matches that could ignite the universe.

"I'm declaring this a top secret situation," Pelligrew pronounced hastily. "No one says word one about what happened here today. I'm calling in the brass."

"Do that," Perry said. "But you might be wise to remember that I outrank you, soldier."

The notion delighted Valerie and she didn't try to hide it, but Pelligrew pointedly ignored him. "And none of you are taking one step off this site until we find out what the hell is happening here," he barked.

At that, a shudder worked through Perry and, as though automated by unseen hands, he turned a blank, almost stunned gaze to Valerie. "You mean you really don't know what happened? You don't know how I came to be here?"

"No," she said, and wished she were as small as her voice felt. If she were, she could slip into one of the cracks on the desert floor and be free of the rising outrage in Perry Deveroux's burning gaze.

"Who's in charge here?" Perry asked, and though his tone was even, the smooth, rich quality was gone. His eyes cut to Pelligrew accusingly. "You?"

For once Pelligrew didn't want any of the authority he so regularly claimed as his own. "The *doctor* there. She's the one with the answers."

Again his direct gaze, as emotionally charged as a live wire, met hers, but this time there was a strong element of doubt and incredulity liberally mixed in. *"You?"*

And suddenly Valerie understood just where the doubt and the shock were coming from. She was a woman. He was from 1945. It wasn't until after the war that women had secured any recognition in their fields. That women even *had* fields. And it wasn't until 1972 that an amendment had been added to the civil rights act outlawing sex discrimination in the workplace, and heaven knew even *that* still didn't carry the weight it deserved. Small wonder that Perry Deveroux looked shocked.

However, with that understanding, she also knew what answer to give him, what explanation would offer him all the answers—the only answer—she had to give, that any of them could give him. She looked at Dwayne who, amazingly, seemed to understand her thoughts. He nodded slowly.

How Perry Deveroux would react to it, what it would mean to him in the deepest realm of his psyche, she had no way of knowing, but he deserved it, and she owed it to him. It had been intimated only moments earlier, was evident in the many lines on Dwayne Roberts's face, but Perry apparently hadn't taken it in then. Now was the time. And that word *time* was, in and of itself, the ultimate irony.

Slowing, watching him carefully, Valerie told Perry Deveroux, a man missing for almost fifty years, the date.

Chapter 4

Perry felt the earth rock beneath his heels. His stomach ached as though someone had sucker punched him. Almost fifty years. Half a century. The addition came easily, but without comprehension. *Nearly fifty years!*

The pretty female doctor was watching him warily. Waiting for something. For what? Some acknowledgment that he understood? How in hell could anyone understand something like this? Something *had* happened; he believed that much, because he had been standing somewhere else just a few minutes ago. And because he could read her belief in her blue eyes.

An odd flicker of memory stirred and was followed by a rapid series of unconnected imageries . . . a beach, a woman's laugh, an explosion, seeing an apparition through a haze of rainbows. Impossibly he recognized himself . . . somewhere, sometime. Hearing a child's voice. And the colors, the amazing spiraling spectrum of colors.

But slipping through time? Impossible.

Was this a nightmare? Yet none of his nightmares had ever come with such clarity, and never with a woman like the one before him now.

Had he been tortured, brainwashed into thinking this was real? It made no sense, but was infinitely more rational than playing leapfrog through time. And the woman, her blue eyes seemed to be trying to tell him a thousand things, a lifetime of messages, truths, which didn't fit the idea of being tortured.

She had told him the date with quiet intensity. She had, with her soft, velvet voice, given him a date in time. It was a date so farfetched as to make this whole nonsense plausible. After all, why would he dream such a bizarre year? Why would she offer it to him if it weren't true?

She was still looking at him as if expecting something from him. Was she waiting for him to simply say, "I see," and walk away? Or was she waiting for him to explode?

He was ready for that one, he could feel an explosion, the H-bomb maybe, boiling inside, demanding release. He thought of the rainbow colors reaching toward him this morning and realized they were the scouts, the heralders of insanity.

Without conscious thought he reached out toward the incredible woman physicist, this woman first to greet him in this strange place, this beauty who claimed she was the instrument of whatever madness was gripping him. He had to touch her. Feel her cool skin, experience the warmth that rose so swiftly to the surface. *He had to know she was real.*

He half expected her to move away, but she stood perfectly still as he touched her face. Feeling as if the rainbow colors were spiraling around him again, he let the blue in her eyes draw him, lure him, and he somehow knew she understood his motive, knew that it stemmed not from desire but from a basic need for human contact. A slight smile played on her full and generous lips.

He didn't know another woman who would have remained so calm, so collected. There was no coyness here, no simpering. She was simply offering him what she thought he needed most. But as his fingertips brushed her silken skin, he found he wanted more, much more.

He had a sudden sense of having been there before, of living, laughing, loving. And from the flicker of her eyelashes, the widening of her eyes, the parting of her lips, he knew that she was feeling it, too.

She remained still. Her eyes neither closed nor looked away, and her lips curved slightly, as though recalling a sweet memory. And if her breath quickened somewhat, and a pulse throbbed in the hollow of her slender throat, she gave no indication she was in any way bothered by his touch.

But he knew differently. He knew, almost as though he could read her thoughts, hear her rapid heartbeats. The touch from him, anything but casual, had inspired an equally responsive chord in her.

Dazedly, he wondered if she was one of a kind, or if all women in this time could stand there so confidently, so trustingly, independence etched on every curve of her face, strength evident, and yet somehow unabashedly vulnerable. She seemed to project conflicting images, defenseless yet strong, unprotected yet guarded, susceptible but inaccessible.

He felt as if he knew her, but couldn't understand her at all. Nothing in his life had prepared him for this moment, this touch. This woman. Did her fears spring from being in charge of a project that had gone awry? Did her strengths come from having run this project? Or did the vulnerabilities and the strengths, too, he suspected suddenly, come from some unwillingness to play games, to fight the age-old battle of the sexes?

Were her lips as soft as they looked? Would she kiss with the same fervor that she displayed when she took hold of his hand? With the same openness she displayed now, looking at him so guilelessly, yet so worldly-wise? Would he be in this time long enough to find out?

If the date she gave him was correct, he hadn't kissed a woman in some fifty years. A glimmer of humor returned to him with that thought. Surely he was overdue.

He realized he hadn't moved, his hand still cupping her soft, soft cheek, gazing into her incredibly clear blue eyes. But more amazing than this aberration of his normally cautious personality was the obvious regret he glimpsed in her eyes when he lowered his hand.

Fifty years? No. It was impossible. His heart argued the reality of that gap in time even as his mind told him that explained the lights, the weightlessness, the dizzying spin through color and air so thick it felt like water.

And the images of different places, different sounds... were they dreams, too, or were they real? That spinning, whirling plunge through color had felt like forever, but *almost fifty years?* No. He could remember what he'd had for breakfast, and that it had been only two hours ago that he had left Dwayne at that flea-bitten motor court in Socorro, New Mexico.

Dwayne. So real that his very presence defied the incipient terror that threatened to overwhelm his mind, yet so changed, Perry wanted to scream out in defiance, denounce the travesty that had apparently happened to his friend.

This can't be, he told himself. It simply isn't happening. A tortured list of possibilities ran through his head: I'm dead, and this is hell; I'm alive, but have been brainwashed—for some reason I can't remember or even fathom; the atomic explosion went off as expected but has had some bizarre aftereffects; this is the longest, most incredible nightmare I've ever had; or, simply, I'm crazy.

Because if none of those postulations were true and this was really the year Valkyrie-Valerie had given him, then Dwayne Roberts would be dead. He's dead, all right, a flat voice in his mind confirmed all too promptly. Where else would an almost forty-year-old man be nearly fifty years later? Toes up and six under, that's where.

Perry fought down an almost uncontrollable urge to rage and scream at this pixie-featured Amazon before him. How dared someone so young, so fresh, so impossibly female be in charge of anything, let alone whatever the dickens Project Anomaly was? He felt like he'd just entered one of those radio programs. *The Shadow Knows,* for example. Or, more aptly, *Buck Rogers.*

This Valkyrie-Valerie Daniels was almost as tall as he, which made her almost six feet in height. And she was slender as a reed, almost too slim, lending sharp angles to her cheek and collar bones, which may have contributed to the elfish or pixie elements in her looks. But she had curves in all the right places, and that snappy little dress she was wearing, a dress that looked right out of the roaring twenties, displayed them to ample advantage. But perhaps more striking than all her other attributes was carriage. She projected that undeniable presence he'd only seen a few times before and then always in famous people, those few gifted souls who were completely confident in themselves. He wished he felt as assured as she looked.

What had happened to him? The mountains were in the right place, the endless stretch of ground, the sky—except for that boiling canker up there—looked the same. But did it? No. This morning, or rather, he thought sourly, this morning *some fifty years ago,* tall grass wafted in the early morning breeze. He himself had been in charge of clearing out the livestock that grazed this broad plain confiscated by the government.

Now a sparsely covered, cracked surface stretched in all directions. Where had all the grass gone? Where were the seemingly endless stretches of succulents and cacti? And he could swear the very earth was warmer, the air somehow different, rarefied, as though the plains had turned to dry desert in a matter of minutes. But it wasn't minutes…it was forty-eight years. *Years.*

He thought of the changes that had happened in his short lifetime. He was born in 1906. He'd seen the first car in his hometown of Denver, Colorado. He'd waved goodbye to his father when he'd gone to war and wept openly along with the other families as the men returned. He'd flown in an airplane, something his father had never done. And now he was standing on a desert floor that bore little resemblance to anything he had ever known or witnessed, grappling with the fact that somehow, in some fashion, he'd lost nearly fifty years of his life.

This was true. This was happening. This wasn't 1945 anymore.

Rage again battered for release and he fought it, as much physically as mentally. The war cost him, however, as his body struggled to accept what his mind dictated. His stomach rebelled and for a very real moment he thought he would be sick. It was only the thought of losing control in front of this Valkyrie-Valerie that held the gates closed.

It didn't take a mental giant to see that they—*she*—was as shocked to see him as he was to be here. But *how* could he be here? *Almost fifty years later.*

Was this some reaction to the atomic explosion that no one had counted on? But the atomic explosion hadn't happened yet, had it? Weren't they at T-Minus twenty-nine seconds and counting? Hadn't the photographer called his name right before then? He'd turned, and behind the photographer had seen . . . Seen what?

Dear God. What he'd seen was—had to be—an omen of his own death. Colors, lights…and that inexplicable omen.

No, that couldn't be right. He wasn't dead. *Or was he?*

He felt disoriented. Was it possible he was in two places at one time? It was not. It was against all laws of physics. But she—was she the one he'd seen before the explosion of color that had seized him?—had said she was a quantum physicist. Quantum, he knew, meant "sum" or "amount." Quandary would have been more accurate, for all this time-switching was certainly a puzzle. A mystery.

She was still watching him closely, but some of the openness had ebbed from her fine eyes. God, were they blue. The same pale blue as the sky. And like the sky, limitless. He read a thousand questions there, but few answers.

He sure couldn't answer any.

He wanted to look at Dwayne again, but couldn't. What could he possibly say to this old, old man who looked at him with Dwayne's blue eyes and apparently still carried memories of days that must surely be only dimly recollected occurrences some fifty years gone?

He held the girl's gaze, almost fearing not to, half afraid she would slip from view in this strange nightmare, never to return again. It was only an ingrained sense of right and wrong, of inappropriateness that kept him from taking her hand again and clinging to it like a child fearful of getting lost at a county fair.

"We'll figure something out," she said so softly Perry was certain no one else but him could hear her. He liked the way she made it a plural. Until she did so, he hadn't realized the majority of his confusion was caused by a simple feeling of helplessness. By offering him the "we" she somehow gave him power to act, to *do*. The concept steadied him, grounded him.

He dragged his gaze away to study the men around him, really seeing them now, noticing their pallor, their repressed excitement, the distended eyes, the nervous twitching at their peculiar clothes. All but Dwayne; he couldn't look at his old friend.

One of them was taller than any man he'd seen before, and he had the idle thought that if it weren't wartime and a college coach could find four more like this fellow, the nation would soon be clamoring for a national basketball association. But maybe the world wasn't at war anymore. The thought rocked him. If they weren't . . . who had won?

They were all young and, except for the captain in the strange yet familiar uniform, scruffy. They sported hair so long it touched their collars, and each wore open-throated shirts without ties, one without even a collar. One of the men had a beard, and another a mustache. One of them looked like he belonged to a gypsy circus, all loud colors and harem-ballooning pants. The sneakers on this guy's feet were bright orange with little black racing stripes.

If anything could have truly convinced him he had shifted to another time, those sneakers might have done the trick. Not even in a dream could he have imagined such a thing. Besides, the head doctors, particularly that Dr. Freud that everyone was nuts over, all agreed that no one dreamed in color. Unless you were insane. Now, there was a cheery thought.

"You aren't," the woman, Valkyrie-Valerie, said softly.

"Aren't what?" he asked, and he was fairly pleased it didn't come out in a squeak.

"Aren't nuts," she answered. She smiled tentatively. And apologetically?

God, did they read minds in the future? In the now? He almost laughed in spite of how he felt. "Is it so obvious?" he asked.

She shook her head, but her smile widened and he could read the relief reflected there. "No, it's just that I know I would be feeling that way. As it is I am feeling off balance."

He didn't know what exactly off balance meant, but the notion was apt. He did feel that his entire foundation was rocking. Violently.

"Somehow, lady, that doesn't make me feel a lot better," he said, and wished he hadn't spoken. It was a phrase that Dwayne Roberts always used when he didn't have anything else to say, couldn't come up with a quick comeback.

He heard a wheezy chuckle and looked up. Dwayne met his gaze, blue eyes twinkling, yet a wealth of sympathy and understanding also lay behind those aging eyelids.

"Dwayne," he said. Deep down it was as if he had really acknowledged him for the first time. He felt the rightness of that simple acceptance ripple through every fiber of his being. This really was Dwayne Roberts.

"All too true, Deveroux," Dwayne answered. And despite the aged voice, despite the lines—and completely overriding all that was sane in the world—Perry knew it *was* true.

This aged man was the same person to whom Perry had served as best man at his and Pat's wedding only three years ago. He was also the same fellow who had broken the news about Perry's folks dying in a terrible automobile accident while Perry lay in a veteran's hospital bed in Washington, and had given him his father's wedding ring, a ring he wore to this day. He was the friend who had helped Perry pick up the pieces of his life after his shoulder was shot to hell in Germany. It was Dwayne...and that meant Perry really was no longer in 1945.

He felt both sick and elated. Questions clamored for release. He looked back to the girl—woman. For the first time he noticed her clothes. She was dressed in a risqué little pink thing that clung to her figure in ways that would make any man's heart pound a little faster, and she had short, sassy hair that seemed to capture every vestige of the sun's rays. And she met his eyes with a directness that left him feeling winded.

According to the blustering captain, she was the one responsible for getting him into this. If she didn't know what was going on, how was she going to get him out?

"What happens now?" he asked, hoping against hope that she had a solid answer.

The captain answered. "You're all staying right here. Nobody is going anywhere until I get some people in here who can explain just where and how the *doctor's* experiment went to pieces."

Perry almost laughed out loud. This strutting peacock was a pass-the-buck man. He'd met plenty of them during his days in the service. He felt a twinge of imagined pain in his left shoulder, heard a voice from the past—the now *distant* past, his mind insisted. "It wasn't my fault, Colonel. I told him the Krauts were in there. Perry just wouldn't listen, Colonel." These were the tough guys who literally got going when the going got tough.

"Why don't you go get them, then?" the woman suggested. There was no mistaking the curdled cream in her voice. She had spunk, all right, Perry thought.

"Don't touch anything out here," the captain ordered before turning on his heel. "It's all evidence."

"Ya'll come back now, hear?" the young fellow in the circus outfit drawled, wholly perplexing Perry, but causing the tall giant to grin.

As if the departure of the sole military presence lifted a pall of silence from the remaining group, all of them, except the woman and Dwayne, began to fire questions at once, none of which he answered.

Where had he been all this time? He honestly couldn't say, didn't know, and above all, he wouldn't have known how to describe the experience of sliding down a rainbow, anyway.

Did he remember any of the experience? All too well and none too clearly. Yet the scent of water and a woman's laugh strangely clung to his mind, to his heart.

Did he have any physical manifestations of his travel through time? What did *that* even mean?

And strangest of all, from the heavy-set Oriental fellow: who won the pennant in '45? The Cards or the White Sox? The young man went on to say that he knew Brooklyn took it '47, but he couldn't remember who had walked away with it in '45.

The question reminded him of the codes they'd used in the trenches in Germany. Who won the Pennant in '38? Who played second base for the Cards? But the 1945 World Series wasn't scheduled to be played for another three months. And *Brooklyn* took it 1947? Impossible.

Just like it seemed impossible to be talking about the future in terms of the past?

Perry felt he was walking a fine line through a mine field. The woman physicist interrupted the battery of questions then, giving him a decided sense of relief that not everything had changed in this bizarre universe: women were still perceptive in this world.

"Cut the man some slack," she said, baffling him with her phraseology, but pleasing him with the immediate effect it had on the avid interrogators. "Why don't we move over to one of the units? The air conditioners would probably feel good."

No one paid any attention. Except Perry. The others moved as one to the P-40 Warhawk. Aside from Dwayne, it was the only thing vaguely familiar in this strange place.

Perry followed them, bare inches from the woman's side, feeling as if he were still floating somewhere. He did want out of the sun. More than anything he wanted to sit down, light a cigarette and just think about the day's—the forty-eight years' worth of days—events. As if reading his mind again, she dragged a couple of lightweight folding chairs made of some unknown substance over into the shade of the plane.

Perry warily eyed the chair she selected as she gracefully claimed its seat. It held her weight. Would it hold his? He turned a questioning gaze to Dwayne and forgot about whether the chair would hold him as he watched his now-aged friend bend painfully to sit. He wondered bleakly if he should offer a hand to Dwayne or leave him be, but Dwayne was seated—with a noticeable sigh of relief—before Perry could make up his mind.

He reached into his jacket pocket, feeling the comfortable sensation of the bulge in his inner pocket. He pulled out a crumpled pack of cigarettes and shook one free.

He knew the moment he held it to his lips he'd done something none of the others expected. Didn't they smoke in this time? But it wasn't the cigarette they were looking at, it was the label on the packet in his hand.

"Luckies," Dwayne said with an odd ring to his voice. "Lucky Greens go to war."

Perry heard the note of awe in his friend's voice, heard the unmistakable ring of nostalgia in his tone. He was suddenly reminded of the way his grandfather had held him high up on his shoulders when Perry was only four or five, telling him to look up. "Look up, boy, it's the greatest miracle you're ever gonna see." That had been in 1910. Halley's Comet. That same note of remembrance had rung in his grandfather's voice. He thought that maybe his grandfather had been wrong. That spectacular blaze in the sky was a piker compared to a fifty-year-old pack of Lucky Greens.

Valerie had to fight the urge to reach out and touch Perry again, to feel his solidity, to encounter that warmth of human flesh. She saw him check his actions, as though aware he was presenting a new mystery and, unwilling to add embarrassment to his surely already dangerously overloaded emotions, she dragged her gaze from the cigarette package. But she couldn't stop watching him.

He stuck the cigarette between his lips, full-handed, cupping the paper-wrapped tobacco in an offhand caress that made Valerie's throat go suddenly dry in memory of his warm touch of her face. He patted his jacket pockets for a lighter, or perhaps a pack of matches. He pulled out an old-fashioned press lighter, the kind she occasionally had found in one of her grandfather's junk drawers. With a start, she realized that it was one thing *thinking* about his leap in time, but it was clearly another matter entirely to witness the proofs; not that he wasn't proof enough all by himself.

He bent forward slightly and depressed the switch. A flame jumped up and Valerie knew that all their eyes were trained on him as the blaze snapped up and lit the tip of his cigarette. She suddenly knew what a caveman must have felt upon seeing an eclipse . . . only in reverse.

He pocketed the lighter immediately, and frowned again at the scrutiny of the group studying him. He said nothing, but after a moment, with a wry smile, held out the crumpled pack. No one took him up on the offer, though Valerie was fairly certain that every single one of them wanted to, smoker or not.

He blew out a cloud of smoke that was instantly caught by the wind and snatched away. He held the cigarette back-handed, hiding it from view. It was a gesture Valerie had only seen in old movies, never in real life. It was the simple gesture of a war-trained man, the hiding of a possible tell-tale glow of light.

A million questions jumbled around in her mind, but she couldn't think of where to start. She remembered all too well the bemused expression on his face as her crew pelted him with queries. He looked relaxed now, but she was certain most of it was pure facade. No one could feel at ease in such an extraordinary situation. If time travel ever became a common occurrence, a thousand years from now, maybe, a visitor would be able to drop his suitcases, stretch and say, "It feels good to get away, doesn't it?"

But this man was, as far as she knew, the first of a new breed. He was merely biding his time, waiting for events to show him a path of action. Without knowing him at all, Valerie knew that *action* was the word that would charac-terize Perry Deveroux. She'd read it in the files, in his Army record. She had heard it in Dwayne Roberts's account of his long-missing friend. She'd felt it in his touch, in the firm-ness of his grasp.

And she didn't think he'd settle for this limbo of non-explanation for very long. Not a man like Perry Deveroux. Not a man who was so strong he'd felt no embarrassment in touching her cheek, clinging to her hand.

But no words came to her tongue.

Almost as one, all heads turned at the first roar of Pelli-grew's light plane. Apparently, it wasn't enough that he simply call in a report of the morning's strange doings. He had to carry the word in person.

Everyone was silent, though Valerie suspected all were relieved when the plane swiftly rose to face the sun. Valerie noted with sour amusement that the captain carefully avoided looking any too closely at that roiling cloud—puncture, hole, whatever it was—in the sky. For once, she was in complete accord with the man.

As usual it was Phil who stepped in with a glib comment. "I guess we'll get our funding now."

Several of the team chuckled, and even Valerie had to smile, but she knew that all their humor was tinged with that same note of hysteria she'd felt rising in her only moments earlier.

George Franklin pushed to his feet and moved to examine the P-40N Warhawk. Valerie watched him as he reached out to touch the plane, as though fearing his hand would pass through it. She knew the feeling all too well. Her own hand still tingled from touching Perry Deveroux.

"What funding?" Perry asked.

"For our project," Jack Chew answered. "Our mission is to seek our new civilizations, to boldly go where—"

"Knock it off, Chow-down," Phil said, his eyes on Perry's frown. He looked at Valerie, raised his eyebrows as if seeking permission, and at her nod turned directly to Perry. "You see, we believe that a lot of unexplained phenomena—like your disappearance, for example—can be attributed to electromagnetic sources."

He stopped, looked at Perry expectantly, and Valerie had to hide a grin when it was obvious that Perry didn't have a clue as to what Phil was talking about. It wasn't humor at Perry but at Phil, for he was talking in what he proudly considered lay terms and still wasn't conveying the concept.

She broke in. "We used modern equipment to see if we could discover a magnetic field in the atmosphere. What I think we've actually found is a . . . ripple . . . in the time continuum. A distortion. We know it's magnetic in nature, but it's obviously a lot more than that."

Phil broke in with some excitement, "It does go a long way toward explaining the numerous disappearances in this part of the world. Just think, if there is a similar electromagnetic field over—''

''We'll get into all that later,'' Valerie said.

Perry's lips pursed as though he was about to argue, then he clamped them shut and shifted his gaze to the boiling mass of color in the sky.

''And that's your ripple?'' he asked.

''We think so,'' Valerie said cautiously.

''It wasn't there before, and now it is?'' he asked.

''And so are you,'' she said. She felt that bubble of joy return, the one that had struck her upon first seeing him, that had threatened to spill over when their palms had met, when his hand had softly stroked her cheek. They had been right, that ripple in the sky was some kind of a portal, some kind of a doorway that allowed passage through that most unknown of dimensions—time.

His eyes dropped and met hers. ''When will it go away?''

She shook her head. The joy ebbed as swiftly as it had risen. Guilt supplanted it immediately.

''And if it does, do I?''

''I don't know,'' she said. Watching his suddenly hard face, his guarded eyes, she felt an inexpressible sorrow. ''I honestly don't know.''

''Hey, guys, look at this!'' George Franklin called.

As one all heads turned, including Perry Deveroux's.

George was bent over that pile of rags that Valerie had noticed earlier.

''What is it?'' Phil asked, rising to stand behind George.

Ignoring Pelligrew's earlier injunction against touching anything, George gingerly pulled back a flap of material—it looked like some sort of leathered animal skin to Valerie. Beneath it was an assorted collection of wooden implements, feathers and stones.

''It's a medicine bundle,'' Phil said, answering his own question. ''Wasn't there something in the files about a missing medicine pouch? Disappeared from an *hechicero's* hand right during a smoke lodge ceremony or something like that?''

''Bet that was one magic maker who had a bunch of true believers!'' Jack quipped.

Valerie's three crew members crowded around the find, even Dwayne pushing slowly to his feet to join them, and all ignored Perry Deveroux for the first time since he'd appeared on the test site.

All except Valerie. She didn't join them, too intent on not missing a single detail of Perry Deveroux's presence, too afraid that if she turned her eyes for a moment he would disappear. She noticed that with the attention of her crew elsewhere, he seemed to relax.

''This isn't some kind of war maneuver?'' he asked quietly, too softly to be mistaken for a casual question. His eyes weren't on her, but rather stared up at the odd mass of color in the sky.

''No,'' she answered simply. ''The war is long over.'' When he didn't say anything, she hurriedly added, ''We won.''

Again he was silent, but finally he sighed heavily and said, ''This is crazy.'' He turned to her and gave a half smile. She felt the shock of his gaze, the penetrating, total-connection sensation she'd encountered earlier. She had the odd notion they had made physical contact, as well. His lips twisted.

She had no illusions, there was no humor in that gesture. Bitterness, perhaps, or even a grim acceptance of his odd fate was reflected on his features, but no humor. She felt a stab of regret—they should have met somewhere else, somewhere normal, sometime they both belonged to—and more than one jab of guilt. This was a man, not a bundle of rags, not an artifact.

She found herself wanting to give him some scrap of reassurance, some glimmer of hope that everything would be all right, but there was nothing she could say; she knew as little as he did about what was going on, for all her vast knowledge of quantum physics.

Phil's voice intruded, broke the grim, unspoken communication. "I'm going to take this over to the barrier, Val. I want to pull a computer facsimile on the bundle that the old chief said was missing."

"Fine," Val said.

"It won't mean much, considering we've got living proof—" Phil broke off as Perry turned somber eyes in his direction. "Sorry. That was tactless as hell."

He started to add something, then broke off with a shrug. George Franklin dropped a long arm across his shoulders and propelled him toward the equipment setup.

Valerie watched them go with a curious sense of indifference. Phil was right, what did a medicine bundle matter in the face of a living, breathing relic? But then, why did the notion leave her feeling soiled, as dirty as the ancient medicine bundle?

Phil and George hadn't gone two hundred yards when Phil suddenly cried out and jumped back. George yelled also, and whirled around, eyes not on Perry or Valerie but up at that teaming hole in the sky as if for an explanation, or as if he expected it to be doing something.

Valerie was on her feet and running toward them before she could think about it. She heard everyone else following, with Dwayne calling out for them to wait for him.

"Stay back, Deveroux!" Phil all but screamed.

Valerie faltered, turning to see Perry not three feet behind her. He slowed and stopped, looking for all the world like a toy whose batteries had just run down. But there was nothing humorous about his expression. It chilled Valerie to the bone. It was the look of a man determined to escape, ready to break free, of a man pushed beyond his endurance.

"It just disappeared!" Phil yelled. He waved Valerie forward while making it abundantly clear that Perry should stay put. "One minute it was here, the next it just wasn't in my hands. It's not anywhere!"

He held out his hands as though Valerie needed proof of his words. George, who had been turning around in circles, eyes on the ground, searching in vain for an item that was no longer there, raised his head. "I think...I get it."

"Tell me," Valerie said, her breath coming with difficulty, not because of the run, but because of the fear of what might happen to Perry Deveroux. Would he also simply disappear? If so, where would he go? Those closed case files told her all too clearly that Perry didn't return to 1945. A cold chill that had nothing to do with experiments, anomalies or living artifacts seized her chest.

"Tell me!" she said again, more urgently this time.

"That thing up there—" George pointed at the whirling hole above them "—I think we all agree it's a doorway. A portal of some kind. And see, while it's open, or whatever, it sets up some kind of energy field, or more accurately, a displacement field."

"I'm not following you, George," Valerie said as calmly as she possibly could. *"Explain."*

"Well, this is just a theory...but let's say that when something shifts in time, it displaces the physical laws as we know them. Okay? Look, take it from a purely physics standpoint...mass-to-mass ratio. With me?"

Valerie was. It was the most basic of physics laws, most easily seen in water displacement. Put an object of a certain mass in water, the water level rises. This is true regardless of the *size* of the mass, it is only relative to the *weight.*

She asked now, "You're going off traditional mass displacement theory?"

"Exactly!" George said excitedly. "Now this—" he waved his hand out to include the items littering the desert floor "—this is the displacement site. Say this plane, our universe, or the earth is the *above the waterline* level. See? But if something gets outside the radius—if it *is* a radius— then it simply isn't in this plane of existence anymore."

Phil yelled excitedly. "Like taking the mass *out of the water!* If we combine that law with the Helmholtz law of conservation of energy—"

Jack cut in, his voice cracking in his attempt to quote the law. "Which states that energy cannot be created or destroyed, but can be transformed or changed from one form to another—"

Phil shouted, "Or *passed from one object to another!* Yeah! That's gotta be it! You see?"

"Not at all," Perry said, relatively equably.

"Well, it was pretty obvious that we triggered a magnetic field up there—" he pointed to the colorful puncture in the sky "—discovering a portal. And it's still open. Somehow, when it opened, you and that bunch of stuff came through. Probably snatched from half a dozen different displacement or holding zones."

Jack interjected, "Stuff is always showing up in different parts of the world, ships in the desert, parts of houses floating in the ocean. All kinds of stuff that can't be explained by any normal means."

Phil nodded, as if Jack had proved his point. "Anyway, now that hole is linked to this area. If we try taking something outside the range of influence, it simply is sucked up by that thing out there. Put back or...no!" He frowned, looked disgruntled. "They didn't go back, did they? They stayed missing from the time they belonged in..." He dwindled off, obviously frustrated.

Jack said, "I got it! They go back to some other displacement zone. Like you said, a holding pattern somewhere else. Some *when* else. That would account for everything!"

They were all silent as the implications of the three men's words sank in.

Phil muttered, "Unless this is just the beginning, and the things out here...and Perry Deveroux...are going to disappear again, one by one."

Valerie whirled to see if Perry had overheard Phil's last statement despite her crewman's lowered tone. One look was enough to tell her that he had. Even as her heart went out to him and her mind screamed a protest that had nothing to do with science, she knew that any reassurances and explanations would have to come later.

In the meantime, it was imperative that they at least determine the parameters of the displacement field—if that's what it turned out to be.

She turned to her team. "George, you and Phil start throwing every bit of data you can think of into the computer. And fetch me the laptop. Don't leave *anything* out. Start with the mass-to-mass ratio theory, add Helmholtz and then try any other theory you can think of, especially quantum. Include the temperature, condition of the soil, whatever.

"Jack, you pick up a scrap of something that came across at the same time Perry did, I don't care what it is, and slowly walk in a rough circumference of . . . say one hundred yards from the airplane. If you feel the slightest tingle or something happens, report at once. We've got to determine the parameters of our safety zone. Got it?"

"Got it," Jack, Phil and George said simultaneously.

"Okay, come up with something!"

She knew by the looks on their faces that she must have sounded nearly as hysterical as she felt. And she knew she was asking for the impossible. But it was an impossible situation, and they had to have some answers. And quickly.

As they trotted off, each to their respective tasks, she turned to face Perry Deveroux. She saw he was watching her with some amusement. For a host of reasons, the notion nettled her.

"What?" she asked.

He opened his mouth, closed it again. When he spoke, Valerie was sure it wasn't what he'd been about to say.

"Are all quantum physicists like you?"

"If you're asking if we are all equally qualified, the answer is yes, more or less. If you're asking if we are all women, the answer is no. George, Phil and Jack are also quantum physicists."

"What does it mean, exactly, *quantum?*"

Valerie smiled, feeling a little foolish. She wasn't usually so touchy about equality of the sexes. In fact, she generally took it for granted. She hadn't in her younger years, when every day in the world of academia and physics was a battle for the right to stay there. But sometime in the last five years, she had been accepted, given her own laboratory and funding, and now she felt comfortable with her own stature as a rising star in the quantum game, as well. It was like breathing or walking.

Perhaps simply knowing he was from another time had triggered her need to assert herself as an equal. He certainly hadn't treated her as if she weren't. But she also knew the reason for the seemingly inane question: he was again biding time, waiting to determine his course of action. The realization made her warm to him. Would she be as strong if something similar happened to her?

"Technically the word *quantum* only means a specified amount. But in our field, it's taken from Max Planck's quantum theory, which works with light, X rays...but most of all, radiation." Seeing that she was losing him, she cut her explanation short and smiled. "Personally, I've always thought the more accurate term would be quantuplicity, which means—"

"It's okay," he said. "It's all Greek to me, anyway." He didn't say it unkindly but rather as if it were simply one of too many things to take in at the moment. He looked from her to Dwayne. "You understand all this gobbledygook?"

Dwayne smiled. It was a faraway smile at best. "Some of it."

"How about putting it in terms an old Army buddy can understand?"

"Want it from the beginning?"

"I guess, from my perspective, that's about a half a century ago."

Dwayne chuckled. He looked at the portal in the sky and sighed. "Yeah, but I always knew you'd be back someday."

"Like a bad penny."

"Too true, Deveroux."

Slowly, in unspoken agreement, the three of them began walking back to the P-40N Warhawk. Valerie listened to the two men, the two contemporaries who looked so different, but didn't really take in their words. She was too conscious of every gesture, every movement of the younger man at her side.

He unfastened the buttons of his leather jacket, then a few seconds later, slipped it from his back with a grimace.

"The shoulder still paining you?" Dwayne asked.

"Yup."

"You'd think it would let up after nearly fifty years," Dwayne said, a chuckle making him cough.

"Seems like yesterday to me, pal," Perry said, but there was no rancor in his tone, and a genuine grin split his face. The sight made Valerie's mouth dry. Until this moment the wariness, the guardedness of his features, had blurred what she should have seen all along. He was a man only some five years her senior, and for the first time, she saw him as Dwayne Roberts must have known him. The smile erased all the tension and revealed him as a man who was capable of living hard, laughing, engaging in all that life had to offer.

Valerie wished he would turn that smile her way. And then was glad he didn't, for she already felt too connected to him, with him. If there was anything she couldn't and mustn't do it was to become emotionally involved with this anomaly from the past.

Grabbing this stricture, she forced herself to look at him as he really was, not as what she believed she could see in him. Perry Deveroux was a man from the year 1945, born in 1906, the days when wagons and horses were still very much in use. All his training would be rudimentary at best, his perceptions regarding science as limited as looking through a mirror and trying to see the bottom of the universe.

"Did Oppenheimer's test succeed?" he asked Dwayne, then, as if sensing her thoughts had flown along a dark path—though luckily not picking up on the twisted road they'd taken—he turned his head slightly to include her in his question.

Dwayne shook his head. "If you can call it that," he said.

"Yes," Valerie answered simply, then, when he frowned, she elaborated. "They used it to bomb Hiroshima and Nagasaki the next month."

Perry neither smiled nor frowned. He nodded. "Everyone hoped it would be the ultimate weapon."

"It was."

"Was?"

"Still is. But it's fission now, not fusion."

He didn't ask what fission was. "You said 'they' used it. Who is 'they'?"

She looked at him blankly for a moment, then realized it was a logical question. "The military. The government."

"Us, then."

Again it took her a moment to realize his meaning. She worked for the government, was used to living the life of a civil servant, but somehow she had always categorized herself as outside the established governmental controls, despite having to suffer idiots like Pelligrew. When had life shifted so that it was automatic that the government and the military were they and the rest of the working class us?

The cigarettes he smoked, the lighter he used, the physical contrast between Dwayne Roberts and him, his very presence here now, these were all evidence of a man out of his time, but his simple shouldering of responsibility for an action the government had taken some fifty years ago, his willingness to accept the credit or blame on behalf of that government, was perhaps the most telling of all.

In this day and age of Watergate, the Iran-Contra Affair, the Thomas confirmation hearings, the attempted coups in a dozen third-world countries, in these times of wanting to crucify the single person responsible for a given event, here was a man who simply intimated, "I am a part of the whole, therefore I, too, am responsible."

Valerie met his gaze and felt humbled. A moment earlier she had been trying to condemn him in her mind as less educated, less informed than she. She had been so dreadfully wrong. What would he be thinking of her? She, and her team of eager co-children, had somehow yanked this man through time and space and delivered him here. At the very least, they had opened the magnetic portal and allowed him through.

And she was responsible. Both for having done it, and for his well-being. As though a sword-sharp blade sliced through her, she encountered the realization of what was to be. She had felt joy, awe, even fear at the discovery of their living mystery. Then, somewhat to her amazement, she'd been aware of him as a man.

Now she was brought, all too forcefully, to understand that somehow she and her team of scientists were accountable and that they had to accept responsibility for it. Had they killed someone today, there would be no fewer repercussions, no less guilt. They had, in essence, done just that. They had *stolen* a man's time, if not his life.

And who was to say that a man's time was not his life?

Chapter 5

Perry thought the young Oriental they called Jack Chew looked as if he'd walked every inch of the some two hundred miles of desert surrounding the test site instead of a single ovoid circumference of some two hundred yards all the way around.

He didn't interrupt the *transfer of data* by asking any questions. He figured he probably wouldn't understand the answers anyway, any more than he understood the *computer* Valerie was typing on or the futuristic cars parked beside the trucklike trailers.

But as he watched, he thought long and hard, trying to extrapolate some semblance of reason out of this peculiar time.

Take this Jack Chew, for example. The young man looked about twenty-two or three. He already knew from Valerie and then Dwayne that the war was over... long over... but this Chew seemed mighty young to have some kind of doctor's degree in physics and still have served his stint in the military. And despite his good humor, and overshadowing his obvious know-how, Perry had the gut feeling that the young man was somehow soft, untried. He reminded Perry of a raw recruit, fresh off the farm, the kind of kid who was scared half to death but all filled with starry-eyed dreams and the stuff the moving pictures painted.

The others didn't carry the padding the young Chew did, but they struck Perry as soft, too, even the pass-the-buck man in the fancy uniform. That softness wasn't anything he could put his finger on, more of a sublevel understanding that not one of the men—Dwayne excluded—had ever really been put to the test. There was no cutting edge to them, no projection of the sharper instincts of survival. He didn't think he'd want to rely on any of them to get him through a trek safely. They looked as though they would have to be carried and babied along after twenty miles or so.

He wondered if they were representative of the rest of the men in this time. The thought depressed him enormously. He had never consciously tried envisioning the future before, but he knew with bitter certainty that he wouldn't have portrayed men weak.

The only one who didn't appear soft, but whose skin pronounced otherwise, was this Valerie. There was something in her eyes that told him she'd faced uncertainty, fear and had stood with her back to the proverbial wall. Something inside her had laid hands on that well of inner strength that people reserved for the most trying of moments and once having discovered it, used it always.

He was mildly curious about what had tested the steel in her, had proved it, but didn't really care to ask. The making of a person was always an intensely personal experience. He might ask her someday, before they sent him back, but for now it was enough just to know that she, at least, possessed that extra something the others lacked.

In the couple of hours since they had met, he'd seen it in a thousand small and seemingly inconsequential ways. She had been the first to reach him, the first to touch. And the first to see him as a man rather than the unique offshoot of an experiment. She had fixed him something to eat, using an oven that didn't get hot, that cooked an obviously prepackaged meal in less than two minutes.

He didn't believe she had taken her eyes from him for more than a minute at a stretch. While he told himself that his unlooked-for presence here was the cause, his awareness of her told him otherwise. Or perhaps it was simply that he didn't want to be a mystery, didn't ask to be one. And when she looked at him, he wanted her to see him as a man, he hoped one she might be interested in personally, and not just as an extension of her damned project.

The others were eager to discover parameters, find out what was going on in this desert, but from what little he already knew about her, Perry was willing to lay hefty bets that it would be Valerie who would pin down the answers.

It was Valerie who was working now, the rest all sitting or sprawling in the dust.

He watched her, fascinated by the speed with which her fingers flew over this miniature typewriter that lit up and made little squeaking noises and emitted beeps and hums. No, he decided, it wasn't her fingers he was fascinated by, long and supple as they were. It was her entire being. It was the way she seemed wholly consumed by whatever she happened to be doing and yet never failed to try explaining to him what that something was.

She was entering the data that Jack Chew had collected. That was what she'd *said,* but the results were unlike anything he might have expected. To his amazement, a picture appeared on the screen on her lap. It was a miniaturized version of the desert floor, complete with tiny mountains and irregular gullies. Graph lines segmented the square footage of the land surrounding the location they now occupied.

Within seconds the image disappeared and a spiraling oval flickered on the glass. Valerie depressed a few more keys and the oval solidified. At the far right of the oval, a remarkable sophisticated rendering of the P-40N Warhawk was displayed.

"How did you do that?" Perry asked, despite his earlier resolve to withhold any questions.

"A macro," she said, answering his question, he was sure, but telling him nothing in the process.

"See?" she asked, depressing yet another button. On the screen, several tiny, humanlike figures appeared beside the airplane, and two more could be seen on the far left of the screen, still inside the oval line, but behind another single curved line.

"What I'm trying to do is set up a solid parameter for safety's sake."

Perry couldn't drag his gaze from the screen. This time, this present, was truly amazing. He felt as if he'd slipped between the pages of a drugstore science fiction magazine.

"Next we'll be walking on the moon," he said, not even bothering to keep the note of wonder from his voice.

Valerie paused and looked up at him. His heart constricted at the rather wistful smile on her generous lips. She said slowly, "We first landed on the moon on July 20, 1969."

Perry could read the truth in her eyes, the almost tender sympathy she felt for his shock, but he still couldn't accept what she'd said. He felt the way he had when she'd told him today's date—sucker punched.

"Twenty-four years ago? We landed on the moon a quarter of a century ago?"

"Two men, Neil Armstrong and Ed Aldrin, Jr.," she said. She went on slowly, "Armstrong said, 'That's one small step for a man, one giant leap for mankind.' People all over the world heard his words. I remember standing with my mother and father, watching the TV, and all of us hugging and crying at the same time. Of all the things we've accomplished in all the years, to my mind that moment is still the single most triumphant testimonial to man's pioneer spirit."

For a while neither of them spoke, and Valerie's words seemed to hang in the midday heat, captured by the warmth yet chilling them both with their import. Perry was overwhelmed by the intensity of Valerie's personality.

Again he reached for her instinctively, understanding so much more about her now, trying to see her without the clouded vision of his past preconceived notions of what a woman was to be, what a scientist did or wanted. Trying to come to terms with her having been a child in a time that was a full quarter of a century in his future.

She might say that the landing on the moon—the mere thought boggled him—was a testimonial to man's pioneer spirit, but she was wrong...she was.

Her hand folded around his and returned his squeeze with sublime confidence. There was so much he wanted to know, wanted to ask, but with her hand touching his, with the smaller palm pressed to his, he was suddenly content to bide his time, to wait for the answers to unfold in their own sweet way.

She nodded, as though understanding his patience, and she let his hand go. He made a fist as if catching her imprint to his fingertips. Unconsciously, he slid his hand in his pocket, still clenched, holding her yet.

He glanced away and met Dwayne's knowing and wholly sympathetic gaze. A slow smile lifted his friend's thinned and wrinkled lips. "A little like Pat, don't you think?" Dwayne asked.

Perry nodded shortly. He couldn't ask about Patty, sweet Pat, Dwayne's wife of fifty-one years now. He didn't dare.

Valerie pushed another set of buttons and the computer beeped once or twice, then one of the human figures detached from the rest and seemingly walked across the screen toward the outer rim of the oval. As the figure crossed the line, it simply vanished.

"Where did it go?" Dwayne asked.

Valerie sighed and looked up to meet Perry's eyes. Perry was stunned by the depth of emotion he could read there.

Guilt, sorrow, a carefully banked desire and other things, things too personal, too intense, to try to unravel at the moment.

And he knew what had transpired on that small screen. "It was me. That little stick figure. That was me, wasn't it?"

Valerie nodded.

"If I cross the line, I'm out."

His heart constricted as she closed her eyes. That single gesture told him more than any little glittering man on a screen.

"And you don't know where it went?"

She shook her head, her eyes still shut. He didn't like it, he felt cut off from her, and she was the only one—Dwayne included—who made him feel he was still a person, still himself, not some relic from the past. But he needed to see her eyes to feel that.

He turned to Dwayne and asked the question he probably should have asked right off the bat, but had somehow never really dared allow to form in his head. He knew the answer, but had to ask it anyway. "You never saw me again, did you?"

"No," Dwayne said sadly. "Not until now." He looked as though he might say more, but shook his head instead.

But I did go back, Perry wanted to protest. *I must have. Because I saw . . .* What the hell had he seen? Perry glanced at Valerie. Her hand was now on her forehead, as if she had a headache or was crying.

"Valerie," he said. "Look at me, Valerie." He was almost surprised at how easily her name came to his lips, how right it felt there.

She slowly dropped her hand and opened her eyes. As he'd suspected, tears pooled in her eyes, though they didn't spill. She blinked rapidly, then made a swipe at her eyes, as though angry with herself.

"You knew I never went back to 1945. And that little demonstration was to tell me I can't leave here, either. Is that it?"

"I'm looking for an answer, not trying to give a demonstration," she said stiffly.

He immediately felt guilty but pushed on, anyway. He had to know the answer. "But it has the same effect, right? You're telling me that I'm stuck here."

"We don't have all the data yet," she said, but desperately this time.

"We don't need to have it all, do we? That oval on that glass is a kind of wall, like your barrier over there. But it's the wall of a prison. And you're telling me I'm the only prisoner. You all can come and go, but I can't. That's it, isn't it?"

She turned away from him then and started typing again. The screen with the oval was eradicated and Perry found himself biting back a protest. He had the sinking feeling that he was being eliminated, also.

She typed furiously, and a sequence of odd symbols flashed across the glass, curlicues, mathematical equations, a few keystrokes that looked like she was just typing anything in for the sake of typing.

Behind her, on the other side, Jack Chew muttered something about vectors, and Valerie nodded, though she didn't slow her furious pace. Perry had the distinct impression she was arguing with the computer on her lap. And the depressing suspicion that she wasn't winning.

Her fingers shook slightly now, and he could practically feel the tension rising from her shoulders. He wanted to rest his hands on them, a sign of faith, perhaps, or maybe just to convey his apology for his sharp tone. She was trying her best. He knew that as surely as he knew he was alive and well no matter how distantly in the future. She didn't deserve his ire.

But did he deserve to be wrenched from his own time and place?

"It could be worse, Perry," Dwayne said from right beside him. Perry could only turn disbelieving eyes in his old friend's direction. "Everybody at Trinity Site died an early death as a result of the radiation."

Perry took more meaning from the look in his friend's eyes than his words. "How long afterward?"

"Some within ten years, a couple lasted as long as twenty."

"At least they lived out their days in their own time, and not as prisoners," Perry said, unable to hide the bitterness welling inside him.

He wanted to shout at them that it wasn't enough for them to tell him he was in a displacement zone, that he was safe inside the circle. It wasn't enough to feel *safe*. The need for a future, the freedom to pursue his own destiny, was too strong in mankind, too intense. His entire future had been stolen, stripped from him every bit as deftly as a pickpocket would steal a lady's purse.

A sharp exhalation from Valerie snared his attention and he looked at the screen as she pulled away slightly, murmured some imprecation—and jabbed a button.

The screen resolved itself into an almost identical picture as before, four human-looking figures, some piles of stuff and the reproduced P-40N Warhawk. But this time Valerie had one of the figures mount the plane and, to Perry's amazement, the plane began to roll across the area inside the oval. The plane lifted from the ground and within seconds had crossed the oval's line. As before, the plane disappeared. Worse, so did the man inside it.

"Well, you can't fly out," Jack said. "Try bringing it back."

Valerie pressed another button, and swore like a sailor when nothing happened. Those words on her lips, on any woman's lips, made Perry turn to Dwayne with raised eyebrows. His friend grinned and looked up at the sky.

"We're going about this backward," Valerie said now. "We need to be looking at that portal. That's what holds all the answers."

"But, Val, we don't know anything about it!" Jack Chew protested. "We don't even know why it's still there. Try flying the plane out with someone else piloting it."

She did so, and the figure remained on the screen, albeit flopping onto the ground, but the plane still disappeared.

"So we can come and go, but he can't. Why is that thing still open?" Jack asked.

"It's still there because I'm still here," Perry said. He had no basis of information for that statement, none of the sophisticated equipment that these people were armed with, but he knew it was true. He *felt* it.

"I think you're right," Valerie said slowly. "But that still doesn't tell us why you're here nor how—" She broke off and bit her lower lip.

"Nor how I'm going to get back or how long I'm going to be hanging around. Right?" Perry asked.

She nodded sadly.

"What happens if it just disappears? Can't you do your experiment, the one that brought me here, in reverse? Can't you just send me back? Won't that close the hole? Take me home?"

Valerie shook her head. "I don't know. I honestly don't know." Perry felt rather than saw her shoulders sag and knew a moment's real doubt. He'd known her less than two hours, but had already come to rely on her judgment, her determination. If she didn't know, and couldn't push herself to magically figure out a way of learning, then he felt he was truly doomed.

To his delight—and profound relief—she suddenly jerked upright, as though mentally slapping herself and looked up at him with a swift, rather mischievous smile. "But we're going to do everything in our power to find out, you and I. And we're going to start right now."

Her eyes lost that shadow of despair, of confusion and met his openly, challengingly, and Perry felt a surge of energy sweep through him as she closed one eye in a deliberate wink.

He smiled broadly. "Tell me what you need me to do, honey. I'm with you all the way."

And with a flash of insight, he realized that he meant it far more literally than he'd originally intended. He found the idea more pleasing than disconcerting.

"Okay," she said. "Let's start with everything you remember about the morning of July 16, 1945."

"This morning," Perry said.

Her smile faded a little, but she nodded easily enough. "Yes, this morning for you, forty-eight years ago for the rest of us."

Just hearing the words aloud did odd things to Perry's gut. But this time he didn't want to scream or rage. He wasn't even angry. What he felt now was more a sensation of stepping off a four-hundred-foot cliff and falling, the world slipping by him at a rate too rapid to be understood.

As he talked, she would occasionally type in a few details on her computer. When he had described everything up to the moment of hearing the photographer call his name, she paused and glanced up at the color portal. She looked swiftly away, as though the beautiful sight was something evil, a cloud that portended nothing but trouble. Perry thought she might really have something there.

"And when you turned, what did you see?"

Perry hesitated. "Colors, like those in that hole up there, but all over."

Valerie made a few notations. "And did anyone else see these colors?"

"I don't know. The photographer was over to the left of the barrier. So was I. The color array was behind him."

Jack Chew said, "There's no mention of anything unusual in the files for that date."

"Except for Perry's disappearance," Valerie added dryly.

Jack flushed. "Except for that, yeah."

"And you saw nothing else unusual?" Valerie asked.

Perry hesitated. That wasn't all that he'd seen, but the rest made no sense. He shook his head.

"And then what happened?"

"I came here."

"Just like that?" she asked. "How long did it feel like it took? The blink of an eye? Several moments? Days?"

"I don't know. It's kind of like a dream," Perry said slowly, remembering. "The kind of dream where there really isn't any sense of time."

He hesitated, aware of the irony in that, taking in, possibly for the first time, the truth of his own words, the reality of his experience. "A dream where you've been somewhere forever and it's going to keep right on going. I remember everything, yet nothing makes any sense."

"Like what, for example?" Valerie asked.

"Well, I thought I saw a beach. There was water all around, anyway. And I could hear a woman laughing, but I didn't see her. And a child's voice. And . . . I thought—" He broke off for a second, not quite certain what he'd thought then, what he thought now. He continued lamely, and not quite truthfully, "All I could see was the water, and the colors."

"You thought . . . ?" Valerie prompted, seizing on his momentary confusion. She was nobody's fool, this spunky woman in pink. She looked up and met his gaze. As before, her blue eyes steadied him. Her eyes were the same color of blue as the ocean of his odd dreamlike experience.

"Like I told you, the whole thing is jumbled up in my head. There were rainbow colors, like a host of rainbows all flashing together. I can't explain the woman's laugh, or the beach . . . maybe I *was* dreaming. Seeing you walking toward me is the first thing, the first really *aware* thought I had after . . ." But was that the truth? Hadn't he felt totally aware and completely whole on that beach, hearing that laughter? And before that, at Trinity, when he'd seen . . .

"After?"

Perry gathered his spinning thoughts. "After the rainbow burst out behind the photographer."

Valerie frowned, and Perry wondered if she suspected him of leaving something out. He was, but it was too damned embarrassing to talk about. People just didn't go around mentioning they'd happened to see an omen of their death. Or maybe what he'd seen had been the start of this strange journey through time, the signal, perhaps.

"And you don't remember seeing anything else during the interval you were actually crossing through the portal."

"Not forty-eight years' worth of memories, no," Perry said.

"I've never seen such a bunch of yahoos in all my life," Dwayne told Perry as they both eyed the four "experts" the pass-the-buck captain had collared from somewhere. At least he hadn't returned.

The Men in Suits, as Perry tagged them, had appeared on the scene some two hours after Captain Pelligrew had taken off in that amazing toy plane. A jollier bunch of jokers never existed. Except they weren't playing any games. These fellows weren't doing a damned thing, but were deadly serious about it. They'd been amazingly efficient at constructing this prison in the desert.

Dwayne said, "I do believe they have a collective I.Q. that registers at room temperature."

Perry chuckled at Dwayne, though he didn't have the slightest idea what an I.Q. was or even what his old friend meant by room temperature. The tone implied that it was a slur. That was enough.

As used as he was to Army maneuvers and bivouacs and the remarkable speed with which the military could set up a modern camp upon demand, Perry nevertheless felt stunned with the production of practically a full-blown town in this patch of dry ground. Yahoos or not, these civilian fellows knew a thing or two about quick establishment of quarters.

Luckily Valerie's motley team of strange quantum physicists had managed to secure a few musts before the suits had arrived. The waterline for Perry, and the rest of the odd collection of artifacts—he still resented the living daylights out of being referred to as an artifact—proved to be one hundred and fifty yards in length and one hundred in breadth from the P-40N Warhawk in an almost perfect oval, with the Warhawk at the far end and the peculiar glasslike but not glass barrier at the other. The area was the real version of what Valerie had managed to magically draw on that little computer screen of hers.

Valerie's team seemed to find the fact that it wasn't a circle, but rather an oval, of great interest, but Perry didn't find anything very fascinating about it. What it boiled down to was that he was as good as a prisoner behind invisible bars.

"Let Me Off Uptown," Anita O'Day's sexy voice crooning to Gene Kroupa's orchestra, seemed to haunt his mind. The whole song flitted through his mind, but it was that one line that tore at his guts. It took on a whole new meaning with the situation he was facing now. There wasn't any uptown for him.

He was more scared now than he had ever been in his entire life. Facing the enemy across a five-foot trench was nothing to this. Flying home on a Douglas C-47 Skytrain, a transporter holding twenty-five other wounded soldiers, scared to death, hopped up on something the doc gave him before the medics stowed him on board, seemed like a picnic now.

There were only two other moments of this kind of soul-stirring fear that he'd ever encountered before: when he first saw the rainbow in the middle of Trinity Site, and when he saw Valerie Daniels for the first time.

But both those times had been filled with a sense of destiny, of strange and glittering promise, whereas now he felt trapped in this present, trapped in a bizarre world, time, place he couldn't begin to fathom. And, as if things weren't bad enough, the suits had determined right off the bat that all nonessential personnel were to clear the area.

They might just as well have handed Dwayne his walking papers, because he was the only one they could have meant.

Perry had volunteered, but no one but a steaming mad Valerie had even acknowledged his meager joke, and all she'd done was send him a quick nod.

"Don't be ridiculous," Valerie had snapped at the men in the three-piece, pin-striped gear, "Dwayne Roberts has been on-site since the first of these tests. He was here when Perry came through—or appeared or however you want to call it in your reports. He already knows everything we know about this. What earthly good could it possibly do to send him away now? And it might do some irreparable harm."

Perry agreed for the most part with everything she said, but if pressed, he would have to admit he was more impressed with how she said it. Four- and five-syllable words rolled off her tongue like a motorcycle from a transport tanker, slick as could be. Another thing he liked was that she didn't refer to him as the major or by his last name. Whenever she used his name, she used his *first* name, like they'd known each other for years.

But no matter how eloquently she'd argued, nor how angrily, the suits had won and Dwayne was going to be escorted to his vehicle in less than ten minutes.

For the first time since he'd landed on this peculiarly familiar stretch of New Mexico, Perry felt the weight of the missing forty-eight years. Dwayne was his only link with a time these people, even Valerie, seemed to regard as being just a few years after the dinosaurs. Although it was irrational, he had the sinking feeling that if Dwayne left, he might never see him again. Or worse, that 1945 and all that was precious to Perry about life during his thirty-nine years on earth would disappear with him.

He wanted to rage at anyone who would listen that he hadn't seen his old friend in nearly fifty years, and they were making Dwayne go away? And staring at his own reflection in four pairs of sunglasses, seeing identical inflexible expressions on four faces, he'd almost given in to that rage.

But Dwayne himself had nodded and agreed at the same time that Valerie had wrapped a firm hand around his wrist. "I . . . I 've got to go, Perry," he'd said. "I've got a ranch to run."

His voice had been choked with emotion, and his gnarled hand had grasped at Perry's other arm with fierce possession. "But you write me, you hear? You write me and tell me everything. Then, when this is all over, you come see me."

Dwayne's eyes had met Perry's like he was again a commanding officer and he had given a direct order. "And you bring this little gal along." His grip loosened, and his eyes roved the broad plain. "You do whatever you want to do, Perry. But don't you forget to write."

"Can Mr. Roberts at least stay with us until you finish resettling the housing arrangements?" Valerie had asked, switching her tactics from vinegar to honey, continuing to hold his other wrist. "He has been searching for Perry for some fifty years. He never lost faith that his friend would be found someday. It seems dreadfully unfair not to let them have a little time together."

The suits conferred, then the one that Perry had decided was chief spokesman, Bob something or other—not that he thought it would make any difference which of them opened his mouth, for the words would all be identical—nodded. When he spoke, Perry was reminded of dry ice, all smoke and chill and scare, with only a chunk of carbon dioxide.

"Mr. Roberts. We realize your concern for Major Deveroux. It isn't our intention to prolong our investigation in any way, but you must understand that a situation exists, and that all precautions must be undertaken with the utmost secrecy in the interests of national security."

"Double-talk," Perry had said. Valerie's hand had tightened on his wrist, and he'd subsided for her sake, though he couldn't help but wonder who these fellows were that they could sweep in here and take over a project and apparently scare even as redoubtable a woman as Valerie.

He asked Dwayne now, "Tell me about those boys. I know you said, 'C.I.A.,' but what the hell is that?"

"Central Intelligence Agency. At least, that's who I'm assuming they are. They act like it, anyway."

"We change governments or something?" Perry asked. Though he'd deliberately kept his tone light, he felt anything but.

Dwayne snorted, looked highly amused. "Not quite so drastic as that, buddy. And don't let them hear you say it. They believe they *are* the government."

"I don't like the way that Bob fellow looks at Valerie."

"Can't say as I blame him all that much. She's not all that hard to look at."

Perry shot him a hard glance, forgetting in that split second what his friend would look like. He looked away quickly, not shocked, and not feeling pity, but uncomfortable because the change in his friend reminded him all too clearly of the half a century of mystery between them. Dwayne had filled him in on history—the world, events, the fate of presidents—but, as if by unspoken agreement, they hadn't covered personal ground.

Perry said now, "Well, whatever they are, they're pretty good at bivouacking."

Dwayne murmured some assent, then said, "I wish..."

Perry waited for Dwayne to continue, his eyes traveling back and forth between the three amazing trailer homes with motors already built in, which the suits were moving into the chalk-lined oval. One of the suits was jerry-rigging a generator of some kind to all three huge trailers.

"You wish...what?" Perry asked finally.

"Nothing. I'm just glad you came back."

"Did you really stop the Army from declaring me dead?" Perry asked him. His fingers played with the dirt beneath his hands, dirt where tall grass should be. It felt as dry and lifeless as his former dreams of the future.

"Sure did. But I imagine you'll have some hell collecting your back pay."

Perry chuckled, feeling some of the tension in him ease. The only other person who made him feel this easy in her presence was Valerie. But when he was near her, he felt a tension of a different sort.

He said now, "Yeah? Well, I imagine they'd have a harder time explaining much of this whole thing. Seems like it might be easier for everyone just to pay me off and let me go home."

Dwayne didn't answer and Perry knew why. No one knew just how to get him back home. And, if they were all right about him being missing for forty-eight years, he never did go back. Which meant only one thing: he was staying right here, not just in this time but in this one patch of desert ground.

He thought of the little house with the picket fence he'd always envisioned having once the war ended. A job, probably teaching, since that's what he'd planned to do before the war, and a wife, a few kids, a life. A real, solid life. A life now as insubstantial as the air around them, or that rainbow cloud in the sky.

Dwayne said, "Looks like they're sparing no expense on your quarters, pal. I'd hazard a guess that not one of those super recreational vehicles sells for less than forty grand apiece."

Perry turned to stare at his friend. "Forty *thousand* dollars? How can anything cost that much?"

"Got a few surprises for you, Deveroux. What did the average house cost in 1945?"

"I dunno, you were the one who was hot to squander your pay," Perry said. "Six, maybe seven thousand if they were building them new, which of course, they aren't. Weren't."

"That would have been living pretty high. You remember, I bought that spread outside Socorro for less than six thousand?"

"Well, that's fair. You got what, two hundred acres?"

Dwayne grinned. "Hang onto your hat. I had it appraised last year so I could redraft my will to include those infernal great grandkids, and the figure came in the six digits.''

"Get outta here," Perry said.

"I'm not horsing around. I'm not telling you this to make your eyes bug out at how rich I am. Though, between you and me, I'm not hurting. But to put things in perspective for you, Dev, I was pretty disappointed in the appraisal amount. If it had been in California, say, the place would have been worth a cool million.''

"Who has that kind of money?" Perry asked, sincerely curious.

"Lots of people do now. Fact of the matter is, I do. Hell, it ain't hard, nowadays. And it ain't that much money, either. And you gotta remember, I spent forty-eight years accumulating that kind of dough.''

"Robbed a couple of banks, did you?"

Dwayne chuckled. "Nah. I got interested in technology a couple of years after you disappeared. Put what little money Pat and I could scrape together in things like television, plastics, microwaves. Things like that.''

"I don't know what the hell you're even talking about."

"You will," Dwayne said. "That's what makes the world go around these days.''

"You telling me I'm going to be rich, too?"

"In forty-eight years, maybe. You're just a punk, not even in your prime.''

Perry was silent, so was Dwayne. He thought perhaps they were both unwilling to state the obvious, that he might not even have a prime to reach. The odds didn't look all that promising at the moment.

"Take that pretty gal over there. She probably pulls in close to sixty or seventy thousand a year.''

Perry mulled that over. As a major, with a sheaf full of veteran's benefits, he'd felt pretty cozy about the future. But the kind of salary Dwayne said Valerie was making in just one year cast Perry's entire net worth into the shade. He wasn't sure why the idea rankled so, but it did.

"But even on that kind of salary, how can anyone afford the prices you're talking?"

Dwayne smiled. "Loans. Not just for mortgages, but for everything. You can just walk into a furniture store nowadays, pick out the set you want, sign the paper and they deliver it a couple of hours later. Or you can buy a TV on time, or a microwave, or anything else. Or else you can charge it on a credit card and pay the card company the interest."

"What's a credit card?" Perry asked.

Dwayne thought for a moment, then said, "Like a coupon book, but you don't have to have the coupons. Times have changed, Perry. Take me, now. Last year I got a hankering for the ocean. You know I always fancied a place on the water. So I called a friend, and he called one, and the next thing you know, I bought into a whole beachfront property. I didn't want to develop it, though, just wanted it natural. It's...well, it's beautiful. When you get out of this pickle, you'll have to come see it."

"I'll do that," Perry said absently. His eyes fell on Valerie, standing behind her team of quantum physicists. They were all studying something. She looked up and across at him and Dwayne, and he knew whatever it was they were looking at pertained to him. For a variety of reasons, he wished she looked happier.

"When did all this happen?" Perry asked, feeling as though there couldn't possibly be an end to the changes he was forced to view.

"The kind of experiment that brought you here, or the differences?"

Perry nodded, his eyes still on Valerie.

Dwayne seemed to understand exactly what Perry was really asking, for he said, "Oh, it took time. Nearly a half a century of time." While his tone was somewhat sad, it didn't carry any regret.

Perry eyed the solid, motorized buildings that had been wheeled across the plain and parked, saw them with new respect and no little trepidation. After the perimeters had been established, he had half expected an Army tent or two, but he never would have imagined—like the orange sneakers on Phil's feet—completely furnished quarters, electric generators, hot and cold running water and kitchen and bathroom facilities indoors, or any of it costing a pure fortune.

He was truly in the future, in some time that made no sense. He didn't recognize anything except Dwayne's humor, and even that held a multitude of nuances and references he didn't understand; and the people, like the strangely uniformed Pelligrew and the men in the suits, baffled him almost as much as the music that blared from something Phil called a "boom box."

He felt there were only four things he totally comprehended. This time wasn't his time; he couldn't go beyond the chalked line; the men in suits didn't have the foggiest notion what to do about him; and Valerie Daniels might be some kind of futuristic woman boss, but she was still a woman.

This last thought steadied him somewhat. This world might have gone crazy, and Dwayne might be leaving, but at least Valerie would be there with him. He could think of worse fates.

He grinned, watching her now across a totally transformed field. She marched briskly across the chalk line and up to Bob what's his name and started talking earnestly. Pretty soon, she was actively arguing. Perry couldn't hear them, but didn't need ears to understand that she was becoming hopping mad. He had no idea what the suit had done to irritate her now, but from the steam all but visibly rising from her skin, it must have been a doozy.

"Feisty," Dwayne said, accurately assessing Perry's smile.

"Are all the women like her now?" Perry asked. He was more than merely inquisitive.

Dwayne shrugged. "Nah. She'd be unique in just about any time, I'd guess." He grinned still more broadly. "Leastways, it seems like it to me. You forget, I don't hang around the young gals much anymore. Even my youngest daughter is forty-five. And your own kids don't count anyway, 'cause they're always sixteen to you.''

Perry didn't turn to look at his friend of yesterday, though after this short session together, talking easily, being brought up to date without having it rammed at him, he didn't think he was still having difficulty coming to terms with the changes time had wrought. "Does it bother you?" he asked finally.

"What? Valerie?"

"No, not that." He couldn't elaborate.

Dwayne apparently had no such qualms. "You and me sitting here, old Army buddies, same age, me looking like I got one foot in the grave, you looking like my grandson? That what you're asking?"

Perry felt a stab of guilt that cut him to the quick. He would never in a million years have put it so harshly. He wished like hell he hadn't brought it up. But having done so, he had to answer. "I guess so," he muttered. He had to look at Dwayne now, face the ravages of time, really see him for what he was now, not what Perry might wish him to be.

Dwayne wasn't looking at him, he was staring fixedly at the ring on Perry's finger. His father's ring, the ring Dwayne had brought him at the hospital in Washington, D.C., right after his folks died.

"Remember that day?" Perry asked now, hoping this might help bridge the terrible gap of time.

"Very well," Dwayne answered. He still didn't look away from the ring.

Perry held his hand out. "I've never taken it off," he said. "Don't guess I will until I meet the right girl." Unconsciously, he looked back at Valerie.

"Perry?"

He turned, somewhat reluctantly, and met Dwayne's intense gaze. An oddly significant message burned in his eyes. His friend swallowed heavily and opened his lips as though to utter the words behind his look. "Just remember that all things have to change, Perry," he said finally, and Perry was certain it wasn't what his friend had intended to say.

"Like you and me?" Perry asked.

Dwayne smiled, and it was more wry than bitter. "I've known for a long time that I was going to outlive most folks." Again that intensity crept into his eyes, then flickered and faded. "The notion has always kept me going when times got really tough."

Perry wanted to ask Dwayne where he'd gotten his certainty of a long life, wanted to ask him about some higher power, God maybe, but it wasn't the kind of thing they talked about. He would give a lot to have Dwayne's faith in the future right now. He looked across the desert at the mountains, purple and stark in the distance.

Dwayne said, "You asked me if it bothers me. I'll tell you. Sure. It's the damnedest thing I've ever seen."

Perry didn't say anything. There wasn't anything to say. It bothered him, too. But in an odd way, it felt good to have it out in the open.

"But it doesn't bug me the way you're thinking it does. Sure, I wish I could suddenly, whoosh bang! be thirty-eight or nine again, get rid of this arthritis, sleep like a kid, but trust me, Deveroux, I wouldn't want to go back and do it all over. Not a chance, pal. There were good times." His voice trailed to a harsh, throaty whisper. "Hell, there were some great times. Times you'd kill to go back and live again, taste again."

Dwayne sighed. "And there were more than a share of bad times, too. There's even more times I don't remember, and that's probably a damned good thing.

"But I'll tell you, when I look at you, I remember Patty and that makes me wish all kinds of things." Dwayne hesitated, then said quietly, too quietly, "Patty's gone, Dev."

Perry wanted to get up and start running. Damn the chalk lines. Damn everything in this cursed place. He didn't want to hear this, would rather have heard almost anything else than that.

"She's been gone these twelve years. And I haven't ever gotten used to waking up in the morning and not having her beside me in that bed. I don't believe I'd like to live through these last twelve years again for all the tea in the Boston Harbor."

Dwayne could talk about Patty being gone these twelve years, but for Perry, the pain was brand new. He closed his eyes against the sharpness of the knife that cut through him. He'd kissed her goodbye just the night before, standing in the doorway of that spread that was now worth a pure bundle of cash. Sweet Pat, hostess at one of the U.S.O. dances, who had taken one look at Dwayne and decided he was the man she would marry. Perry had introduced them, feeling more than a little envy of his friend for getting the girl with the rayon dress and stars in her eyes.

Dwayne was silent for such a long stretch that Perry could see that Valerie had already rousted the suit, had turned and was walking in their direction. Perry didn't say anything, wishing he knew *what* to say. But all he could think about was the sheer unfairness of never having seen Dwayne's kids, never seeing their mother grow with age, mellow with years.

"So here I am," Dwayne said. "An old man with grown kids. I've got six grandkids, two great grandkids. You ain't known hell till you have a passel of kids charging through your house thinking they can do any damned thing they want just because you're so old and doddering they think you can't catch 'em before they set the house afire. But they're mine, and I love 'em because I loved their grandma, and I love my kids. I wouldn't want to think about having missed that."

Perry's heart took in Dwayne's meaning, but his mind rebelled against accepting it. He watched Valerie instead. She walked like the desert floor was made of air and she floated, Perry thought. She had a fine pair of legs, and no stocking seams marred their elegant line. Her hair captured the glow of the sun and came alive, a riotous mass of golden curls that was a vibrant testimonial to all that was fresh, independent and unfettered in this world.

"The only thing I envy you about your youth, Deveroux, is that young gal walking our way," Dwayne said, and Perry turned to look at him. Dwayne winked and time collapsed in on itself, and he was a young soldier again. "And it's a damned good thing I'm not still that kid. I was always the better looking of the two of us."

Perry snorted and looked back at Valerie.

"Patty told me, oh, must have been five, six years after we had Jimmy, that she never saw another man after she saw me that first time."

Perry grinned, shifting his gaze to Dwayne, trying not to think too much on Valerie's graceful approach. "Patty was the best liar I ever met," he lied.

Valerie tried cooling off as she drew closer to the two men sitting in the shade of the airplane. She was relieved to see Perry was with someone, and that the someone was Dwayne Roberts. What she had to say was hardly the best news.

If only the data had coughed up other possibilities. Any other news. Ever since that blasted medicine bundle had disappeared—and she had to be thankful her team had disobeyed Pelligrew's orders, for if they hadn't it might have been Perry Deveroux who mysteriously vanished and not a hundred-year-old collection of feathers, stones and pipes—they had all been on edge. Perry most of all.

She wished there was something she could say to erase the shadow in his eyes, a shadow that had appeared as soon as he took in the implications of that disappearance. A darkness that had deepened when Bob Fenton had told Dwayne he had to leave the area. She had tried arguing, but to no avail.

She slowed and stopped just this side of hearing distance of the two men and glanced up at the now hateful portal in the otherwise unblemished sky.

The doorway was growing smaller.

Phil had told her so not twenty minutes earlier. And that was what she'd been arguing about with Fenton. He claimed that the shrinkage was negligible and that it wouldn't change any of the tests they had proposed for Perry Deveroux. Just the notion of the tests they had in mind was enough to make Valerie shiver. And she had been sidetracked into arguing about those, too.

Fenton was wrong on all counts, but most particularly about the altered data relating to the portal. The shrinkage of that bizarre still-opened portal to some other time or dimension was terrifying. And certainly not just because of its presence in the sky. That alone was a frightening thought. But added to that fear was the simple stark fact that as it shrunk, in almost perfectly direct proportion, so, too, did Perry's chances of survival on this earthly plane.

What would eventually happen was anyone's guess. It was also what she'd really been arguing about with Bob Fenton. He wanted Perry installed in a lead-lined transport vehicle and removed from the site. That was when Valerie had snapped at him that she'd turn the damned lasers on again before she'd allow a single person to try taking Perry out of the compound.

Every scrap of information the computer released showed that if Perry tried crossing the chalk boundary, he would simply disappear. Where he would go, what condition he would be in when he got there, was a total blank.

The trouble was, turning on the lasers, aiming them at the color cloud, might well be the only thing that could return things to normal. The data and projections showed there was every likelihood of electromagnetic stimuli closing the portal as simply and as apparently easily as they had unwittingly opened it.

The bigger trouble was that if they did, history showed all too clearly that Perry Deveroux didn't return to 1945. He was never seen nor heard from again. The only scraps of evidence that he'd ever been at Trinity Site were a few faded photographs and that satchel long since given to Dwayne Roberts.

But the biggest trouble was that in Valerie's heart of hearts, she wasn't all too certain that she wanted Perry to leave. His departure meant the disappearance of a thousand dreams, wishes of finding a living, breathing anomaly, one that not only produced more questions, but could provide intelligent, coherent answers. And it meant more, too much more, but she wouldn't allow herself to consider that frightening avenue of thought.

Because now, there wasn't even a chance he could stay, however restricted, however confined the parameters might be made.

The prison walls were closing in. Not swiftly, but closing nonetheless. If her team's calculations were right—and no one seemed to doubt that they were—then Perry Deveroux was soon to be squeezed out of this dimension, or at the very least out of this time frame.

If only they had some scrap of proof—of hope—that the medicine bundle had arrived somewhere...some *when*...safely, then she wouldn't feel so horrible, so guilty. So scared. But they didn't have that hope, and there was no guarantee it had been displaced to some location that would even tolerate it.

Atomic particles trapped in the earth's magnetic fields were thought to come from the sun. What if, by some horrible quirk, turning on the lasers catapulted Perry to the sun's molten surface?

There were too many variables, too many uncertainties. Perry Deveroux had been gone for almost fifty years and yet only clearly remembered the morning of the Manhattan Project test at Trinity. His following memories—a glimpse of a beach, a woman's laughter—were sketchy and inconclusive, and even if they had been in glorious technicolor, filled with a million minute details, they could hardly hope to explain away nearly fifty years of absence.

He had told her everything from the moment the photographer had called his name to the moment he'd seen her "in that spunky little dress." But it didn't add up to much more than a few minutes, possibly even seconds in linear time.

If only there was more, she thought. If only he had seen something. She'd said as much and had seen an odd flicker in his eyes . . . a memory? She'd snatched at this farfetched hope, but he'd dismissed it as nothing, telling her his eyes must have been playing tricks. What did you see? she'd wanted to know, but he'd shaken his head. Nothing. Nothing at all.

The worst factor of all to Valerie was that Perry Deveroux had only been in her time for some seven hours, and she found herself responding more to him than to any man she'd ever known before. She'd tried telling herself it was simply a matter of a scientist's reaction to a fascinating anomaly, but she knew it was more than that. Perry touched her not simply as a bridge across time but, more deeply, as a man.

He was a man without a home, a drowning victim without a life raft. But that wasn't what called to her sympathy. It was more the way he was struggling to accept his odd fate, swallow the more than normal anger and dampen his pride that called to her, made her soul stretch to his in deepest empathy.

And it was something even greater than that, some intangible strength or inner aura that he projected without even thinking about it, that she recognized, that she understood, that beckoned her as nothing else, no one else, could have.

And now she had to tell him that the displacement zone, this strange fourth-dimensional storage shed, was getting even smaller, and would, according to the data, continue to do so until there was no displaced area left. And when that went . . . so would Perry.

"Quite a tussle you were having with the man in blue," Dwayne Roberts said as she finally stepped within hailing distance.

Valerie tried to smile and knew she failed when Perry asked calmly but firmly, "What's wrong?"

If only he would wear sunglasses like everyone else, she thought. Then she wouldn't have to continually drown in that brown gaze. Thank heavens the brim of his hat occasionally shaded his eyes. Unfortunately, it wasn't doing so now.

"The portal is shrinking," she said. There wasn't any kind way to put it, no softening that would carry weight with this man.

She could hear the voices of the CIA men behind her, and the now-querulous pitch of Jack Chew's questions. The trailers were in their new places, and Jack's postulations that they were well within the shrinkage zone only made Valerie think of the days of circling the wagons to avoid attack. Only what they were guarding against weren't raiding Indians, but the vast unknown. And there was no dodging this particular onslaught.

Unless they, she and her team of baffled scientists, came up with something, Perry Deveroux would cease to exist here.

She thought fleetingly of her condo in Virginia Beach and wished, for the first time in two months, that she could be there, flopping facedown upon her cool, untroubled bed, never having come to New Mexico, never having met Dwayne Roberts or his youthful friend Perry Deveroux.

And yet meeting Perry was the single most significant encounter in her life.

The portal is shrinking. Time was running out for Perry Deveroux. The thought refused to be laid to rest, resisted any attempts to thrust it aside.

"Meaning this fancy prison they're setting up here is going to shrink, too," Perry assayed correctly.

Technically the land, and the items in it, wouldn't shrink because all items brought in would, according to their projections, stay just where they were, but the invisible walls were already closing in. So, in effect, he was right. "Yes," she answered slowly, too baldly.

"How fast?" he asked.

She was struck anew by that core of inner strength in him. He wasn't going to go nuts on her, wasn't going to scream at the injustice of it. He only wanted to know how long he had. Like a condemned man, she thought bleakly.

"Ten days. Maybe... less."

Chapter 6

These people in the future—in the present, Perry's mind tried in vain to correct—must take some kind of super vitamins. Everyone was still hard at it, while he felt like he was the bottom slab in a hot icehouse.

But Perry knew why at least two of them seemed so peppy. They were spelling each other. Two went after him while the other two were absent from the luxurious travel trailer. Snoozing, no doubt. Or thinking up new tortures.

The two men with him now had finally shed their jackets. Unfortunately Perry realized that didn't mean they were going to settle back and order a soda, it meant they were getting down to business. And still more unfortunately, the business was Major Perry Deveroux.

He glanced at the only other person present, Valerie Daniels. She was the only reason he'd gone along with all this nonsense. As long as she was in the same room, he didn't have that immigrant feeling, that man-without-a-country sensation of having walked down corridor B when he meant to head for some other place. And as long as she was there he was able to subdue the more murderous thoughts about the men in the suits.

He'd felt that way ever since Dwayne Roberts had walked outside the white-chalked line and headed for a vehicle that looked, for all the world, like a Wehrmacht staff car.

Dwayne had looked at him for a long, long moment and then had said, "I don't care how long or short you make it, pal, but you'd better write. Don't let me down, now." With that, he'd walked stiffly to his car, only turning briefly to raise a fragile arm in farewell.

"Everything will work out okay," Valerie had said then, but the luminous quality to her eyes had told the truer tale. "We'll get him back here," she'd also said.

But Perry didn't believe that. From what she'd said earlier, he didn't have much more than a few days. What difference would it make to pull Dwayne back in on all this? Except for a last goodbye. They'd already had too many of those during their years together. But this one might prove the hardest.

Besides, everything was not going to work out okay. Perry didn't believe that, and neither did Dwayne or Valerie.

But for some odd reason, Valerie Daniels did believe that something was going to happen for the good. Perhaps not that everything would be okay, but that some kind of a solution would magically dance across that piece of glass she called a screen.

He wondered if she still thought so. Because now, even she was showing the strain of the long day and night. Her eyes were half closed, and her fingers, on the keyboard that seemed an extension of her body, had slowed considerably.

"How was his blood pressure at last reading?" one of the suits asked his colleague, who was handling the medical equipment. They had introduced themselves with brief flashes of odd-looking badges with their pictures and some kind of emblem on them, but that had been early on in this nightmare, and Perry couldn't remember what names they'd thrown at him.

He was getting so tired, he thought, that in another few minutes, he might have difficulty repeating his name for the hundredth time.

The medic picked up a clipboard and rattled off a couple of numbers. "It's been an hour since last reading. I'd better check it again."

Perry saw Valerie look up from the computer screen and frown at the two suits. That was enough of a signal for Perry. He'd decided he'd had a snootful of their shenanigans a couple of hours back.

"I'll tell you how his blood pressure is," Perry said, neither knowing what that pressure indicated nor caring. "It's ready to boil." Though he wasn't looking specifically at Valerie, he felt her eyes shift to him.

The fellow with the equipment ignored him, however, laying the cuff with its black pump on the table and switching to busily preparing yet another of the many needles they had poked at him, and though Perry should have been used to it by now, he found he wasn't able to let it pass any longer.

"You come at me with that sticker, and you're going to have to explain to your mother why you have pierced ears."

He didn't raise his voice, or even speak in a tone other than conversational, yet the man with the needle glanced his way, meeting his eyes for the first time since he'd arrived. Perry felt it was the only time any one of them had met his gaze directly since their sweep into the desert some ten hours earlier. And he had a fairly clear idea, when the man hesitated then slowly lowered the needle to the shiny new table, that the cold message in his eyes had been received—loud and clear.

"You've drawn enough of my blood to fill up a dead man," Perry said.

"Now, Major Deveroux—" the other one, the one Perry had designated as spokesman, began.

"I'm talking now," Perry said. "You've poked, prodded and you've X-rayed. You've asked questions a second grader

could answer. Then your cohorts have had a go at me. And I'm telling you, *really nicely* . . . it's enough."

"Major—"

"Are you with me here?" he asked. He didn't dare take his eyes from the suit, but he could sense Valerie's sudden alert concentration.

"Now, Major—"

He didn't stop to wonder if her attention was based on worry or approbation. He had to do this. "I said. . .*are you with me?*"

When both men remained silent, Perry leaned back. He was enjoying himself for the first time all day. No, that wasn't quite true; he'd enjoyed watching Valerie Daniels at work, had spent a couple of good moments wondering if she applied that same concentration in other areas of life. And he'd liked touching her hand, and the way her fingers felt around his wrist. But this was something different. This was something he could *do*.

"I'm going to call the shots for a while," he said, and suddenly smiling. He knew if Dwayne were here, he'd be advising the suits to hit the deck while he escorted Valerie from the room.

From the blank look on the two men's faces, Perry suddenly understood what they were all about. Just like the captain—who had turned out to be in the U.S. Air Force, a still foreign concept to Perry, since, as far as he knew, fly-boys were part of the *Army* Air Force and not in any separate command—he recognized these men in the suits.

These were the shout-and-fury boys. They came on strong, shoving their weight around and barking orders, but let something go wrong, let someone buck their routine, and they all but crumpled. Perry wondered what had happened in the last fifty years that men like these could get away with all that bluster. Couldn't people see through that bull by now?

This realization of what they were, something he'd instinctively known since first laying eyes on them, made him truly wonder if times had really changed that much after all. They, these people of the future present, had all sorts of gewgaws, little gadgets for this and that, machines to do practically anything he could dream of—and for all he knew they had movie theaters installed in every house—but they were still willing to be bullied by glory boys. He would have thought that the First World War and the War to End All Wars would have ended that particular tyranny.

"What is it you wish us to do, Major?" the spokesman asked calmly enough.

"First, I want you to tell me your names. Slowly this time. And your ranks."

The spokesman looked at him as if Perry were a raw recruit and still wet behind the ears. "My name," he said too slowly to be anything but patronizing, "is Robert Fenton. And this is Aaron Janes. And we carry the military equivalent of full colonel."

"Okay, Mr. Fenton . . . and Mr. Janes . . . I want you two to clear out."

"Look here, Major—"

"Now."

Perry watched as the two men exchanged long and obviously meaningful glances. Finally, Fenton nodded at Janes, who began packing up the array of medical equipment and charts.

Fenton spoke, and there was no mistaking his pomposity. Perry wondered idly if it was for his benefit or simply to save face. Then, as the man's eyes slid sideways toward Valerie, he understood exactly who it was for.

"We understand that you're tired. It's been a long day for all of us. I'll tell you what, we'll knock off for the night, but resume our tests in the morning. One of us will accompany you to your quarters and stay there with you—"

"No," Perry said.

"But—"

"No," he repeated, with greater emphasis. "I'm staying right where I am."

"Someone has to stay on the premises with you."

"She will," Perry said, cocking his head in Valerie's direction, but not taking his eyes off Fenton. "This is her place, isn't it? Well, as of right now, she has a houseguest."

He hoped Valerie would remain quiet. He had no desire to compromise her, or any intention of ruining her reputation, but he'd had more than his fill of these men. All these men. He was tired and wanted to think, needed desperately to just think.

Again the two men exchanged a long, silent look.

Finally, Fenton said, "Very well. There's no point in arguing. As I said, we'll resume our tests in the morning."

Perry knew better than to press that particular point now. There would be no more tests, and he suspected they already knew that, but bluff-and-bluster types needed to believe they had at least one finger of the upper hand. He said nothing, nor did he move. He simply waited.

The screen door leading to the cool desert night opened and shut and they were gone. He could hear them walking away, not talking, and then couldn't hear them anymore. The relief of their departure swept through him like a mountain wind, and he actually shook. His knotted shoulders, particularly the one he'd injured a couple of years ago—a very long couple of years ago—ached with a grinding heat.

He closed his eyes, absorbing the quiet, the stillness, the reduction in the level of tension in the room. He could hear nothing but the sound of his heartbeat and Valerie's shallow breathing.

He opened his eyes, turned slightly and met her widened gaze.

Valerie felt as though the earth had stopped spinning and she had somehow been thrown clear of any gravitational pull. She had already recognized Perry's strength, had seen firsthand his incredible patience and durability. But not since she was a little girl and her father had routed a gang of teenagers that had been tormenting her had she witnessed such implacability.

He was studying her now, a slight smile playing on his sensuous lips, and nothing beyond a slight weariness and an easy camaraderie showed in his eyes. But she knew a different side of him now. He was tough in a sense of the word that she was unfamiliar with. Fenton had recognized it, Janes had even quicker. So had she, and now she felt a frisson of fear—strangely mingled with delight—work its way up her back and across her arms.

Masterful. The word bounced like a Ping-Pong ball in her mind, back and forth, making her hands tremble. In all her life, she would never have attributed the word to anyone. But it was the only word that fit Perry Deveroux. She wondered if it applied in all areas, then, perhaps because he was watching her so closely that he seemed to be reading her thoughts, she blushed to her very core.

He'd flatly stated that he would be staying the night, in this mobile home, with her. The notion jarred her, jolted her into an alertness she'd been far from feeling only moments before. But there was a sofa, she reminded herself firmly. Strangely, it was a depressing thought.

"Is there something cold to drink around here?" he asked.

It was such a mundane question, it should never have made Valerie's throat go suddenly dry. But it did. Her already unruly imagination pictured him lifting a cold bottle to his lips, eyelids lowering, corded muscles shifting.

"I'll get something," she said hoarsely. She set her laptop aside and rose unsteadily. She felt as though she were on a ship or a bucking plane, despite knowing that the trailer was securely installed and sturdy. She pulled open the refrigerator door and stood staring at the contents for several blank seconds.

She hadn't heard him move, and jumped what felt like a mile when his hand dropped to her shoulder. She couldn't have turned around for anything. She closed her eyes, conflicting sensations assaulting her mind, her body. The cool air from the refrigerator stretched toward her face, her chest, while the heat from his body bathed her back. The hand on her shoulder was gentle but solid, causing a molten heat to rise within her.

She was too vulnerable to this man, this mystery from the past. She wanted to know everything about him. *Everything.* The very idea made her knees go weak and caused a knot of tension in her stomach that tightened with every breath she took.

From the moment their eyes had met this morning, she had felt this tension, this inexplicable yearning for something she didn't dare put a name to, didn't dare even allow herself to fantasize over.

But as he had that morning, he was touching her, his warm hand branding her.

He's leaving.

Her mind fumbled with the meaning behind the words her heart was throwing at her. But with him so close, close enough to feel his heat, smell the faint traces of his cigarettes, she could barely think. Just knowing that he was only inches away from pressing against her made all thought flee, desire filling its void.

"I've got less than ten days," he said, not so much speaking as breathing the words into her ear. Her heart scudded in reaction. As if sensing her reaction, his hand tightened on her shoulder.

His breath played against her ear, the nape of her neck, hot, tickling, arousing. He murmured, "And I'm not saying that like a ship out with a come-on line."

He spoke so slowly, so deliberately that she knew he was telling the raw truth. Yet she also knew the deeper reality, could feel it in his grip, could hear it in his ragged, too rich voice. He was shipping out in the truest sense of the phrase. He was heading for an unknown destination, a point of no return.

All my life, she thought. All my life I've been looking for a man like this, a real man, a man strong enough to show emotion and strong enough not to fear my strength.

Why now? Why this way? Why was fate so terribly cruel? Why have him appear only to yank him from her grasp in less than ten days?

Better this man for ten days than any other for a lifetime, a small, utterly selfish voice insisted. Who knew how short or long life would be, anyway? She caught her lower lip between her teeth, fighting the urge to lean back into him, to feel his body pressed against hers.

"Valerie?" he asked, and her name was a host of questions, some primal, others as ethereal as the fabric of dreams.

"Yes," she answered, not even bothering to define the perimeters of her response. Like his question, it was too elemental, and stretched to meet the infinite promise she felt trying to burst into flames between them.

His hand released its fierce hold on her shoulder, and with no more than a fingertip, he slowly, gently turned her to face him. The heat from his body leaped toward her, enveloping her, invading her senses with its heady male scent, the warmth of a man pushed to the very limits of endurance. His hands lifted to cup her face and draw it upward. She looked up willingly, and knew her lips parted, though she felt oddly numb.

His eyes met hers and, as before, she felt as if she were drowning in the depths of richest mahogany.

"I've never met a woman like you," he said softly.

"No," she agreed, knowing it was terribly true. In this time, perhaps, there were many like her. Women who had battled the world of science, commerce or industry. Women who had overcome the effects of ridicule, child abuse, wife battering and rape.

The women of yesterday were gone. Even the most dependent of women now exhibited strengths and had rights

the women of yesteryear had never dreamed of. But in his
time...

He said no more, only nodded, as though understanding
where her thoughts had taken her, or perhaps, more realis-
tically, he'd taken her long silence as acquiescence.

Achingly slow, his face descended, and those firm lips met
hers. Feather soft at first, lightly questing, his mouth
brushed hers, as though testing, tasting the possibilities. He
murmured something indistinguishable, a mere breathing of
words, and she yearned to catch them, wished that she
could, just as she wished she could do something, anything, to stop his prison from shrinking.

At her moan, as her limbs trembled and that knot of tension coiled to its breaking point, his hands slid to tangle in
her curls and he brought her hard against him. She gave
herself to the moment, to the kiss, and she arched to him
willingly.

Kissing her now with passion she suspected had been
contained for far too long, using the electricity that sparked
between them to erase the day's trauma, he conjured utter
magic with his lips, his tongue, his hands. With hard, driving desire, his need called to her, and he groaned, a near
growl that Valerie could feel in his chest, could taste against
her tongue.

She had thought him masterful before, but now she could
feel the mastery, could smell, taste, touch the determination, the urgency, the power that drove him. And it fanned
her own desire like a hot wind to a forest fire. Without conscious thought, with totally matching fervor, she pressed
tightly against him, grasped his once-starched shirt with
both hands and clung to him, pulling him closer, deeper.

You'll be hurt, a small, uncertain voice whispered inside
her. *He's going to disappear, but literally, and you're going
to be hurt.* But in his arms, feeling his hands tightly gripping her hair, then lowering, following her curves with a
strong, forceful need, there was no hurt, only joy; no future, only now.

* * *

Holding her, kissing her, losing himself in an embrace like none he'd ever known before, Perry felt as he had when the strange array of rainbowed ribbons had swept through him—disassociated and totally complete all at the same time.

Her body against his felt so right, so perfect. Taller than most women, she curved into him in all the right places. And perhaps because she was taller, or maybe it was because she wasn't playing coy and innocent, Perry didn't feel as if he would break her. He'd never encountered such matching passion before. The very newness of the sensation threatened to dazzle him every bit as much as that rainbow cloud had done.

You can't do this, an inner voice cautioned. From the way that she felt, by the way that she tasted, it was obvious that she wasn't a woman for half measures, and in this hell that he'd come to, there were no guarantees of futures or even glimmers of green and bright tomorrows.

The other part of him, the baser, seize-life-while-you-can part, insisted that with the future a complete blank, he should take what he could while the taking was good. And how he wanted to do just that, to sweep the madness from his life in one swift, completely mind-obliterating night with this woman.

With her lips, her tongue against his it was so very hard to think, so very difficult to do what was right. But the thoughts had already intruded and Perry felt the furious first flare of passion giving way to something deeper, a stronger desire, a more gripping demand, a need for the total woman, not merely the incredible magic that sprang so readily between them.

Deliberately, reluctantly, he slowed his questing, molding hands. As in tune with him as she'd been from the first moment they had stared at each other across that lonely plain, she also gentled her fierce grasp of his shirt.

But though he knew he must, he couldn't relinquish the heady taste of her lips.

He thought he heard her whisper, "why now?" against his lips, the words as elusive as a butterfly's touch, and as poignant. He wasn't certain what she meant by them, but inwardly agreed all too sadly that fate, in their case, seemed worse than fiendish.

He had long held onto the thought that somewhere, sometime, he'd find a woman he'd want beside him forever. That was how nature worked. His parents had found each other, Dwayne had found Patty. He'd thought the process simple, that it was just a matter of time. That was all too ironic now. The one single thing he didn't have was time.

And that made things all the more damnable. For instinctively, he knew that nature's process *was* simple. Here was the woman he'd waited for. Wanted forever. It was that starkly clear to him. That plain. If he'd met her in the hospital recovering from his shoulder wound, he'd have courted her and eventually made her his wife. Because that was how life worked. Or how it had worked in his day, in his life.

But here, in this odd world, in this strange time that ticked minutes and lives away, cast him upon this peculiar shore for only a brief moment and offered him no promise of a future, there wasn't a prayer in a foxhole of having her.

Because he wouldn't settle for less than everything. All day long, lines from songs—the songs he and his buddies had clung to with every desperate measure of their heart and soul—had run through his mind, like reminders that he didn't belong here. Another did so now: "As Time Goes By." He'd heard it sung in a motion picture with Humphrey Bogart just a year ago. But the world didn't always welcome lovers. Not in wartime, and certainly not now.

What flared so brilliantly between them had to be left alone, couldn't be tampered with, because *he had no future*. And therefore, *they* had none. It wasn't in his nature to lure, to entice without promise. And he knew just from the way she kissed that it wasn't in her nature, either. And that was as it should be, even if it felt so brutally cruel. Some of the fundamental things had to still matter, had to still apply.

He raised his head with the greatest reluctance he'd ever known. But he couldn't bear to let her go from his arms. For the first time in all that long, long day, he felt safe. Felt he'd come home, was harbored from fate's dizzying storm.

He heard her shallow, rapid breathing, could feel her heart beating both through his hands and against his chest, giving him the oddest, most wonderful feeling that he'd somehow managed to draw her inside of himself.

Pressed so tightly to him, she'd have no misconceptions about how she stirred him, but what he couldn't tell her was how much more deeply she moved his heart, how much more he wanted from her than merely touching her, holding her, kissing her.

He'd seen one too many war-time affairs, known too many men who let the fear and loneliness and "the moment" carry them right into revealing the secrets in their hearts, and then, when they didn't come home—lost to a bullet or a bomb somewhere—a girl was left with the hardest memory of all: that she'd been loved and was now alone.

After being sent stateside, Perry had had to deliver too many dog tags, too many foxhole-written letters, not to know that it was better that a girl found someone else rather than carry that sad and lonely memory all her days.

But, dear God, how he wanted this woman.

"If we don't close this refrigerator door..." she began, and trailed off.

Yes, the lady had spunk. She wasn't any fool. She could see right through him. And she was giving them both a reason to break this too-sweet embrace and step apart. Aching for her, wanting her in a thousand ways he'd never dreamed he'd ever want someone, he managed to find the strength to lower his hands and let her go.

Perry turned away before Valerie could do more than catch a glimpse of his rigid-jawed profile. She was relieved.

The moment had been too intense, too fraught with a million wishes and longings for her to be able to look him in the eye. Where she had been vulnerable to him before, she was now raw. Where she had felt mere sympathy before, she was now thoroughly involved.

As before, she turned to the refrigerator, but this time didn't stare blankly at the array of drinks and foodstuffs inside. She couldn't see them through the haze of tears that stung her eyes. She grabbed something, anything, and stepped back from the cold, hoping he wouldn't still be standing there, praying that he would.

He wasn't. The door to the refrigerator swung shut, slicing through the chill air, cutting the pale blue light that had dusted his hair, played on his face. Valerie looked at the ceiling of the modular unit for a moment, willing the tears to subside, forcing her trembling body to obey the command of stillness. It took no more than a few seconds, but it felt like years before she was able to turn around.

She needn't have worried. Perry was across the room, sitting forward on the sofa, elbows on his knees, head in his hands. He was the very picture of a man in torment. She knew exactly how he felt; it was mirrored in her soul.

She crossed the room and pulled one of the dining chairs to face him. He didn't look up.

"Here," she said, holding out the bottle she'd taken by chance. It proved to be a beer.

He lifted his head then, and she saw his eyes focus on the squat, brown bottle. A small, bitter smile twisted his lips. "Beer. I was half afraid that would be gone, too," he said. He took it from her hand, turning it around to read the label.

Valerie didn't know what other things he'd decided were gone from his world. She wasn't sure, giving the tenor of the last few minutes, that she wanted to ask. She waited for him to speak, to let her have some glimpse of what was going on in his mind, if not his heart.

"Valerie?"

She wished then that he would look at her. "Yes?"

"How am I supposed to drink this?"

She frowned. "What do you mean?"

He looked up then, a gentle smile on his lips, the bitterness gone, the passion still there but carefully banked, ruthlessly shoved to some nether region of his heart. She knew such a sharp regret that it stole her breath.

"It's not open," he said. His smile broadened, but more in forgiveness and understanding than in any real amusement.

She took the proffered bottle and with a sharp twist of her hand, removed the screw-top lid. She handed it back solemnly. Such a little thing, she thought, opening a bottle. *But he hadn't known how.* How many proofs of his linkage with another era, with another time, would she witness in the coming days and nights? How long would it take her to forget them? *Forever.*

He stared at the open top for a long, thoughtful moment, as if thinking along the same lines as she, then lifted it her way in a somewhat apologetic salute before bringing it to his lips.

She had no need to imagine the way his lips would move now, or the muscles in his throat. She had felt them, had massaged the throbbing pulse in his jaw, had bent to the strength in his hands. She looked away.

"You saw something else before you left in 1945," she said. She was careful not to make it a question. He didn't answer. "Something you didn't want to tell me about this morning."

He made some noncommittal sound.

"Want to tell me about it now?"

"No," he said.

"Because it really wasn't important, or because you don't want to talk about it now?"

"Because I want to talk about you, about this time . . . about what happened over there by that icebox."

She looked his way now and was instantly sorry, for his gaze had been waiting to snare her. "It . . . it could be important," she stammered.

"Oh, it is," he said. "It's very important."

She realized he wasn't talking about whatever it was he'd seen on that 1945 desert floor. He meant something else entirely. And what she saw in his eyes took her breath away.

Finally, he spoke, and to her vast relief, his question was innocence itself. "Tell me more about this time of yours. Do you like it?"

She smiled. "Like it? I don't know. Does anyone notice the time they're living in?"

"I did," Perry said. "I noticed it. And there were a lot of things to like about it, wartime or not." He leaned against the sofa, dropping his head back, and shifted his gaze to the bottle in his hand.

His eyes glazed over and Valerie knew they were clouded with memory. "I heard some noise coming from Phil's machine this afternoon. It reminded me of the foundry back home, a million different screeching metal components all striking bare metal at once. He called it music. Punk rock...something like that. If that's music today, I think I'll pass. There's no romance to it, no urge to pull a pretty girl into your arms and swing her around a hardwood floor."

He swallowed some beer, then sighed.

"Phil's kind of music isn't the only kind nowadays," Valerie said, feeling oddly defensive of this era. "You can find almost anything at a music store."

"And dancing? Do you still dance?"

"Of course we do," Valerie said, but she no longer felt defensive now. She felt sad. He'd said the word with a note she'd never heard before, was positive she'd never hear again, a veneration, an earnest love that perhaps had been missing all her life. Had anyone ever simply taken her dancing? Just to dance? The answer was a wistful negative.

He met her eyes. "I'd like to take you dancing, Valerie. I'd like to see you on a golden dance floor, stardust in your hair. I'd hold you in my arms...we'd listen to Goodman. Yes, only the best..." He closed his eyes and hummed a long-ago, well-known theme. "And I'd tell you all the things..." He trailed off, then was silent.

Valerie watched him, knowing from the steady rise and fall of his chest, from his parted, suddenly vulnerable mouth, that he'd fallen asleep in mid-sentence.

Slowly, quietly, she removed the half empty beer bottle from his slackened grip. Unable to resist, she lifted it to her own lips, tasted him upon the rim and swallowed a small sip. It felt cold and strong, and tasted like the bitter tears she was shedding somewhere deep inside.

She took the bottle to the kitchen, drained it in the sink and set it aside. She moved on to the bedroom and gathered a pillow and blanket. She felt curiously on hold, as though her emotions had gone through too much and had checked out. Her mind felt sluggish and uncertain. The unfairness of this night, this day, chased the dog tail of her thoughts.

After arranging the pillow on the sofa, she tugged lightly at his shoulders, easing him to a prone position. His eyelids flickered and he murmured something too low to be discernable. She lifted his legs to the couch and swiftly undid the cumbersome laces on his shoes. He sighed deeply and gratefully as she slid the heavy shoes from his feet.

She made a mental note to see about getting him some new clothes to wear the next day. A slightly hysterical giggle threatened to escape at the sheer magnitude of the notion that he'd been wearing these for almost fifty years.

She spread the comforter over him and would have pulled away, but a stray strand of his short and sandy hair caught her attention and she bent to smooth it from his brow. It was softer than she'd imagined and silkier than it looked. And like the man beneath, it eluded her delicate touch.

"Don't leave," he mumbled, though his eyes were still closed.

"I'm not leaving," she murmured.

"I have the feeling that when I wake up, this will all have been a dream."

I'm afraid, too, she wanted to tell him. "I'll be right here," she said instead.

"Kiss me again," he said.

She leaned down and pressed her lips against his forehead. He was already warm with sleep. His brow furrowed beneath her lips.

"It's not fair," he said, his voice blurry with weariness.

"What's not?" she asked, though given the circumstances and her own torn and battered feelings, she could think of a hundred unfair things at the moment.

"We never even got a chance to go dancing, did…" Again he trailed off and didn't resume his sentence. He'd fallen asleep, slipping into his dreams and leaving her behind. As he would do all too literally in the near future.

Valerie straightened slowly, aware of how long she'd been awake on this remarkable day, how much she wanted and couldn't have, and depressed beyond belief. She pulled the string on the floor lamp and stood for a moment in the dark, disoriented, lost in thoughts so intense, so chaotic, that she felt she might never find her way out.

But finally, she turned and sought the solace of the large, too-empty bed in the adjacent room. She tossed her clothes into her plastic hamper, washed her face, dealt with her teeth and then, for a long while, simply stood staring at her bemused reflection.

It held no answers, only more questions.

When she slipped between the cool sheets, her flesh contracted and momentarily woke up, reminding her all too painfully of how she'd felt in Perry's arms. She willed herself to sleep, but perversely, despite the late hour, it eluded her. All she could do was play and replay the day's events, rerunning everything Perry had said or done, every gesture, every facet of his personality.

She wondered what he was dreaming about. Was he back in 1945, a million light-years away, listening to the music he missed, doing things the world had long ago forgotten? She lay in the dark, hearing not the crickets or the lonely far distant wail of a coyote, but Benny Goodman's orchestra.

And if she dreamed, it was of Perry Deveroux, and he had stardust in his hair and eyes only for her.

Chapter 7

Even after nearly fifty years, the desert dawn was still an amazing spectacle, Perry decided, almost as remarkable as his slide down the rainbow of time. First the night appeared to shyly retreat, slowly, sadly, like someone cast from the room, a pall left behind in his wake. Then, emulating the hundreds of thousands of waking folk, the sky seemed to stretch, and upon its limbs danced wondrous morning colors, rose, gold and richest violet, all heralds of the sun yet to be.

How could everything seem so peaceful, so calm, when his entire life had been turned upside down? He wondered if there weren't some sort of message in this; but which platitude served to decode it? *All good things come to him who waits. Time teaches all things . . .*

Perhaps the only timeworn phrase that really applied was one he had scorned as a young man but had understood readily enough just before the bullet that shattered his shoulder took him from the danger zone: *To everything there is a season, and a time to every purpose under the heaven.*

I don't understand, he thought, gazing out at the roseate horizon, looking up at the rainbow's end still very much in evidence in the sky above him. Where is the purpose? What is it? Why have I traveled so many years from home, from everything I knew?

If it were the purely selfish reason of connecting with Valerie Daniels, it would make sense in some queer fashion. It would make all the sense in the world. If that was the case, the magic, the rainbow's end would truly be gold. But he was denied even that solace. His sentence was short in this bizarre twentieth-century prison that wasn't of his own making. Ten days, he'd thought. Less now that a new day had dawned.

Why?

A musical motion picture that he had seen a couple of years ago captured his mind. A young girl, hit on the head during a tornado, believed she'd gone to another place far removed from her home in Kansas. She hadn't liked her home, but all she'd wanted to do once she was in this other place—an incredible, beautiful place—was to get back home.

Perry knew now exactly how she must have felt. This world was also incredible, strange and exciting. But the little girl in that movie didn't have the conflict that raged in him; she hadn't fallen for the cowardly lion, the scarecrow or that man of tin.

He remembered the actress in the movie. She'd been new, but boy, could she sing. She'd sung a song about going over the rainbow. Patty and Dwayne had run out and bought the record, playing it over and over. "Somewhere Over the Rainbow." Was that what he had done? Had he literally gone over that rainbow?

Had he traveled so far from home, so distant from all he knew, only to be teased with something he couldn't hope to find in his own time? And to be denied it here in this one?

Remembering the feel of Valerie's lips, recalling the way her vibrant body had curved to meet his, was he all that sure he even wanted to go back? No, he wasn't sure, but it apparently wasn't a matter of wants or human wishes. The prison—which, given Valerie's presence, mightn't have been so bad at all—was shrinking. He had less than ten days in this strange time. Less than ten days to come to terms with whatever it was he was feeling for Valerie Daniels.

However, there were a few things that human wishes could dictate, and one of them was the tests the boys in the suits intended to run on him today. They were definitely out of the question. Or, as he'd heard Phil say yesterday, "No way, José."

Valerie had to feel sorry for Bob Fenton. He didn't stand a chance against Perry Deveroux's smiling denial. Perry simply folded his arms across his broad chest and said, in much the same way he'd refused the night before but much more mischievously, given a good night's sleep, "No more."

Fenton had protested, but as Perry ventured, "Short of hog-tying me and pumping knockout drugs into my veins, I don't see that you have a whole lot of choice. And I'll guarantee it'll play hell with you if you try..."

No, the man didn't have much choice.

Fenton's crew had arrived shortly after eight o'clock, just after Valerie had initiated the automatic coffeemaker that intrigued Perry so. She'd sent him to the shower while the water ran through the filter and had smiled when he'd wanted to play with every gadget and device in the bathroom, laughing over some, frowning over others.

A night's sleep had apparently restored his good humor, his willingness to handle this strange new world of his. And this made Valerie even more determined to find some solution to his predicament. It wasn't often that she'd met someone who could face change with such easy good spirits, let alone changes this monumental.

The coffee was done long before he even closed the Plexiglas, shatterproof door and set the turbo shower in motion.

He appeared from the bathroom looking like a new man, complete with a nick on his jaw, a rueful look in his eye and a slightly dazed smile on his lips. Valerie had to look away, because the blush in her cheeks—partially caused by imagining him in the shower and somewhat engendered by an unnerving desire to fluff his slicked-back hair—would too readily betray her reaction to him.

She wasn't sure if she'd been relieved or annoyed when Bob Fenton and Aaron Janes had knocked, then entered their trailer.

But their visit didn't last very long. Armed with only a cup of scalding coffee, Perry routed them as offhandedly as a busy mother sends the kids to the backyard. Both men looked like children deprived of their favorite toy.

But Perry didn't send them away empty-handed. He gave them something new to play with: how to keep the news of his arrival quiet.

"You keep talking about secrecy," he said. "And you bellow about this and that ramification. Then you go right out and send away somebody who witnessed everything, not to mention that portal in the sky. Somebody must see it, if we do. I'm not the trouble, fellows, I can't go anywhere. At least not for about nine days, by everybody's reckoning. But I know Dwayne Roberts. He's a yakker from way back."

Bob Fenton actually had the grace to smile. "I suppose you're suggesting we bring him in."

Perry's eyes twinkled, but his lips didn't so much as twitch. "Well, *I* would. But then, I don't rightly know what all you boys have in mind. All I know is it doesn't involve any more of your medical and who-took-the-pennant-when-I-was-a-kid tests."

Nobody, least of all Valerie or Bob Fenton, was fooled by Perry's drawling, I'm-just-a-hick-from-1945 attitude.

"But I can tell you this, and seeing how good you are at organizing things, I think you can handle the job. I could do with a clean pair of duds and—" he held up one foot and wiggled his toes at Fenton "—I wouldn't mind a pair of sneakers. I notice you have them in adult sizes these days. Just not orange," he added wryly. "And some more of those lightweight razors. They are incredible." He rubbed his obviously nicked jaw and smiled. "But maybe some shaving soap."

Bob Fenton smiled in return and suggested—too innocently to be taken for anything but camaraderie—that perhaps Dwayne Roberts might still have some of Perry's gear at his ranch. "After all, he was the one who wouldn't let the Army declare you dead."

Perry winked at Valerie behind their backs. It was a wholly devilish gesture, and one that sorely tried her composure. How could he be taking all this so well?

And why wasn't he the slightest bit put out by what had transpired between them the night before? Lord only knew, she was.

In an odd way, once the pressure of trying to run a series of nonsensical tests on an obviously well man was off, Bob Fenton and his men seemed to relax. They got down to the business of trying to keep the ripples of rumor from spreading, and after some discussion, Aaron Janes was immediately dispatched to find Dwayne Roberts. The remaining two were assigned the duty of running the camp, a task that apparently suited them completely. They became so cheerful that for the first time, Valerie suspected she might actually end up liking one or two of them.

While all of this went a long way to lifting everyone's spirits, the news from Phil, Jack and George wasn't going to make any lips curve into smiles, least of all hers...or Perry's.

The chalk line was getting smaller. It was already two feet shorter in circumference than it had been the night before. And Jack Chew had startled them all by announcing a more rapid shrinkage than earlier anticipated. Unfortunately he hadn't kept his voice down, and Perry had overheard. From the glint in his eyes, Valerie expected trouble any minute.

She didn't stop to consider how she knew this, she simply accepted it. Her knowledge was akin to trusting the sun to come up or the stars to shine in the sky at night. Nine days of waiting would seem an eternity to a man of action.

Unfortunately the few number of days was also an eternity to a woman whose heart had been touched by that same man.

The three of them, Bob Fenton, George Franklin and Valerie, were all seated around the makeshift headquarters at the rough center of the oval, going over the new data presented by her team.

Perry shamelessly eavesdropped while pretending to fumble with what Phil called a pocket video game. The little, hand-held device reminded him a lot of Valerie's computer, but it seemed the macros were already stored in the case. The case itself was mystery enough. Phil had told him it was plastic. It looked nothing like the door to the shower, but that's what Valerie had called it, too. Unlike the shower door, though, this plastic didn't seem terribly durable in that it couldn't withstand high temperatures or extreme cold. Still, it was truly amazing, lightweight and apparently able to be molded into anything. He could see why Dwayne had invested in the stuff.

On the plastic case's miniature screen, little men ran around, charged buildings and bushes, and pictures in the game actually asked typed questions of the player. The questions were usually posed in medieval language. "Gentle Knight, wilt thou enter this castle?"

What kind of a world was this? The men were soft, the women strong. Windows, doors, barriers and computers were made of lightweight plastic, and houses had motors to take them anywhere. A small ranch was worth a bigger amount of money than he could even contemplate, and loans were freely available on something called revolving credit. From what he'd learned from Phil and George, the latest war had a romantic name and was largely fought via computer. And games like the one he held in his hand were supposedly played by adults and children alike. Hooey. He felt like he was stumbling through a forest of sickly sweet flowers.

And yet, there was something amazingly fun about it all. Then he glanced over at Valerie and changed his mind. There were certain aspects that weren't so fun at all, but downright terrible.

Earlier, George had hooked up something called a VCR and slipped a cartridge in. And there, on the screen, was a rendering of the arrival of one Perry Deveroux in full and glorious color. And there was Valerie, holding out a noticeably trembling hand, the expression on her face rapt with wonder and more than a hint of fear. How slowly he'd held out his own hand and taken hers. It hadn't felt all that slow at the time, Perry thought. And somehow, it had seemed far more important than this recording indicated.

This veesee-are showed what happened, but couldn't begin to reveal the depths of emotion. Perry had wondered then, and he wondered now, trying to get this silly game to do something besides what it wanted him to do, if this time also had machines capable of plugging in emotion. He hoped not, for that would be the final indignity. These people relied on far too many things, fascinating and intriguing those might be.

Take the printed sheets of data Valerie, George and Fenton were looking at now. There must be ten pages of numbers printed out in neat little columns, and what did they all mean? Every one of those numbers said that the original guess was wrong, that in less than seven—not ten—days, Perry Deveroux was either a goner, or going someplace, some *when* nobody could even predict.

He handed the game to Phil, who clucked commiserat-ingly when he checked the score. "Didn't get past the guard at the castle, huh?"

"Didn't want to go in the castle," Perry said absently.

"Eh? Why not? That's the object of the game. Go through the castle, fight the bad guys and rescue the prin-cess."

"The problem at hand's a little more challenging," Perry said, walking up to Valerie. He touched her elbow and wished he hadn't, for he was abruptly reminded of the way she'd felt in his arms the night before, the way she'd re-sponded to his kiss, the way he'd responded to hers. Hell, without her even turning, and her remarkable eyes not yet meeting his, he could already feel the sizzling energy run-ning between them.

He'd half-expected her to show some nervousness, maybe even a little anger this morning, especially in front of the others. But she hadn't. She'd only smiled at him easily, as though kissing with that kind of passion was a common-place occurrence for her. He'd been somewhat relieved by this reaction, but more than a little piqued by it, as well. Any woman he'd ever known would have been upset at what had happened between them.

She turned to face him now, that easy grin on her lips. But when her eyes met his, Perry suddenly understood that the smiles, the offhand comments, were nothing more than a facade, that she was again trying to match his moods and had masked her feelings every bit as carefully as he had. He knew, with absolute awareness, that while she might not feel any remorse or embarrassment—and certainly shouldn't—about the night before, she was far from unmoved by it.

The realization that she was just as affected by what they'd experienced, was, in fact, holding back on showing it to spare him, went a long way toward improving his day. He might not be able to do anything about the jam he was in, any more than he could ignore that unusual connection between the two of them, but he sure as hell didn't want to be the only one feeling it.

"What about turning those lasers of yours back on?" Perry asked her now. "Aren't they what opened the rainbow cloud in the first place?"

Valerie looked up at the portal in the sky. Perry followed her gaze. Though the data showed it was shrinking, to Perry it seemed just the same. The end of the rainbow, he thought again. And this time frame was the pot of gold? He looked down at Valerie's crown of golden curls. Could be. Could just be.

Bob Fenton suggested they try it.

"No!" Valerie said, and her voice carried a wild note of panic in it.

"I still say it's our only option," George said. He tossed an apologetic glance Perry's way. "After all, that's what opened the damned thing in the first place. Maybe the lasers could close it again."

"And what about Perry?" Valerie asked angrily. "If we do manage to close it, what happens to him?" She slapped at the printout in George's hand. "When that portal closes, so does this displacement zone!"

"You can't know that for certain," Bob Fenton said, looking at Perry not unkindly. "And it may just save his life."

"I categorically refuse to experiment with a man's life," Valerie said flatly. "Unless we have some idea of where *and when* he might land safely, those lasers stay *off*."

"Valerie," Perry said.

"What!" she snapped at him. When he didn't say anything, she took a deep breath and said, "I'm sorry. I just don't want to do anything rash."

"Look at it from my perspective, honey," he said, and immediately wanted to rewind his words, as George had done with that recording he'd shown him earlier. He'd unconsciously used an endearment he meant with every fiber of his being, but under the circumstances it was unfair to use it out loud—it only served to remind them both of the hopelessness of their situation. More than that even, she *was* looking at it from his perspective, and she had spoken out of fear for his safety.

But there was one little detail she was overlooking. "One way or another that portal is closing up. I'd just as soon take a stab at getting somewhere before it either shuts me out or decides I'm not worth shoving in some other corner of time."

"None of you are getting it," Valerie said desperately. She took hold of Perry's arms as if by touching him she could convince him. He didn't mind—quite the contrary—but she was wrong, he wasn't the one who wasn't getting it.

She shook his arm a little. "We just can't take that kind of chance. We'd never know if it worked or not."

"You might," Perry said. "Maybe you'll eliminate the portal altogether and I'll stay right here. You said it yourself, you don't know."

"But you might just disappear," she said, and now her voice was pleading, her eyes wide with distress.

He wished he could wipe the worry from her face, but there wasn't anything he could do or say that would accomplish that. Except what he'd done the night before. There had been no worry lines creasing her forehead then, only a dewy, heavy-lidded acceptance of whatever magic worked between them.

"Valerie, in less than seven days—and I would hazard a guess that it's going to be a lot less than that considering the rate of shrinkage—I'm more than likely to disappear, anyway. I don't know about you, but I'm not much of a man for sitting around smoking cigarettes and playing patty cake while waiting for the end. I lived through your laser-thing once, and I'll most likely do it again. But I don't want to hang around and just wait for it."

He wanted to add that he also couldn't stand being near her and not having her; and that was what the lack of future dictated for him, for them. But there were too many other people listening.

"I can understand that," she said, "but—"

"Somehow your experiment got me here. I'd feel a whale of a lot better if you were running the show to get me out. This piddling around doing nothing is like chanting in a drought, waiting for a rain cloud. I'd rather put my trust in some of these machines you people have in such abundance."

"He's got you there, Valkyrie," Phil piped up from behind them, and Perry could have throttled him.

He shot the man a quelling look. Startled, but receiving the message loud and clear, the young physicist stepped back a full pace.

"I'm sorry, Perry," Valerie said. "I can't, in all good conscience, agree to such a plan without knowing something more, something that will tell us you jump somewhere safely."

Perry thought for a long moment, a thousand images flitting through his mind, then, making a decision, said softly, "What if I can offer you that proof?"

The silence from the three people facing him was so intense that Perry could hear the beeps and blips of Phil's pocket game.

"You did leave something out, didn't you?" Valerie asked softly. She didn't sound particularly angry about it, but Perry avoided looking directly into her eyes. He knew her too well already. Her kiss had told him how she would react: without reservation.

He shrugged, trying to be casual. "It didn't seem important. No, that's not exactly true. The truth is, I saw something, and when I saw it, I thought I was either losing my mind or—don't laugh—I thought it was some kind of an omen for my death."

"What did you see?"

"Myself."

"What!" The others echoed Valerie's shock.

"I saw myself. Standing there, not twenty feet away, but through some kind of mist, or haze. Right after the photographer called me." Perry looked up at the portal, and added, "It was as if I were seeing something through that."

"You saw yourself," Valerie repeated, frowning heavily, chewing on her lower lip. Did she have any notion how sexy that was?

"There you have it, Dr. Daniels," Fenton said.

"I don't have anything," Valerie said. "Yet!" She leveled a hard look at Perry. He could well imagine that such a look would subdue most people, particularly men. For some reason he didn't bother to analyze, it had just the opposite effect on him. He had to bite his cheek to keep from grinning.

She fired rapidly, "How long did this vision last?"

"I don't know," Perry said, firing right back and enjoying the exchange tremendously.

She gave an exasperated sigh, and he added, "That's when you folks invited me to drop in."

The glance she shot him then was pure venom. He couldn't hide the grin this time.

"You saw yourself, but before your other self disappeared you came to this time," she said slowly.

Something about the entire bizarre conversation made Perry want to laugh. They accepted everything so easily in this time. *His other self.* "That's about the size of it."

"That doesn't prove anything, then," she said.

"It sure as hell does. It means I was *there* after I was here," Perry said, any thought of grinning wiped out.

"Yes, but—"

"But nothing, Valerie," Phil had to put in, "I agree. He went back. It's that simple."

Valerie turned on her staffer with all the frustration and uncertainty she'd obviously been holding in since the previous morning. Perry thought that if she hadn't, he would have. But he didn't much care for what she had to say.

"Perry Deveroux was never seen or heard of again after July 16, 1945! I don't care how many images of himself he saw that morning. He didn't stay there!"

"How do we know that for sure?" Jack asked, joining them.

Valerie turned with exasperation. "*Et tu, Brute?* I suppose you're going to rewrite history?"

"Well, actually, until yesterday, I would have said that while time travel was theoretically possible, the odds against making it happen were astronomical. But Perry's here. So if time travel's possible, why can't the past be changed?"

"Because if it could, the files on Perry Deveroux wouldn't say that he'd disappeared but that he was right there along with everyone else. And we wouldn't have done all the research for this project, and Dwayne Roberts wouldn't have spent so much time looking for his friend, and none of us would be where we are right now because Perry Deveroux wouldn't be here and—"

"And you're confusing me," Perry said. "This is that paradox thing you were talking about this morning, George?"

"You got it. Don't get mad at me, Valerie. I was just posing a theory."

Valerie sighed. "I know. I'm just frustrated. There's got to be something that'll give us a clue as to what we can do to insure Perry's safety."

Perry was all for that, but he was also for taking charge of his own fate. One look at that narrowing series of chalk lines was enough to give him the willies, and he, for one, wasn't about to sit around and wait for his body to do a disappearing act. He wasn't any Harry Houdini, but like that famous escape artist, he wanted to have a hand in breaking out of this squeeze.

And the only way he could see of accomplishing that was to have Valerie turn those lasers back on.

"Could we talk in private for a few minutes?" he asked, hoping that if he talked with her alone, just the two of them, she might listen.

She shook her head, as if suspecting that his methods would be less than scrupulous. Arms wrapped tightly across her chest, her jaw squared, she looked like she was digging in her heels. Clearly he had his work cut out for him.

"Please," he said softly.

Finally, searching his eyes and seeing the desperation under the request, she nodded and allowed him to propel her to her mobile unit. He didn't say anything until they were inside and out of the blistering heat. The chill of the air-conditioned room was not only a welcome relief, but still somewhat of a miracle to Perry. This was one thing he could get used to, he thought.

Valerie was another.

"I can't do it," she began before he could say anything, and for a split second he thought she'd been reading his mind. He half wished she could, it would make convincing her so much easier. And then he was doubly glad she couldn't, for she would see all the things he was hiding from her, trying desperately to hide from himself.

He held out a chair for her, then sat down at the table facing her. Placing his hands on the table, he said urgently, "You've got to try, Valerie. Please."

"Perry...don't ask me to do this. It's not fair." The plea in her eyes was almost enough to dissuade him. But this was his future they were talking about, his need to *do* something, not to simply let fate gobble him up without putting up a fight.

"Nothing about this is fair," he said.

She looked down at her hands, her dejection underscoring his words.

He continued, "Look, here's what I see happening. You turn on the lasers, I go somewhere. Or you turn them on and nothing happens. But if you don't, what's going to happen? This little prison is going to get smaller and smaller until the very ground I'm standing on is going to swallow me up. Phil was saying just a few minutes ago that the chalk line is already so close to the Warhawk that it's likely to slip away any time now.''

At her convulsive, instinctive rejection of the reality, he hesitated, then decided to go for broke. ''God, Valerie, I feel like I'm on a raft surrounded by sharks. And any day now, the raft isn't going to be there.''

''So you'd rather jump in the water and swim for it?'' she shot back sarcastically.

''That's right.'' There was no other way to put it. ''Believe me, I'm not too keen on the idea, either, but it beats staying on the raft watching fins circling me.''

She shook her head, though whether it was in negation of the idea or his imagery, he couldn't have said.

Finally, she said, ''But what if there was a way to rescue you?''

''Name one,'' he said. He hated pushing her. It not only wasn't his style, it wasn't totally fair, but she had to see this from his point of view.

''You know I can't. But—'' she held up a hand to keep him from interrupting her. He fought the urge to take that slender hand and clasp it tightly to his chest.

She continued, ''But we can at least try. Jack is working on a program right now that projects the scope of the portal, approximates what might be on the other side of it, how far and wide it might stretch, if it stretches at all. If he succeeds, and if we reap some more data on that thing, we may be able to at least have some idea of where to go next.''

''And how long will this take?'' Perry asked.

''Tomorrow, the next day, maybe,'' Valerie said. She chewed on her lower lip. That betrayal of her worry decided him.

''I'll make a bargain with you, Valerie,'' he said. He longed to reach across the short span separating them and touch her in some fashion, but he refrained. He had the strong feeling that if he touched her now, he wouldn't be able to stop.

"Here's what I propose," he said instead. "I'll stop pushing you—and stop Fenton and everyone else, too. Until day after tomorrow."

The look of relief on her face almost made him decide to forget the rest of his bargain, but he knew he couldn't do that. "But if no new data turns up, we do it my way. Okay?"

"But—"

"Is it a deal?"

"I don't like it," she said.

"Hell, Valerie, do you think I do? I don't like any of this. It goes against everything I've ever known," he exploded. At the stricken expression that crossed her face, he shoved to his feet and turned to look out the window.

He couldn't let her think he'd included her in that dislike. If ever there was a time that he had to go against his instincts and let her know what he was feeling, it was now. He groped for the words and suddenly knew there weren't any right or wrong things to say, only the truth.

"I didn't mean you. You know that. And if you don't, you should. But you're also the one aspect of this whole thing that confuses me."

"Why?" she asked. He could hear the pain in her voice, and it wrenched at his heart.

Damn. What could he possibly tell her but the truth? Raking a hand through his hair, he said, "Valerie, when a man kisses a woman like I kissed you last night, there should be some kind of future to take her to. Not only do I not know where—or *when*—I'm likely to be in less than one week, I don't even know if I'm going to be alive!"

"Is that why you pulled away last night?"

He didn't dare turn around. She'd see every raw and tangled emotion spelled out on his face. "Mostly. Yes."

"You want to know why I let you?" she asked.

If she'd thrown a bucket of ice water on him, he couldn't have been more surprised by her question. Why *she* let *him?* He turned around.

"I knew what you were feeling. I *knew*. And I also knew that tomorrows matter to a man like you. I realize we barely know each other, but I believe I understand you." Her eyes blazed with a fiery combination of anger and want and an almost tangible deep, deep well of pain.

She continued, "I'll tell you something, Perry Deveroux of 1945. I need tomorrows, too. And promises, and possibilities, and . . . and all the things that mean s-some kind of a future."

"I know that, Valerie. Why do you think I stopped when I did? Why do you think I've been going crazy trying to stay away from you? To joke, laugh, anything to keep from spilling my guts?"

She drew a deep, shuddering breath and met his gaze with a rock-bottom sorrow. "What happened yesterday made me realize I've been so caught up in trying to unveil the mysteries of the universe that I've forgotten, or maybe plain lost, the sense of wonder I used to have over the fundamental mysteries of life. But you brought those with you, Perry."

"What mysteries?" Perry asked, thinking he knew but needing to hear them, anyway. He purposely ignored the part of him that warned he was playing with fire. He should stop her now, halt any further intimacy between them, before it was too late.

"Things like futures, the day-to-day details of life. Love. All the fundamental things that no one can predict, no one can promise."

"But there has at least to be a sense of future before any of those things can work," Perry said intensely. They were no longer talking about vague concepts.

Valerie nodded, her eyes closing, then opening again, glittering with tears. "And I know we c-can't have that. I *know*."

Her voice cracked, but she resumed hotly, as though angry with herself for crying, angry with him for forcing her to such a state. "I can almost face knowing that you're going to go away, but I can't face not knowing if you're going to be safe, not knowing if you're even going to—"

She broke off, tears all but leaping from her eyes. She sprang from the table, turned her back and swiped furiously at her face.

Valerie would have said that yesterday was probably the worst day of her life, if not also the most stunning, the most fascinating and the most confusing. But today was worse. And what Perry wanted her to agree to was against every tenet she held dear, every truism she adhered to in her scientific research and experiments: safety first.

And yet, he was right. There was—at this point—no safety zone. His analogy about the sharks circling the raft was all too horribly appropriate.

Now she was standing with her back to him, the memory of his tortured bargain indelibly printed on her heart, the vision of his shocked features when he'd turned to face her forever etched on her soul.

How could she have bared her heart to such a degree? She would never have done so under normal circumstances. But then again, these could hardly be considered normal, and Perry was anything but an ordinary man.

"Valerie...?"

Despite the softness of his voice, she knew he was mere inches behind her. It was as if her entire body responded to his proximity. She could feel the current that ran between them pulling her. *Don't touch me,* she willed, *because if you do, I'll come completely unglued.*

She hated to cry, hated to break down. She despised the lack of control. But again, this wasn't an ordinary circumstance. What he was asking her to do was intolerable. What he assumed about her, that she couldn't see things from his point of view, was so very, very wrong. Why couldn't he see it from hers?

"Valerie, do we have a bargain?"

Much as she didn't want to attempt any more experiments—this was Perry's *life* they were talking about—and much as she wished she could simply say no, this was Perry asking. He didn't ask for much, hadn't asked to be brought here, had tolerated all done to him, hadn't even raised protests that might be considered his due.

Surely he deserved the right to dictate his own fate. She couldn't deny him that. Couldn't, in all honesty, deny him anything.

Even if it meant that he might go away that much sooner.

Heart heavy, her throat closed with suppressed emotion, she managed to choke out, "All right. Yes. You've got your damned bargain. You let me have two days to try... and if I fail... you can swim for it."

Valerie had steeled herself for the metallic whisper of the door opening, had already ached in preparation of hearing his departing footsteps, so she wasn't ready for the touch of his hand at the base of her neck.

A low moan escaped her lips and she felt a shiver run across her shoulders. She knew she should step away—jerk aside perhaps, or whirl indignantly—and snap at him for using this unfair advantage. Wasn't it enough that he'd asked her to all but throw him to those sharks he'd painted so vividly? Did he have to torment her, as well?

"Valerie...?"

He'd only spoken her name, letting it fade from the air in a question, yet the very timbre of his voice, the rough, choked quality in that single word told her more clearly than any impassioned soliloquy might that he was as tormented as she. If not more so.

She could no more have resisted the question, the poignantly unasked query, than she could have lashed out at him. As if sensing her equally unspoken answer, his fingers trailed up her neck, lightly, scarcely touching, as slow and delicate a graze as a dream and just as elusive.

She shivered. Her body seemed both chilled and over-heated. Her breath tangled in her throat, and her lips were suddenly dry and trembling. Instinctively, reflexively, she leaned into him, needing to close the distance separating them.

"Valerie," he whispered, and this time no question punctuated her name, instead she heard decision, a ragged note of desperation that matched the fervor his touch had roused in her.

His lips replaced the tracing fingertips and the very heat emanating from them made her dizzy. He brushed his teeth along her sensitive nape while his hands ran the length of her suddenly leaded arms only to sweep back up and into her hair, across her flushed cheeks and gently, smoothly across her exposed and vulnerable throat. And lower, no longer with fingertip delicacy, but with firm, bold strokes, actively questing now, molding her form with the surety of a master sculptor.

Her head dropped against his shoulder, granting him even greater purchase. His lips continued their slow and deliberate onslaught, moving over her shoulder and pressing against the throbbing pulse in the sensitized hollow of her throat.

Involuntarily she turned to face him, her head thrown back, her throat bared to his lips, her fingers clinging to his arms, seeming to rise of their own accord to encircle his neck, draw him even closer.

It wasn't fair, she thought hazily. No one should have such power over someone else. But an inner voice insinuated that power wasn't the real issue, it was the awareness that she was vulnerable to him and that he would soon be leaving. One way or another, he would be gone from her life. That was what wasn't fair, that he should be the one to open this glorious feeling for her and have to leave.

With a groan, he dragged her against him, holding her tightly, raising his head and pulling at the cool air like a man who had run a hundred miles to be with her. Hadn't he almost done the same? Hadn't he come forty-eight years worth of miles?

He lowered his eyes slightly, meeting hers, and in those brown depths she could clearly read his need, his confusion and a multitude of things he would never fully express. He couldn't. Not as things stood between them, not with his all-too-imminent departure creating a veritable wall of uncertainty.

Unable to withstand the agony in his gaze, she closed her eyes and pressed forward, her lips parted, her ache beyond reason, her need for his kiss beyond rational consideration. She'd tasted him once, had met his confusion and weariness with dazed wonder. She had to know him now, at this moment, when determination warred with uncertainty, when tomorrow loomed too greatly on the horizon and yesterday was fifty years gone.

He held her almost angrily, and a low growl escaped him as he fiercely seized her lips with his. Roughly, as if impressing her with his entire being, he kissed her, his lips grinding against hers, his tongue stealing every vestige of her secrets, his body pressed so tightly against her she would have felt bruised had she not been doing the same to him.

This wasn't a kiss, she thought wildly, it was denial. It was the hard, raging denial of the knowledge that they were, in some cosmic reality, meant to be together and that fate wasn't playing fair. It was the atavistic, primal scream of two people driven beyond endurance.

He dragged his lips from hers and held her away from him, and she could feel the intensity of his emotions through his fierce grip, the trembling in his hands. His eyes met hers, his gaze darkened, shadowed with the unvoiced rage, the unspoken fears. What was he reading in hers? Was he seeing the matched anger, the desire, the sorrow over the sheer magnitude of the unfairness that would soon separate them?

"I hate this, Valerie," he said. She knew he didn't mean the kiss, the feelings that ran too strongly, too easily, too fiercely, between them. She knew he meant the lack of future, the unfulfilled, molten ache that nothing could assuage.

He released her slowly, the anger draining from his face to be replaced by a hard despair, an almost weary acceptance that it wasn't enough to want, to crave with every fiber of his being what she so obviously wanted also. A future had to accompany that need.

Gravity pulled at her, and reality reasserted its heartless control. She longed to stop him from retreating, to step back into his arms, forget tomorrows and promises of pretty futures and keep him with her until all dreams were laid to final and penultimate rest. But she held herself still, clamped her lips against the cry of protest.

She had brought him here, and she had to let him go without causing him any more heartache than she already had. But she couldn't watch him leave now, couldn't stand there knowing that the only real passion she'd ever known would be leaving permanently in less than two days' time. She dragged her gaze from his, and slowly, feeling as if she might be making the single biggest mistake of her life, she turned her back toward him, hiding her suddenly filled eyes, her breaking heart.

She didn't turn around when she heard him leave the trailer. It would have been too much like watching him disappear from this time. Their time. It would have been too close to saying goodbye.

Chapter 8

The trouble with bargains was that you all too often regretted them within minutes of making them, Perry thought. And this one was no exception. It wasn't that he no longer wanted to control his own bizarre destiny; he did. But the strain of waiting was getting to him, and the dark shadows beneath Valerie's blue eyes all too clearly told the tale of her inability to come up with answers.

The two days were nearly up, and everyone seemed testy. Tempers were noticeably short. And for Perry, patience felt like something other people possessed. Granted, he probably had the most to worry about, since it was patently his hide that was in jeopardy, but he knew there wasn't a soul on this flat stretch of desert that hadn't tried to put themselves in his place, even Fenton and his boys. But none of them could.

Unlike him, the rest of them had the future to secure, careers to uphold, jobs to maintain. He was the only one who had nothing, an absolute blank nothing to look forward to. And he'd had two days of living hell just being around Valerie, wanting her as much as he wanted that sense of future restored, but not being able to give in to that want because the hereafter was as dark and mysterious as that damned portal.

Yesterday Phil had woken them all with screams to get outside quick, to *look!*

The P-40N Warhawk was gone.

The crusty sand was still dented where the Warhawk's wheels had rested, grooved by the tail gear, but the plane was nowhere in sight. The chalk line had eaten it, stripped it clean from the suddenly not so safe zone.

Its disappearance had put a damper on the team's enthusiasm, depressed their youthful spirits. It had done a lot more than that to Perry. Every time he glanced at where the plane had sat, a mystery just like himself, he was struck anew by the sensation of falling off a cliff. He had to look away swiftly, trying not to add to that dizzying spiral of fear with an even greater despair.

Now that the oval was notably smaller, chalk lines closing in and the Warhawk noticeably missing, Perry was all too conscious of a general avoidance of his eyes. No one wanted to come right out and say that they didn't know anything more than they had from the first moment of his appearance, but it was painfully obvious that this was the case.

Adding to his own personal frustration were the nights. It was bad enough to be standing around in Dante's limbo all day long, but the nights were the worst. That was when homesickness slipped in and hit with all the force of a Shoeless Joe pitch. That was when a million wants and needs he didn't dare consider came to haunt him.

And, of course, since he was trying to be wholly honest with himself, the true cause of all his frustrations, day and night, was one Dr. Valerie Daniels. She was both the sole delight and the darkest part of his days in this curious place. Having to watch her throughout the day, near enough to touch her, often close enough to catch a hint of her elusive scent, was slowly driving him insane. Having to witness her failure to find answers to his dilemma smudge her eyes with sleeplessness, and the futility of her search bow her shoulders as if the proverbial albatross hung around her slender neck, he felt constantly tormented.

At night, a single thin wall separating them, hearing her vain efforts at respite, he was all too aware of her body. Always remembering the sympathy, the surging electricity that inexplicably ran between them, he found himself digging his hands into the sofa to keep himself from going in to her.

He'd been as careful as she, in these past two days, not to come into physical contact, even to the point of deliberately placing either Phil, Jack or even Bob Fenton between them whenever they talked. Unfortunately, two days of such studious avoidance only served to increase the need within him to give in to his desires. And it was showing. Just this morning he'd caught Bob Fenton's speculative regard as the man slowly looked from Valerie to him. He hadn't said anything, but it was obvious he was aware of the tension between them.

And Phil, whom Perry had initially written off as a prime example of comic relief, had actually grabbed hold of his arm last evening with so total a sympathy that Perry had found himself inwardly apologizing for his earlier thoughts about the man. To his surprise, it was also Phil who had rounded up some extra clothing for him.

Phil had first offered some of his own clothes, and since they were close to the same height and weight, the exchange made sense. But Perry couldn't bring himself to put on what he still thought of as circus pants or island shirts. Unoffended, the young man had taken some notes and given one of Fenton's boys a list of items for Perry.

"I have an older brother," Phil said when Perry expressed his somewhat chagrined relief over the set of clothes the man had secured for him. "A real yuppie type. A lawyer. He wears the new style like you."

Perry was stunned by the word *new*. But the clothes Phil had sent for had fit amazingly well, if a little snugly across the shoulders. Four plain cotton shirts, happily with button-down collars, and three pairs of tan cotton trousers with tidy pleats and cuffs, assorted socks and underwear comprised the inventory. He'd tried one of Bob Fenton's ties, but as it was much shorter, wider and brighter than he was used to, he'd passed and gone back to the one he'd brought through time.

No one else in this area seemed to be constrained to wear one—much as they seemed to have given up the wearing of hats in favor of plastic sunglasses—but he felt more comfortable wearing both. And with the use of the world's lightest disposal razor, which he still found amazing, Perry felt dressed and able to face these odd days.

There were, he decided, a few good things about this time.

But external trappings didn't make him feel any better about his situation. And the worst part of his situation was his feelings about Valerie Daniels.

He wished again that Dwayne Roberts was here. Dwayne was the one man Perry could honestly talk to. The only contemporary who spoke the language of his youth, understood the words of his time. But the agent sent to fetch him hadn't yet returned.

And now, T-Minus fourteen hours to his departure—Valerie's end of the bargain soon to be paid—he might never be able to see Dwayne again. Or this time. Or Valerie.

He watched her now, aware of her refusal to meet his eyes, understanding her more after the scraps and bits he'd caught of George and Phil's films, after having devoured the magazines and books they'd brought with them for entertainment. His favorite book, though, was a paperback copy of the *World Almanac*. He'd discovered that most of his catching up on fifty years' worth of history had been focused on social issues, on growth and decline of cultural mores. Real history, not merely the spanning of time.

Coming from a pretelevision era—something Perry had already discovered made him an alien in this time—he was fascinated by the changes he could see in the attitudes and sophistications of almost five decades of his fellow man . . . and woman. So much was indicated in these tapes and programs, about man's search for meaning, woman's striving for identity. He could see it clearly, and yet his mind rebelled against the comments that his generation regarded women as chattel, that men like him, men from his time, had taken them for granted.

In both wars, World War One and Two, women had been a necessary and vital force to the American and British efforts. The Women's Army Corps and the others were an integral, working part of the tide turning in favor of peace. And the women who had worked in the factories, sewing parachutes, or in the hospitals, the paper refineries, had worked toward peace every bit as hard as the men had. When did they begin to feel undervalued? When did men begin to treat them as though they had no brain, no depth?

And yet, he had to wonder if he would have allowed any wife of his to continue working. Would he? On the other hand, was it really a matter of permission back then, or had it been more a reflection of a particular thought process that had pervaded his time? And was it really so negative, the desire to provide? Was the real problem that it could be taken too far, that there was a fine line between providing for a woman and treating her as a child?

Valerie was so far different from any woman he knew that he had to concede there was some vital change in how men and women related. She reminded him most of women he'd known in the twenties, headstrong and brash, a generation of women that had known where they were going and how they were going to get there. But Valerie didn't have any of the wildness that had seemed to go hand in hand with the flapper girls.

She was utterly feminine, but with no coyness and seemed sublimely indifferent to the covert looks of all the men present—with the possible exception of himself. At the same time, she possessed an innate confidence that had immediately intrigued him, then, as these three days progressed, commanded his utmost respect. Her honesty, her integrity cried for equal honesty from him, from everyone around her.

She was a new breed of woman, the kind of person who would not only be a mate but a partner, not merely a wife, but an equal.

He'd heard stories from friends, men coming home to find their wives had managed perfectly well without them and recalled how daunted some of those men had felt, how confused about their roles, about their manhood. He thought of them now with sorrow. If only the men of the past could have seen what a woman could really be, could have gotten one glimpse of the women of the future, of Valerie Daniels, surely they would have embraced their strange new lives with enthusiasm.

And it was thinking such thoughts that made Perry realize just how far he'd traveled. Somehow, in just three days, his mind had come to accept the gap that he had crossed in time.

Two days ago he'd been almost shocked by how readily these people of the future accepted the notion of other selves, of time traveling, of his very presence in this time frame. Each new gadget or machine had not only thrown him, but made him feel dizzy and out of reference. But already he himself was separating the two eras into distinct categories: then, and now. In three short days, this odd time had become his present.

He no longer fought the mental battle with "today." He had somehow, shockingly, accepted this year as *now* and looked back on his former life as *then*. A very long ago then. Another lifetime that already seemed as though it belonged to someone else.

And for the first time, he found himself identifying with this era, this time. If it wasn't for his shrinking prison, he thought he could probably learn to like it here, to carve a life for himself.

Especially if that life involved Valerie.

But ifs were like wishes, and wishes were mere dreams. Because all the wishes in the world wouldn't stop that rainbow hole from shrinking, and all the dreams he might dream couldn't fix it so he could share a future with Valerie. It was that simple. And that sad.

In less than an hour, darkness would descend again and his last night on what Valerie called "this earthly plane" would slip away. The morrow would bring the lasers and his one chance of escape.

The trouble was, as it had always been, escape to where and when. And the terrible ache inside him wrenched anew at the thought of the sheer loneliness of his departure from this time . . . and one woman.

Valerie felt desperate. Two whole days and nights had passed and she was no closer to a solution than she had been the afternoon she'd agreed to let Perry jump in the shark-infested waters and swim for it. She hadn't slept in what felt like weeks, and her eyes were gritty with sleeplessness and the interminable sand. Numbers swam before her eyes, and her heart had long ago constricted to the point of unconditional pain.

No hope. Around and around in her mind the two words chased each other, driving away rationality, flailing her with her failure, with her inability to solve this particular puzzle.

Not five minutes ago, watching Perry light one of Bob Fenton's cigarettes, staring off into the distance he couldn't even walk to—didn't dare to attempt to stride toward—she'd had to choke back a sudden, overwhelming desire to kick and scream, to throw down all the negative data and storm at her crew for not finding an answer for her. At herself for not being able to wave a nonexistent magic wand and fix everything.

She'd only been able to swallow the rage when her mind had grasped the significance of her own thoughts. Somewhere between two nights ago and now, she had stopped searching for an answer for Perry and begun looking for one for *herself*.

Because it was no longer enough that he just be safe. She wanted to be with him wherever it was that he would go. *Whither thou goest...* Or she wanted him to stay. Either way, it didn't matter. But she simply couldn't face not knowing. Couldn't face never seeing Perry Deveroux again.

Her heart cried a protest, and her body responded with a muffled sob.

She'd failed him. She'd failed all of them. Herself most of all. There was no answer in the miles and miles of data they'd thrown into the computer. There were no promises, no threads of hope, no delicate whispers of tomorrow.

"I give up," Phil said now. His eyes were as strained and tired as hers. He stretched, a testimonial to the long hours, short supply of sleep and utter futility of their endeavors.

"I can't," she said tersely.

"Valkyrie," he said softly, almost too gently for Phil. "We've been over this data a thousand times. We've tossed in everything from the missile testing the morning of the test, to the position of the stars that day.

"And no matter what we do, each time we get the same answer. The portal is shrinking, and so is the displacement zone. We know the Warhawk's gone. And it's got to be somewhere, its mass can't simply have been wiped off the face of the earth, but we still don't know where.

"Perry's right and the data supports it. Turning the lasers back on is our only chance for a controlled jump."

"That's not good enough," Valerie argued. "Our data shows that if we turn on the lasers, we would possibly be sending him to the sun, or to a total vacuum. Or back to 1945—but we *know* he didn't stay there."

"Val," Jack Chew said sadly, "we're fighting a losing battle here. We can continue to give the computer input of everything under the sun, and including it, and we'd still have no measurable data... What's happened here has no precedent. *Time travel has never happened before.* The most we're going to do is what any scientist can do when faced with a total unknown, just record it and say we don't know *why* this is happening, it just is."

"That's not good enough. Let's go over the law of conservation theory again," Valerie insisted.

"Give it up, Valerie," George said, his deep voice harsh with unspoken sympathy. "The law only applies insofar as we've assumed that's what we've got here. It works only in the older, more concrete concept of what makes our universe tick. Obviously, this portal shows that there are other, completely unmeasurable phenomena at hand. This isn't so much the law at work, as the law dysfunctional."

"So where there is a dysfunction, there is a cause. If we determine the cause, we can—"

"You might as well say, knowing rain is possible, we can create it out of thin air," Phil snapped, then hung his head. When he looked up, Valerie was half afraid he would start to cry. Had she been pushing them all too hard, too fiercely? She knew they were trying their damnedest, were giving this their all.

But it wasn't good enough. They had to work even harder. None of them had a choice, least of all her. This was Perry's life, Perry's *future* they were talking about.

Phil said softly, almost pleadingly, "We've always known time travel was theoretically possible, but even with it staring at us in the face, we don't have the foggiest notion of how or why it happened. All we can do is repeat the procedure, or in some ways reverse it, and hope for the best."

Valerie swallowed her arguments. Her team was right, no matter how wrong it felt. Close to tears, and more frustrated than she had ever been in her life, all she could do was nod and wave a noticeably trembling hand at the equipment, indicating they should shut it down for the night. All except the ones monitoring that terrible portal.

Perry wasn't the slightest bit hungry, but he sat down to one of the microwaved containers of food he had managed to heat for the two of them. The contrast of the two distinctly different smells rising from the two dinners assaulted his nostrils. Getting used to the idea of eating hot dinners that put off no scent even minutes before getting to the table was still a difficulty. The food was good enough, especially to someone who had spent several years on K rations, but the lack of odor prior to eating was tough to get used to.

He'd never thought about it before, but half of his appetite was inspired by anticipation. He realized that he'd rather eat it cold, right out of the container, than suddenly have instant hot food. The scent of a meal in preparation was fully half of the pleasure.

He risked a glance at Valerie and wondered if some part of what he'd felt for her wasn't engendered by a measure of that same type of suppressed anticipation. Watching her pick at her food, her face tense and unhappy, he suddenly and bleakly knew that anticipation had never entered into what he felt for her.

For there was no anticipation.

Anticipation implied *later,* offered some notion of future, of coming together another time, and between them there was only the bitter certainty of never.

"I can't bear this," Valerie said abruptly.

Perry didn't demean the raw confession in her voice by asking her what she meant. He knew very well what she was saying, and more, what she wasn't.

"Don't, Valerie," he said softly, unaware until he said it that he was sincerely pleading with her not to go on. If she did, all the resolve in the world wouldn't be able to stop him from taking her into his arms again and spilling every drop of the emotion he had for her.

She fell silent, and though her throat worked for several seconds, as though she'd swallowed something so bitter, so unpalatable, she wasn't sure she could contain it, she relaxed somewhat.

After a few minutes, she asked in a controlled, tight voice, "Was there someone?"

"Back then?" he asked, not dodging her question, her obvious need to know, by pretending any obtuseness. It was as if they were on the same wavelengths. Even using such imagery vaguely pleased him. It was a future word in the mind of a man from the past.

She nodded. "Someone special, I mean."

He started to say no, then remembered that laughter he'd heard in the rainbow time on that faraway beach. He sadly realized at that moment that he'd never heard Valerie laugh, never heard her give in to the delight of simple humor. He knew she was capable of it, had witnessed it in the mischievous glances that first day, the look she'd given him when he couldn't open one of this time's bottles, didn't know how to work the multitude of lights in the bathroom or how to open the shower doors.

"There's never been anyone special," he said, wanting to add *until now,* but knowing how terribly unfair it would be. Thinking how unfair it was not to be able to say it, to be forced to silence by a scruple, he didn't elaborate.

"When I saw your picture in the files, the one of you looking out beyond the photographer—"

"The one he must have taken of me must before I disappeared," Perry interjected, and Valerie nodded again.

"That one, yes."

"What about it?"

She said slowly, "I took it home with me. I used to look at it before falling asleep at night."

Perry felt his breath catch in his chest. His heart started a slow, painful thudding. An image of his photograph on her bedside table, warmed by the glow of her night lamp, teased at his mind, taunted his heart.

"Why?" he asked, almost wishing she wouldn't tell him, despising himself for asking.

"I don't really know. I didn't stop to question it then."

"But you do now?"

"Yes," she said, but she didn't explain any further. For myriad reasons, the thought of her staring at his photograph at night, alone, her eyes blurred with sleepiness, her body beneath the covers of her bed, stirred him too deeply for words.

She said, "I thought...you looked lonely. Or maybe not lonely, but *alone*. Outside the others somehow. I thought the same thing when I first saw you here."

Perry couldn't think of anything to say. She was so right it knocked him sideways. He'd always, *always* felt that way. He'd been close to a few people, his parents, Dwayne, even a couple of Army buddies, but never, until this time, with this woman, had he felt connected. He had never had that odd sensation of bonding with another.

"It's funny," she said.

Nothing is funny anymore, he thought. "What is?" he asked, his voice sounding ragged even to himself.

"Until I met you, until I touched your hand that day, I had never felt alone. Lonely, sometimes, but never alone."

She looked up and met his gaze directly. The shock of the impact felt like a physical blow. Her eyes were sad, windows to her aching heart.

"Now I do," she said. "Now I feel so very alone." Her voice broke on her last word, but she neither cried nor looked away.

He no more could have resisted taking her hand in his than he could halt the strange destiny that awaited him on the morrow. On what would likely be his last morrow.

"I need tonight," Valerie said quietly. She said it without passion, without hunger, but with absolute conviction.

His hand tightened on hers convulsively. "Valerie," he began, but trailed off as her gaze continued to meet his unwaveringly.

She said, "I know in my heart of hearts that we were supposed to have a tomorrow. That we were supposed to have a future. *I know that.* And I know we both shied away from the lack of it the other night. It made sense then."

It still made sense, he wanted to tell her, wanted to silence her with the sheer, unbridled sense of it. But he couldn't speak.

Her eyes never wavered, never slipped from his. Her face was a study in vulnerability and strength, two seemingly opposing characteristics, but so thoroughly and perfectly blended that they made a mockery of all other emotion.

"Valerie . . . don't say anymore," he said suddenly, painfully, unable to bear this. No man could withstand such an onslaught, he thought, but, at her prolonged silence, he found himself nodding for her to continue, because he was just a man.

"Somewhere, in the back of my mind maybe," she said, "I think I was still hoping, assuming that there would be some kind of future. That everything would come out all right, that time and space would bend to accommodate us."

When he would have spoken, she lifted a soft hand to his lips and pressed lightly. It felt like a kiss, and again his breath caught, snagged in a web of desire, a snare of her making.

"But it hasn't. And I think I know now that it won't. There isn't any future for us."

It was so much of what he was feeling, so close to what he railed against with every fiber of his being, that he had to look away.

She let a sharp moment pass, then continued, "So I want the present. I need the present."

Her hand slipped from his lips, but his voice was frozen and his heart was pounding too raggedly to allow an answer. But her silence demanded that he again meet her blue gaze.

"Please . . . Perry," she said, all but unmanning him with the raw request, "if we can't have tomorrows . . . please give me tonight."

Chapter 9

Maintaining his hold on her hand, never releasing her tortured gaze, Perry rose, unsteadily he knew. Never in all his days had he been asked so sweetly, so hauntingly candidly for something he himself wanted beyond all thought.

His body ached with his need for her, and his mind churned with a thousand denials, a hundred had-to-remain-unspoken promises and vows. Her logic was wrong, her truth undeniable. With her asking she cut through every principle he'd ever had or lived by.

He let his want for her be his answer and felt as though he drowned in her acceptance.

Slowly, achingly slowly, she rose to her feet and stood facing him. He could feel her trembling, yet at the same time sensed her absorbing his own tremors. She remained still, motionless, as if poised on a sheer precipice, ready to fall at any moment into the deepest abyss ever created. Perry knew that fall all too well. And understood that she was ready to plunge headlong into the unknown, into a short, poignant present with him, for him.

Inch by inch, he closed the distance between them. He released her hand to cup her face and, almost fearing the fire that would flare between them, slowly lowered his lips to hers. Once there, he thought he could willingly die at that moment.

Stop now, that interior voice tried to roar, but it rose no louder than a whisper and faded at the touch of her hand on his cheek.

Softly, lingeringly, as though time was meaningless and this moment was an eternity in and of itself, she returned his kiss, letting him fully understand how great her fear was of the morrow, how much he was truly losing tomorrow morning, how precious she considered the present.

His hands slid to her hair, caressingly, and he reveled in the texture of her soft curls, the fullness of the short golden mass. Like silk, her curls slipped through his fingers, and he gripped more firmly, unable to resist giving in to the craving inside him.

Her hands massaged his cheeks, his neck, then gripped his shoulders with an unhurried and fierce possession, driving him mad with need, with the magnitude of the moment.

On her lips he couldn't taste the bitterness of the next day, the death of certainty, only the promise of their interval, the timelessness of togetherness, and he drew her honeyed taste inside like a parched and dying man clings to a single droplet of moisture. Her tongue was an anodyne to the pain inside him and her strong fingers a cure to the wound his psyche had suffered by the peculiar twist in his fate.

Valerie didn't feel the need to breathe, lost the last vestiges of any thought of a tomorrow. She gave herself over completely to the forever quality of Perry's touch, of his embrace. Their bodies pressed together in a primal, elemental rightness, meeting, all but melting together.

Ruthlessly, she shoved all thought, all fear of the future to the deepest recesses of her heart. For tonight, for all of tonight, he was hers, he was here, and she knew he would deny her nothing, just as she would give him anything, everything, in the brief span they had together.

This was their time. Their now. And if it was to be their only time, she would strive to make it as rich and as full as a lifetime. Tonight would have to be their forever, their eternity, and she would savor every second of it.

She moaned as his hands gently roamed every curve of her body, caressing, exhorting, demanding what they both so desperately craved. His breathing was ragged and harsh, and she delighted in this, and the way his brow furrowed, then smoothed, the way the planes of his face shifted as he kissed, as his desire raised, increased.

She felt all powerful and knew he felt the same, could taste it on his lips, feel it in his questing hands. And she felt all woman, and wanted him to know this, to touch this, to indelibly etch the knowledge on his very soul.

He groaned softly, more of a growl, and shifted to pull at the air like a man drowning. He buried his lips at the sensitive hollow of her collarbone, creating a riot inside her. His hands continued their quest, and he mouthed the buttons of her blouse, fanned hot breath across her already aching breasts and turgid nipples.

She felt as if she was naked already, as though the material of her blouse was as insubstantial as air and her body was no more corporeal than light itself. Oh, but how he could make that light dance.

His body arched and his lips trailed down, caressing the skin he'd bared, searching, seeking, making her weak with want, with need. He didn't fumble with the catch of her bra, but instead raised his hands to her shoulders and pushed the straps aside, trapping her arms in a tangle of blouse and brassiere. She could only moan as his lips snared a nipple and gently, firmly drew it into his hot mouth.

Her legs quivered and, at her apex, she felt sharp, molten need grow and spiral, coiling in her like a clock too tightly wound, desperate for release. His tongue laved, and she felt the rough-smooth touch of his teeth. She gasped for air, clung to the need to remain erect despite the sudden sensation of antigravity.

He dropped to one knee, his mouth transferring to her other breast as his hands, strong and sure, molded her waist, explored her buttocks, dipped lower and met between her thighs, pulling her to his chest, all but making her faint in the deep surge of desire he was commanding.

She murmured his name, or perhaps said it like a prayer, and he raised his head, his eyes glazed and heavy with need. She knew that want, that incredible ache was echoed in her own gaze. She could feel it drawing her lids closed, weakening her legs, her back.

Perry knew with absolute certainty, vowed it with everything inside him, that if there were to be no tomorrows, this single night of union was going to be the most important, the best of all he had in him to give.

Staring up at her, he felt as though he were seeing her again for the first time. Her glorious breasts, tip-tilted and full with want, teased his mind, taunted his tongue. Her bared, slender shoulders seemed to be begging for touch, asking for his kiss.

Her legs trembled around his hands, unconsciously squeezing together in a restless attempt to end the ache he'd created, and he gripped her more firmly. When her eyes closed and she moaned, not, he was certain, in any kind of hurt, but in the most elemental of pain-pleasure, he pushed urgently to his feet. He wanted to see her. All of her. And this odd dining room, with the remnants of an uneaten dinner on the small table, wasn't the right place.

She was nearly his height, this Valkyrie of his, but he felt invincible, completely masterful. Ignoring the slight protest of his once-shattered shoulder, he gathered her in his arms, not even able to laugh at his queerly quixotic romanticism.

There would be no future for them, no wedding night, no time to carry her over a threshold, so in this gesture, in this fashion, they were truly sealing all bargains, putting paid to all dreams and promises. Tonight he would carry her, hold her dear, cherish, honor and obey.

And tomorrow be damned.

Carrying her, feeling her body absolutely, but not conscious of any strain, he slowly crossed the kitchen and carefully walked through the doorway into the bedroom. Watching her eyes, willing her to understand the significance of this moment, he saw in her gaze her comprehension, saw in her sad smile her acceptance of their inevitable parting. And spiritually as well as literally, Perry carried his lady across the threshold.

He knelt and released her on the bed. With the light in the hallway still on, he could see her clearly and saw that her eyes were liquid with a combination of understanding and desire. There were other things there, as well, but they belonged to another time, a different place, and the determination to drive such thoughts from her mind shook him anew.

"You're such a beautiful, beautiful woman," he said, unfastening the last of her blouse's buttons and pulling apart the material to reveal her splendid body. He slid the blouse free of her arms, taking the bra straps with it, and then ran his hands along her silken arms, caressing her shoulders, her throat and finally her glorious breasts.

A sigh escaped her and she raised her hands to his chest, kneading, then trembling, working at the buttons of his shirt. He echoed her sigh and her long fingers trailed across his bare chest, nails brushing his mat of chest hair, his nipples. Desire flared in him, hot and urgent. God, how he wanted this woman.

He caught her hands, drew them to his lips and kissed her fingertips, drawing one into his mouth, sucking lightly, his eyes never wavering from hers. Her lids lowered still more, until the narrow apertures revealed only the softest hint of blue. He pressed her hands to the bed, holding them above her head. She lay as he placed her, arms stretched fully above her, trembling body beneath him. He slowly unbuttoned her trousers and undid the zipper. Like a man's trousers, they zipped in the front, but there was nothing manly about what lay beneath the silky material. Lacy underwear, as soft as her skin, concealed what he wanted to see, but he left it in place, confident that the time they had together would soon give him what they both wanted, needed.

She raised slightly to allow him greater ease at slipping the silky trousers from her equally silky legs. He tossed them somewhere, neither caring where they landed nor concerned with what might happen to them.

She lay on the bed, a golden shadow, the rainbow's end, arms still above her, her lithe body taut and waiting but with infinite patience. Her lacy bra, loose around her waist, hid her navel from him as her panties concealed other delights. He dropped his hand to her side, stroked softly, urging her to roll over. Slowly, taunting him with the lustrous profile of her body, she obliged him, leaving her arms high above her, fingers curling into the bedspread.

He swiftly unhooked her bra and pulled it free. He imagined he could hear her heart beating, but knew it was his own thunderous applause. The delicate, elusive scent of some kind of flower teased his nostrils, encouraging him to pull more deeply at the air, almost as if he were drawing her very essence inside him. He had to feel her, touch her, and he lowered his hands to her back, massaging slowly, learning her body, searching every curve, every nuance of her. He raised himself to the bed, straddling her buttocks, almost groaning aloud as she arched to meet him.

Perry's slow and careful massage told Valerie more clearly than anything could have done that he was totally in sync with her in trying to make this night last forever. Like her, he was ignoring the next day, refusing to acknowledge the hopelessness of the future. He was creating a tomorrow for them in the dark here and now.

A stray thought intruded. What if she were to become pregnant? She bit her lip, trying to resist the lure of this notion, of this latent promise. But it saddened her beyond reason because the very idea implied futures, and they had forsworn the vague uncertain hereafter for tonight. She regretted having given it an opportunity to intrude.

Perry's hands continued to mold, knead and stroke, and soon all thought was a jumble of pure sensation. The heat of his hands, the promise in his touch, a million dreams of life, loving and trust seemed to pass from his fingers, through her skin and into her heart.

Here in this bed, hearing his soft breathing, worries and the day's tension melting beneath his ministrations, she cast away doubts. No questions were allowed to linger. This was right in the truest sense of the word. Somehow, in some mysterious fashion, he had been brought through time for this one magnificent moment.

And the fact that he was leisurely, almost agonizingly patient about it only stressed the magnificence. Every stroke, every subtle shift in pressure was testament to his veneration, his adoration of her body, of what they were sharing, of what they already shared in spirit.

He shifted, pinning her legs, resting lightly on the back of her calves, and his hands lowered, as well, kneading her buttocks, sliding beneath her panties, his touch smoother now, no longer relaxing, but subtle, erotic and utterly enticing.

He slowly slid the silky fabric down, pulling it clear of her skin, and she felt as if it were not her body he bared but her soul. He shifted anew, and her heart pounded as he removed the final barrier that separated her from his gaze. Though she couldn't see him, she could feel the heat of his eyes, devouring her, burning her with his intensity. His hand lightly trailed across her buttocks, making her tense with anticipation and shiver with want.

The bedsprings creaked softly as he shifted yet again, and she wanted to cry out at the butterfly touch of his lips between her shoulder blades. Her hands bunched the bedspread convulsively, but he didn't move away. His lips, his tongue explored the highly sensitive areas on her back, the nape of her neck, the juncture of arm and shoulder. As if she were the very earth and he an explorer, he searched her hills and valleys, trailing her, leaving a moist, shivering path in his wake. He needed no map, prospecting freely, lovingly, wandering here and there with total regard, absolute adoration, seeking every treasure she possessed.

Her body became fluid and wholly responsive, her mind a mass of quivering jelly, neither thinking nor thoughtless, only receptive to his every touch, every flick of tongue, press of firm lips.

Finally, even timelessness ceased to matter. All she knew and wanted was this man. Love and desire commingled, intertwined and melded together, fusing into a need so intense, so strong that she could no longer be passive partner in a mating that was obviously and truly destined to take place.

She rolled over, and when she would have reached for him, he began his quest anew, investigating in earnest now, a controlled urgency firing his search, melting her, driving her nearly insane.

His hands cupped her face, and she opened her eyes to his burning, glassy gaze. "You will never know how much this means to me," he said. His voice was ragged with a thousand emotions, and his eyes told her even more.

"I know what it means to me," she answered, and saw by the jumping muscle in his jaw, in the suddenly liquid brown eyes how rightly she'd spoken. She longed to tell him more, to add the single phrase that would seal this moment, but knew she couldn't say it without crying, without shattering the brief time they had together.

For *love* was future, was commitment. And the only commitment they could make now was this totality, this sharing of heart, soul and body. One time.

She faced him, quiescent, totally aware of the covenant they were creating between the two of them. Her body thrummed to his, a harmony to a melody, the moon to the sun. Lines from a hundred love songs flitted through her mind, coalesced in her heart. There was nothing she would not do for this man, nothing she would not give him.

He slowly released her, pulling back, his hand deftly freeing his tie. But his eyes remained on hers, a slow, heated seduction even greater than the one his hands had achieved. She pushed his already unbuttoned shirt from his shoulders and imitated his earlier actions by trailing her fingers up his arms and across his shoulders.

His ragged breathing testified to his reaction, and though shadows hid his face, his dark eyes blazed with a fierce, raging need. Never taking his eyes from hers, he lifted first one arm then the other, unfastening his cuffs, letting the shirt slip from his arms. Her breath caught at the sheer force behind his want, the ache she read in his eyes.

He flung the garment aside as if it were offensive, and his hands blindly sought and found her bare breasts, cupping them lightly, molding them to his grasp, nipples trapped between thumb and forefingers, rotated gently, urged to even greater hardness. And she reached for his belt, for the zipper of his pants.

He looked momentarily surprised and Valerie smiled, knowing his conceptions of the past were asserting themselves, and she smiled even more broadly as he accepted that women had assumed greater significance in the bedroom, as well. But her smile faded and her mouth dried in aching need when this realization served to fan his desire, to increase the burning heat in his eyes.

He rose then, shedding his pants, his under things, and as he stood over her, his face turned away, his muscles rippling with the swiftness of his stripping, Valerie could see for the first time the scars railroading his left shoulder. He'd received a bullet in the trenches in World War Two.

Even as the sympathy rocked her, so, too, did her resentment of this reminder of the fact that he was a man out of his time, here for a few days only. Rising swiftly, holding out

her arms, suddenly chilled by a thousand lonely tomorrows, she moved eagerly into his embrace.

"Hold me," she murmured. "Don't let me go."

Perry held her tightly to his chest, folding his arms around
her, cradling her, molding her to his body. "I've got you,"
he said, and even to himself, his voice was harsh with the
choked promise of never letting her go. There were no
promises; nothing could be said that wouldn't be undone in
the morning, in the cold daylight.

For a shocking moment, his resolve wavered. What if he
didn't pursue his end of the bargain in the morning? What
if he simply decided to hang around and wait until the
shrinking portal finally snatched him from this time? He
would have at least another three or four nights with Valerie. He could have them. He knew it. He felt it, tasted it
and could breathe it.

One night . . . or a handful more. His body rocked with
indecision; his mind reeled at the torture. Any more and it
would kill him to leave her. It was killing him already.

His spirit raged with the sheer unfairness of having met
Valerie now, of falling in love with a woman who, in his
time, hadn't been born yet. A woman who, when he went
back—if he got back—he wouldn't meet until he was eighty-
six years old.

"Tonight is all that's important now," Valerie said, res-
cuing him from the agony of thinking about the future.

"It can't be enough," he said.

"It has to be," she answered, raising her golden face,
pulling his head down, meeting his lips with hers. "It has to
be everything."

He kissed her with the rage still warring within him, with
the fierce need to eradicate the future, eradicate the past,
their separate tomorrows. As if sensing his hurt, his anger,
she met him equally fervently, pulling him down, down,
drowning his hurt with her desire.

She was right, he thought dazedly, this was their moment, this had to be everything he had ever wanted to say,

do, believe with a woman. She was the one, the single woman he'd been waiting for, searching for all his life. And if they had no tomorrows together, this one single night would have to last forever.

No matter how unfair it was, no matter how selfish, he wanted her to feel him each time she closed her eyes, to remember his kiss, his touch each night when sleep overtook her, and he wanted to spend the rest of his days with her scent in his nostrils, her taste on his lips.

He bent her back, over his legs, sprawling her luscious body onto the bed. He slid down, conscious of the throbbing of his manhood, the echoing thud of his heart. He wanted to see her, to taste her, to give her the very best of himself that he possibly could.

Her already parted legs quivered at his touch, trembled at his kiss. And as he stroked her heated core, she gasped and spasmed slightly. Dipping a finger into the hot, sweet liquid that told him, as clearly as if she'd spoken, her need of him, he slipped even deeper into her. At her moan, as her body arched toward him, he lowered his head and finally, gratefully, tasted that which he wanted most.

As vibrant and vital as he'd thought her before, it was nothing to what he discovered in her now. Her silken legs wrapped around his shoulders, and her body thrummed to the rhythm of his tongue, of his lips. Never before in his life had he felt so strong, so masculine, so humbled, so gentle, so certain of the rightness of things.

His fingers inside her, he could feel the building of her tension, the strong, overwhelming compulsion to absorb, to open to him fully, totally. She tasted so sweet, so rich, and his own desire elevated as hers strove for completion.

"Please..." he heard her whimper, but he was too wrapped up in the wonder of her to stop, to ask what it was she wanted. And he didn't need to ask, he *knew*. Her entire body was shaking now, responding to his every movement, his every touch. Dewy and damp, her skin glistened in the soft light, and he wanted to drive her insane with want, delirious with culmination.

She murmured something incoherent, pleading with him mindlessly, her body bucked sharply, and still he didn't stop.

Valerie, lost in a universe of sensation, aware only of his fingers, his tongue, the cool air on her breasts, the love in his gentle, fiery touch, felt the too tightly wound coil in her snap. She couldn't hold in the convulsive shudder, the bucking beginning of her release. But he didn't slow, didn't shift, he only took her higher, his tongue finessing her to greater peaks, apparently not content to satisfy her with a mere mountain but needing to give her the entire range.

When she came down to earth, she found her hands were splayed on the bed, her legs limp and shaking, her head as light as if she'd been consuming champagne all evening. Nothing in her life had prepared her for such an emotional, physical onslaught. Her head spinning, her body still twitching, mewling hungry noises emitting from her lips, she shifted away from him.

He raised his head, his eyes darkened to black, a muscle in his jaw jumping with his fiercely checked desire. She raised leaden arms and beckoned him, grabbing onto him, pulling him closer, tighter, arching to meet him.

His eyes met hers as he slowly entered her, then he closed them and uttered a rough groan as she thrust upward, enveloping him, wrapping her legs around his, drawing him deeper, tighter, pulling him completely inside her. He muttered some imprecation as she pushed his locked elbows free and took his weight against her chest.

Reveling in the pressure of him, in his slow, deliberate, rhythmic thrusting, she dug her fingers into his buttocks, pulling him even deeper, driving him upward, inward. His face burrowed into the hollow between shoulder and throat and his lips mouthed her name, his want for her.

She felt joined to him not merely physically, but completely, soul to soul, a total exchange of everything they each had to offer. His scent became hers, her taste his. It was as elemental a communion as existed in this dimension. There was no sense of separation, no feeling of distance, only this rhythmic, spiraling sensation of slipping out of this time and space and melding together as though actually sharing atoms, molecules.

Faster and faster they rocked together, chasing the rainbow fabric of dreams, a culmination of some other reality, a reality that this one night would have to be all that could ever be.

She could feel, then hear, Perry emit a low, prolonged growl, and she clung to him, traveling with him, mindless, sobbing with exquisite need. Her body, so perfectly attuned to his, shook, and she knew he was going to take her over that glorious edge once again.

And faster, harder, deeper he drove, mindless himself now, completely caught in the snare of this alternate dimension, a place known only to lovers who truly love, a universe comprised only of ecstasy. Then, abruptly, he ceased all movement, a groan of deepest pleasures, wildest agony rippling through his body and into hers, through her heart, triggering her own staggering release.

Truly and really blending now, Perry arched above her, his face a mask of pain, his lips pulled back in a grimace, his arms shaking. And as they shook, her body convulsively enveloping his, shudders running through both of them, they each spiraled away from that divine universe of total union.

Still connected, bonded by both body and soul, they nonetheless were once again separate, and the sounds of the night again intruded on Valerie's consciousness. She could hear Perry's harsh breathing but no longer felt as if it were her own. She could feel his skin, but it was once again his, not an extension of herself. And once again her heart was heavy, heavier than before, perhaps, for tomorrow had grown that much closer, that much nearer. And knowing him now, having melded so thoroughly with him, the lack of a future seemed all that much bleaker, all that more painfully forbidden.

He opened his eyes, the trembling tension supplanted by an awareness of time. He opened his mouth as if he would speak, but closed it again at something he read in her gaze. A twisted smile hooked his lips, and he shook his head slightly.

She slowly stroked his face in answer, and his eyes closed again as he pressed his lips to the sensitive center of her palm. There was no mistaking the reverence in his kiss and no misunderstanding the farewell quality of his touch.

Her legs trembled as she untangled her locked grip and he, with a groan, pulled free of her. Valerie had the clearest sense of his slipping away from her, not merely physically, but forever, in all ways.

He gathered her gently in his arms and pulled her close, pressing her face to his shoulder, murmuring sweet nothings, a toneless hum that conveyed sorrow, pleasure and the too sharp awareness of goodbyes.

Wanting to cling to every precious second, Valerie nonetheless felt the first tendrils of sleep claiming her mind, her spent body, felt them taking him, as well.

And she dreamed of the coming dawn, of recreating the experiment and of the wish that Perry could simply stay in her time, that their one time together could truly last forever.

In her dream, Perry was excitedly juggling glasses of water, pouring them from one to another, then making them disappear up his leather-jacketed sleeve only to reappear. "It's the answer," he kept saying, and in the dream, Valerie knew he was right, that it was an answer, that somehow his safety would be insured by carrying the water with him.

She even woke once, suddenly certain that she'd found a solution, a means of providing proof of Perry's whereabouts, of making certain he would be safe in the somewhere, some when. Perry stirred beside her, his arm unconsciously wrapping around her, pulling her close, as though even in his sleep he was totally aware of her presence, still needing her touch, still seeking her warmth.

But as sleep overtook her again, her brain teased her, taunted her with visions of their joining, of a melding so complete that she felt she knew what Perry's rainbowed journey through time must have felt like.

And she dreamed of a deserted stretch of beach and saw Perry there waiting for her, calling her name and cried because it was a dream and not the future.

Chapter 10

Perry stood in the shower, hating the soap and water that stole Valerie's scent from his body. Everything about this not-yet-light morning seemed wrong. Was wrong. Especially in the wake of the night before, in the afterglow of what they could truly have together.

A look out the window had shown that it was still too dark for Jack Chew to have been busy with his infernal chalk lines. But Perry had no doubts that the area of confinement would be some fifty yards smaller in circumference than it had been the first day. The Warhawk was still missing and now so was the mysterious car engine. The sharks were much closer; his raft was all too rapidly eroding.

Valerie was already up and gone, with only a rumpled pillow and the lingering hint of flowers and a richer, deeper scent to prove she had ever been there. It was reaching for her and finding her gone that had awakened him so early. Perry fought against a sense of abandonment, an anger over the promises never spoken but so readily and gloriously given the night before, now snatched away by fate's jealous fingers.

The hot water beat on him, forcing him to come to terms with the fact that this could very well be his last day on earth. He was the only one among this collection of people to actually have seen himself in 1945, and as Valerie had disquietingly pointed out, he was officially listed as missing from that day on. He'd never been heard from again. Until now. And it was a pretty sure bet that he wouldn't be around here very much longer, either.

As it had the night before, the notion of simply staying as long as the portal remained in the sky seemed all too enticing. But the thought of meekly awaiting the inevitable disappearance made Perry feel like a cornered rat. He needed to make his own run for it, his own statement, his own fate.

What was last night, then? Wasn't that the biggest, strongest . . . and most empty run of them all? He had gone along with her every whim, his every whim, their mutual need to grab at least one precious moment of time. Now he was leaving her with nothing but memories. He had damned her for all time with nothing more than a single night of memories.

He turned off the shower and furiously toweled dry. He would miss these huge fluffy bath sheets, he thought angrily. He would miss the snazzy little razors. He would miss a thousand amazing gadgets and trinkets this time had to offer.

"Damn!" he shouted at the miraculously unfogged mirror. "Just damn," he murmured, the echo of his yell still reverberating in the small room.

Ah, Valerie. What he would feel for her once he'd gone was too strong to be categorized with a mere *miss*. That was far too weak a word. He would forever crave her, yearn for her, seek her in his dreams, in the loneliness that would make up the void where his heart used to be.

If, by some odd quirk of time, he did survive the jump they hoped to provide him today, he would be living in a time, breathing air that she wouldn't begin to encounter for another twenty or thirty years. Or worse, he might wind up in some time in the far-flung future, and she could be long gone. In either case, every day the knowledge that he couldn't have her, wouldn't grow old with her, would eat at him just a little more, like the canker in the sky ate at his current prison. Life would have lost its essential meaning.

And, standing there, nothing between him and the stark truth, he realized that if Valerie wasn't to be a part of his world, the jump didn't matter. Because the future had no meaning for him at all. Not without her.

He remembered what Dwayne had said, about how he would never wish to go back because it would mean reliving the past twelve empty years without his Patty. Perry had thought he'd understood Dwayne's comment then, but now he knew he really did. He was facing an unknown future with the knowledge that he would be living it, every lonely day of it, without Valerie.

Silently he regarded his set face in the mirror. He knew it so well, yet there was a new element in his eyes today, a profound despair. Inwardly raging, he wanted to smash the mirror, wipe out this hopeless image, but the face in the reflection remained impassive. He was leaving, and not all the theories and dreams in the world could change that.

It was no good railing against fate, damning his destiny. All he could do was take the reins of that uncertain future in his own two hands and hope for the best.

But the best was Valerie, and he was being forced to leave her behind.

The memory of the night before, the leisurely yet intense passionate encounter they had shared, stirred him anew and made his decision to actively pursue his own fate that much harder to accept. He wished he could see Dwayne, talk to him about that faith he had, wished that he'd asked Dwayne more questions that afternoon.

Dwayne had told him to write. The sudden resolve to pour some of his thoughts out to his old friend spurred him to

finish shaving and dressing. The thought of telling someone about this steadied him.

But when he sat down, at the dinette table, the electric
lamp dispelling the gloom of night if not mood, it wasn't
Dwayne he started writing to, but Valerie. Valerie, girl of his
dreams, woman of this time, this reality. The night before
notwithstanding, he still believed he shouldn't say the words
that would bind her to him forever, but she had to know that
their one time had meant everything to him.

Always before, until this very moment, in fact, he'd
thought that those men preparing to ship out, the ones who
stole a night's love and told the girl every fear they had
within them, as well as every loving term they could come
up with, were little more than heels. He'd strongly believed
that the time to tell the woman you loved how you felt about
her was when you came back. But now, the future too uncertain even to contemplate, the stark realization that he and
Valerie would never see each other again, made him understand that the words were not only a release for the departing one, but a gift beyond price for the one left behind. They
might not have a future, but she had given him last night,
and the least he could do was give her the knowledge that
she had fully touched his heart.

Three pages and a weary heartache later, he folded the
letter, then dashed off a quick note to Dwayne, telling him
how much it had meant to see him again and asking his old
friend to please give this letter to Valerie someday when the
hoopla died down. He stared at the short, terribly terse note,
and added another line: *Patty told me she was going to
marry you before she even knew your name.* He signed it
with an angry flourish and, with a twisted smile, scrawled
the current date across the bottom.

He stuffed the letters in an envelope he found in Valerie's
bedroom, and then, without stopping to think about it,
tugged his father's ring from his finger and shoved it inside. He licked the envelope, grimacing more at the quix-

otic gesture than the bland taste of the gum. He scrawled
Dwayne's name across the outside.

It was time to find Valerie. She was out there in the night
and with the dawn's first rays, he'd be leaving her forever.
Perry slipped on his leather jacket and slid the folded envelope into his inside pocket. He would slip the letter to one
of the boys, George Franklin or even Bob Fenton, just before Valerie turned the lasers on.

He had just reached the front door when it was wrenched
open from the outside, Phil and Bob Fenton bursting in.

"She's got it!" Phil shouted.

Fenton, out of breath, eyes dancing with a wild excitement, puffed, "So-solution. Valerie. Come."

Perry didn't wait for more, catching the infectious hope
from the two men he'd once believed he would never get to
know, never appreciate. He grabbed his hat and was out the
door ahead of the two men. He dashed across the narrow
enclosure to where Valerie and her remaining team of physicists were huddled around a couple of kerosene lanterns, all
gesturing madly, furiously discussing something.

"What?" he asked and was rocked by the haunted shadows in Valerie's eyes as she turned his way.

"Heavy water," she said.

He was sure it had to be significant, but it meant nothing
to him. "I don't—"

"Deuterium oxide," Jack elaborated, but the words still
held no answer for Perry.

George Franklin grinned broadly, his smile almost as wide
as his considerable length. Whatever was eating at Valerie
wasn't affecting the rest of her team. "If we're right about
this being a displacement zone of some kind, then all we
have to do is use a substitute for you. Heavy water."

Perry felt much as he had the first few hours in this
strange time, more than mystified, wholly confounded and
as though everyone here spoke a different language. Heavy
water? "This is something that will take me back to 1945?"
he asked cautiously.

Some of the joy faded from their faces.

Valerie turned away, her teeth gnawing at her lower lip, her hands clenched together. As usual, it was left to her to break whatever the bad news was. "We think...we hope...that it'll take you back. Yes. But you won't stay there. Not if we're right."

"So we're back where we started," Perry said, defeat in his voice.

"Not necessarily." She spoke so softly, he almost couldn't hear her. "If my theory is right, you won't stay there. You see, we all know that you never went back, at least not permanently. This way, if I'm right...and the projected data seems to indicate that I am, you'll come back...*here.*"

"Here," Perry said slowly. His heart began to pound in an erratic, disjointed rhythm. He thought of the letters in his pocket, of the ring inside the envelope. He thought of the night before, the dreams, the bitter taste of having no future. "Tell me. Explain it, please."

Phil took over. "You remember we speculated that when you came through time, a displacement zone was created. And we based much of our data on the old axiom of mass-to-mass ratio—"

"The law of conservation theory, yes," Perry said impatiently.

"Well, right. Now suppose that we fired up the lasers again, and aimed them at the portal. Like you wanted."

"Yes?"

"Well...what if you carried something that roughly equalled your weight in mass?"

"I don't know," Perry answered slowly, but he thought perhaps he did. What he didn't know was how he could be hearing Phil's voice over the thundering of his heart, the cautious, too carefully banked hope in Valerie's glittering gaze.

"One of the masses would stay, the other disappear. Now since we have historic accounts to show that you didn't stay, and that you obviously didn't stay there to supplant yourself—besides, that would be a paradox—then something must have offset the mass. *You.* You must have carried something to displace yourself! But what could you carry that wouldn't have been left behind, that wouldn't have caught everyone's attention?''

George took up the tale, his tall, thin frame shaking in his excitement. ''Valerie came up with the notion of heavy water. See, we turn on the lasers, you blink out, dump the water on the ground and scoot right back.''

''Theoretically,'' Valerie amended.

Perry met her eyes. For once he couldn't read her thoughts in her clear blue gaze. Too many shadows, too much caution masked whatever it was that was troubling her about this.

''What's the catch?'' he asked.

''Whaddaya mean?'' Phil asked in return.

''Well, it sounds too simple. There's got to be some kind of hitch.''

Phil, George and Jack exchanged long glances. Bob Fenton was the one who answered. ''There's no way for us to know if it will really work. It's a shot in the dark.''

Perry met the man's eyes and saw the truth, even a measure of real sympathy. There was no sound and fury now, just a man's respect for truth, for clueing in another man to the dangers of a particularly unpredictable mission. Perry nodded, accepting all that Fenton wasn't saying.

He'd already faced the hard fact that he probably wouldn't survive this experiment. At least this way there was a chance. A chance to have a future with Valerie. He turned to her, wishing they were alone, wishing he could ask her why the shadows, why the fear. Didn't she understand that this was the glimmer of hope that had so eluded them the night before?

But they weren't alone. ''You thought of this? When?''

''I dreamed about it last night,'' she said, blushing. ''Sort of. But it just might work.''

"Let's do it," Perry said. He wished she would meet his eyes.

"You'll be stuck here," she said, her voice curiously muffled.

Jack jumped in. "But not like this. The portal should be gone. You'd be able to go anywhere."

"*If* it works," Valerie said. Her voice was so tinged with pessimism, Perry could almost believe she was someone else this morning.

"Think you'll like this time?" Phil asked.

Perry frowned, hating Valerie's tense shoulders, averted face. He couldn't answer. An hour ago, there had been so little hope of him even surviving that the idea of actually living in any time was boom enough, but living in her time... No, he couldn't even trust himself to give in to the miraculous hope of that. He thought he understood her pessimism now; it was too dear a dream to even contemplate.

"You have to tell him the risks," Bob Fenton said.

George supplied them. "You have to understand that all we have to work on here is theory. It's only *theory* that turning on the lasers will trigger the portal to swing open and shut. And it's only theory that we can displace your mass by using heavy water—"

Phil interrupted. "And it's only *theory* that that hole up there is even a portal. All theory, but I'm sure we'll prove one of them!"

Jack grinned. "We're trying to recreate every possible factor that happened on both July 16, *your time,* and July 16, *our time*—four days ago. The only difference will be the deuterium oxide."

"The risks...?" Fenton prompted.

George and Jack Chew exchanged meaningful glances. George said slowly, "The risks are about the same as before. Meaning to say, we really don't know anything for sure. What we theorize is that you'll have to dump the water within seconds of your arriving in 1945. But we know you went back, because you saw yourself. Do you remember what your other self was doing?"

Perry frowned, trying to think. "Looking at me about the same way I must have been looking at . . . well, me."

"You . . . he didn't move at all?"

"Yes," Perry said slowly, shaking his head. "But I can't tell you what he . . . I . . . was doing. Something with my hand, I think." He held his hand out now, staring at it as if it belonged to that long-ago vision and not to himself. It even looked different, but he knew why; it was because it carried no ring.

"Isn't heavy water radioactive?" Fenton asked.

George nodded, not worried about it. "That's the beauty of this," he said, and the note of excitement was back in his deep voice. "Every single thing we've been doing out here points to electromagnetic forces at work. Radiation, in effect. Deuterium oxide is a measurable, highly condensed mass that not only is portable but safe to carry, and once it's dispersed, holds no directly discernable ill effects to the terrain. A good point-oh-two-percent of all ordinary hydrogen atoms are deuterium. Besides, even if it is a problem, since he'll be carrying it back to the exact location of the first atomic explosion, its radioactive properties won't matter diddly. This whole place was one big glow-in-the-dark zone."

"And the greater risk?" Fenton urged.

Valerie stiffened, as if his words were whips and she was being flayed by them. But she answered Fenton's demand for full disclosure. "When you came through the portal before, you weren't carrying any additional mass. Though the flask will be small, it will still be a significant difference."

Fenton, apparently having decided that everyone was dodging the issue, broke in, "The weight displacement might occur prior to your landing in 1945. There is a very real chance that you might actually merge with the heavy water during transition. Or that by sending radioactive material into the portal, we may trigger some kind of explosion."

Perry met his gaze again. "What are the odds?"

"There aren't any," Fenton said steadily. "You're the guinea pig in the world's first time-travel experiment."

Perry understood the shadows in Valerie's eyes now. There was less certainty of a future now than there had been before. At least before, all had assumed he would land somewhere, some when. Now even that negligible possibility was in jeopardy. Apparently he wasn't the only one to have figured out that the odds were already nearly nil.

But if this bizarre theory succeeded, he might just wind up right here, back in this time, Valerie waiting for him. Valerie, eyes bright again, hands outstretched, reaching for him.

He knew the hope that seemed to flicker and die in everyone else's eyes suddenly flared blindingly bright in his.

For Perry, the other men gathered around them ceased to be there, faded into the early morning air. He saw only Valerie. "I'm willing to take the risk," he said firmly. "I want to try this."

She blinked, and Perry could see tears of guilt, tears of fear, perhaps even those of abject sorrow well in her eyes.

The sky was lightening, gray replacing black, shadows creeping back against the trailers. He had to say something now, something that would make her understand the reasons he was willing to try this, to not make the plunge into the unknown, but rather to risk a dangerous attempt at coming back here. To her.

If he were dancing with her, silken cheek against his, he could allow a song to say it for him, to allow his hand on her back, his heart thudding against her soft breast to say all he needed to say. As he had done last night. But they weren't dancing, weren't touching, and they were standing in full view of six men who seemed to have nothing better to do than listen in on the hardest words he'd ever had to utter in his entire life.

"Valerie . . . ?" he asked, and her eyes again lifted to his, blurred by tears, but meeting his gaze nonetheless. He took a deep breath. To hell with his audience, he had to tell her what was in his heart. "Honey, better the chance of seeing you again than a lifetime of living without you," he said. "All we have in life are risks. And I'd risk anything for a future with you."

Hope and a wild, childishly exuberant longing spread through Valerie, warring with the sharp pain of knowing that Perry was in even greater danger now. She had told him just three nights ago that not knowing where he might land, not knowing if he would be safe was the worst. She'd been wrong.

What you don't know might be able to hurt, but it didn't rip everything apart in the process. Knowing he was willing to risk all, everything, on the slim chance that her conjecture might possibly return him to her, was infinitely more painful.

She was a scientist. She, of all people, knew how easily, how often things went wrong; experiments failed, subjects died. *Died.* This attempt at displacing his mass in a time they couldn't even see, an invisible world that had long ago faded into dim memory, could mean the total destruction of Perry Deveroux.

She wanted to cling to his words, that it was better to take the chance than have no hope of living with her, but she couldn't. The risks were too great. They would be flying blind. There was no time to test the procedure, no time to check it out. It was a one-time shot and it meant Perry's whole life. Hers.

If they tried closing the portal by firing up the lasers and just transmitting the mass of heavy water, the data indicated that the portal would indeed close—but everything that had come through it before would also disappear, including Perry. And the data seemed to suggest that an explosion would most likely occur, an explosion roughly equal to the atomic explosion in 1945.

There was another factor. This wasn't the same date. The avenue of coincidence was considerably narrowed. They had no instruments, no science-fiction time machine that would permit them to spin a fancy dial to July 16, 1945, at the sun's first finger of dawn. They had only a team of curious onlookers and a bank of sophisticated laser equipment run by an inhuman computer. And a woman who wanted it to work so badly that the pores on her skin contracted with that need, that her tongue could already taste the bitterness of failure.

"Hey!" Jack Chew called out, jolting her from her dark reverie. She turned to see what he was yelling about. A pair of headlights strafed across the broad plain.

She watched as Perry held his hand over his eyes, shading them, she suspected, not so much from the glare of the headlights but from the others, for she could see they were suddenly luminous with unexpressed emotion.

The car slid to a dusty stop, and the motor ceased its rumble. Dwayne Roberts, his long-time friend, waved furiously from the passenger side of the Chevrolet sedan.

Valerie knew that until that moment Perry had believed he would never see Dwayne again. She wondered how often Dwayne had thought that about Perry. The fact that he had always maintained faith in his friend's eventual discovery was as much a mystery to Valerie as it seemed to be to Perry. She wished she had some of that faith now, for she seemed to be floundering in a deep sea of pessimism.

George turned to Valerie, then looked quickly at the halting car. "It's only right that he should be here," he said. "He was in on it from the get-go."

Perry glanced at George, took in Valerie with a slow appraisal, then went back to the view of Dwayne stepping from the car. "Longer ago than that, pal," he said and crossed the distance separating him from Dwayne.

Dwayne arched his back stiffly, turning to face Perry. "Well, son, I can see I got here just in time for the party. It's been a nasty three days pacing the floor, wondering what you were up to out here."

The two contemporaries, one frail, the other looking his age of thirty-nine years, stood perfectly still for a poignant, bittersweet moment, sunlight glinting off tawny brown and snowy white hair. Then Dwayne lifted his arms wide and Perry stepped into an embrace that had been some fifty years delayed.

Valerie turned swiftly to look at the array of equipment in front of her, but couldn't see through the tears blurring her vision. The men's embrace had been both hail and a deeply felt farewell. She knew with sour certainty that she wouldn't have the courage to hug Perry goodbye. She might have many kinds of strengths, but that was the kind of total courage she didn't have.

"You brought the deuterium oxide, Aaron?" Bob Fenton asked behind her.

Valerie surreptitiously dried her eyes before turning around. The young man who had been sent to fetch Dwayne and procure the heavy water long before Perry awoke, pointed to the trunk of the Chevrolet.

As one, the group moved to the back of the car, waited impatiently as the young agent opened the trunk. In a single, lead-lined container, roughly the size of a quart fruit jar, Perry's instrument of redemption, or destruction, lay nestled in a foam-packed box.

"It looks like a thermos bottle," Perry said. He still had a hand on Dwayne's shoulder. Valerie risked a glance at Dwayne. The older man's eyes were clear, no sign other than a glimmer of excitement giving any clue to his emotions.

"Now what?" Bob Fenton asked.

"Battle stations," Perry said, unaware he was striking the severest of blows to Valerie's already battered heart.

"Let's do it, people," Phil said, imitating Captain Pelligrew's voice the morning of the fateful test. When Valerie shot him a hard glance, he shrugged and grinned. "Somebody's got to lighten this thing up."

There was no way on earth anyone could lighten it for Valerie. But she gave a wan smile and waved him to his station at the Plexiglas barrier. She conferred for a few moments with Fenton, explaining that since the mobile homes had been moved into the displacement zone, it would probably be extremely wise to move them out prior to turning the lasers on. A significant glare at the Eastern horizon made the need for haste all too clear. As he dispatched his men to carry out her suggestion, she caught Perry looking at the trailer they had been sharing the last few days. The last few nights.

"If I...*when* I come back, I want one of those," he said. "We could drive all around the country and I could see how everything's changed." He turned to her and said gravely, "Somehow the notion of settling down in one place after all this seems difficult, a little too close to the feeling of being trapped. Think the government will give me one in exchange for this jumping around in time?"

Valerie choked back a slightly hysterical chuckle.

Luckily, Dwayne answered for her. "Sure. I imagine the feds will be willing to give you just about anything you ask for. And if they won't, pal, I will. I happen to own one of the companies that makes 'em."

Perry smiled and Valerie had to wonder how he could appear so casual, so *easy*. She'd seen the evidence of his inner strength, seen his ability to master, control, his environment, had *felt* it. But this, this was a situation that went beyond normal boundaries, was completely without precedence. How could he smilingly accept what was about to happen, what could happen?

He shifted his eyes then, meeting hers, and she nearly rocked with the unbridled emotion in that mahogany gaze. He wasn't insouciant. Neither was he in any way unmoved. He was merely desperately controlled, checking a veritable flood of mixed emotions by sheer will, by force of character. That muscle in his jaw that jumped when he was upset betrayed him. The flattening of his lips, still smiling but pulled tight against his white teeth, gave him away. The raw hunger mingled with a thousand fears and dreams told the story of his rigid need to act as if everything was normal. Oh, but she could see the wild hope of the future in his eyes.

How could she allow this experiment? How could she possibly permit this to happen? Better he be snatched away, sent some other where or when than that she be the *cause*, be the one to give the order that would possibly destroy him.

Her knees sagged with the weight of sorrow that settled on her shoulders, that sapped the energy from her body. Last night he'd made her languorous with desire, with the fire in his eyes. Today those same eyes, a trust she didn't deserve shining in their depth, made her languorous with fear, her limbs sluggish, her mind dull.

"Where do you want me?" Perry asked.

Here, oh here, she wanted to cry. *I want you right here!*

George answered for her. "Since you appeared some ten yards from where the Warhawk was, right about there, we've got the program set to take you from that spot." The tall man stopped, frowned, then shrugged. "We think."

Dwayne asked, "What happened to the Warhawk?"

Perry answered him tersely, "It disappeared a couple of days ago."

Dwayne's quick inhalation was fully audible to everyone, but he made no comment on how Perry must have felt about that. "How do you all know *when* to send him back to?"

"We don't," Valerie said dully. "All we have to go on is that he saw himself. He knows he went back. We don't have any way of accurately sending him anywhere, let alone back to July 16, 1945."

Dwayne started to say something, but George interrupted him. "Since he hasn't changed in forty-eight years, we have to assume—just as fourth-dimension theory has always speculated—that time, as we know it, linear time, has no meaning in that dimension. We're trusting the portal to do that for us.''

Perry's eyes lifted to the noticeably smaller, still busily roiling cloud of color clearly visible in the pre-dawn sky. Valerie imitated him. She hated that portal, hated everything it seemed to be stealing from her. Hated the danger of it, the threat. And yet, somehow, magically, from another time, another place, it had brought Perry to her.

And now she was sending him back through it, possibly away, probably into death.

Valerie was grateful to Dwayne who, with far more volubility than usual, asked a host of questions about the details of their experiment. How long did Perry have in order to dump the heavy water, when would they expect him back and how would they know if he had been successful?

The questions served to defuse the team's tension, with the exception of Valerie—for her each question was like a key being turned that wound the coil within her tighter and tighter still, until she was sure she would be the one to explode, not Perry.

"What are you going to carry that thing—" he pointed to the container of heavy water sitting beneath the table they'd huddled around earlier, shaded by the top "—in when you go over, uh, back.''

Perry shrugged. Phil piped up that he had a backpack Perry could use. Dwayne grinned and waved the young man to stay where he was. "I brought something along. I had a feeling it might come in handy.''

He moved over to the Chevrolet and, after a moment's rummaging in the back seat, withdrew a somewhat battered, army-green rucksack. The kind used by some soldiers in World War Two. Valerie stared at it, her heart unaccountably thundering. She'd seen it before. In the photographs in the files on Perry Deveroux. Not in the picture of Perry himself, but in separate photographs, the ones logging the few personal effects left behind.

This had been all that was left of him, given to Dwayne along with the few personal items inside. Her mind swirled with a single shocking question. How could Perry have left it behind if Dwayne was intending for him to take it back with him now?

Perry looked at the satchel with a frown. "Think it'll be big enough?" he asked. He took it from Dwayne, swiftly unfastening it. He didn't appear the slightest discomfited by seeing it here.

Valerie tried putting it together in her mind, but couldn't. If the pack was left behind in 1945, and Perry was now taking it back to 1945, where had the pack come from? It was like staring directly into infinity and trying to make sense of the enormity, the never-ending stretch in all directions of unlimited possibility. The ultimate in quantum phenomena.

She met Dwayne's eyes. He looked happy. Tired, and old, but so very happy. Would he still feel that way in less than one hour? Would her excited team, would Bob Fenton's agents? And would this terrible fear, this gnawing uncertainty still be with her, or gone forever? *Forever.* The mere word, concept, chilled her soul.

"It'll do," Phil declared. "But you gotta realize, Perry, you're not going to be able to simply sling this over your back and proceed from there. That *thermos,* as you called it, looks light, but it weighs...well, it's going to weigh what you do, though it's a hell of a lot easier to manage. Speaking of which, did anybody think to bring a scale out here? We've got to have it down to the fraction of an ounce. Hey, George!"

Phil trotted off, seeking a scale. Jack, behind the plexi-barrier, double-checked the computer's program and checked it yet a third time. The trailers were well out of the safety-danger zone, and Bob Fenton's men were behind the barrier, watching Jack's careful administration.

Dwayne touched Valerie's arm. "You walk him to where you want him. I'll wait for you behind the barrier."

Valerie started to protest. She couldn't do this.

But Dwayne gave her a little push. "Go on, now, Valerie. Sun's coming up. Show this young fellow here some of that feistiness you got plenty of. I already paid my respects. It's your turn, now."

She reluctantly allowed him to propel her toward Perry, but at the last minute, she turned back to look at the older man. His eyes were an open book of sympathy for her, and showed clear understanding of how far she and Perry had come in the last three days. Without either her or Perry having said a word to him, to anyone, about what had transpired between them the night before, this man seemed to know. He had accepted it with gentle joy. And with sorrow and sympathy for both of them. All of them.

"Walk with me, Valerie," Perry said softly, taking her elbow. "And tell me a little more about this world I'll be coming back to."

She couldn't look at him, didn't dare cling to his gaze, could only cleave to his arm. She didn't trust herself not to show him the million doubts she harbored, the nonbelief, the despair, the fears she had for him.

"It'll soon be getting warm," Perry said, slowing.

Treat this normally, she commanded herself. Make small talk, act as though someone travels through time every day. The memory of his first day here, his first few minutes, the touch of his palm against hers, the feel of his warm hand on her face, that monumental feeling of having bridged time and space, suddenly all warred with the need to give him what he craved most right now.

He shrugged free of his leather jacket, and Valerie had to restrain herself from burying her face in the warm, soft folds, inhaling his essence, reawakening all the memories of his touch, his scent, his passion the night before.

The entire time with him, lying in the semidarkened bedroom, her soul absorbing everything he had to offer, she had known this moment, this goodbye was inevitable, had tried saying it with her hands, her kiss, the whole of her. But this was really the moment.

They might have tried to lock away their future in one glorious night, but the soft New Mexico dawn's light was stripping the illusion away, and now there were only words, only two separate and needy people who would have to say the hardest of goodbyes in full view of eight watchers.

And there was nothing she could say. If she pleaded, cried, tried to stop this, it would be to no avail. Perry had two choices: the risky unknown, or the dangerous unknown. Either way, he was still going to disappear. If she begged, cajoled and sobbed against his chest, he would still opt for the chance, however narrow, of returning. Because he wanted to come back to her.

The thought should have made her happy. Instead it filled her with the most terrifying despair.

Gratefully, she heard George and Phil running up behind them, panting over the deuterium oxide, a set of scales and the satchel Dwayne had brought for Perry.

"Okay," Phil puffed. "Here it is. Jack's got the program set for T-Minus twenty." They set their burdens down on the sandy floor.

"Want to get on the scales and see if you need to go on a twenty-minute diet?" George asked, gesturing for Perry to stand on the scale. Perry obliged, and after a few adjustments, George had him get off, hold his jacket and the container of deuterium oxide and then try it again without the deuterium oxide.

Out came the pocket calculator and after a few seconds and a few more on and off the scales, he declared the amount of heavy water too great by three pounds. He gave the calculation of disbursement to Phil, who grimaced and winced as he unscrewd the container.

Valerie met Perry's eyes in surprise. She knew that in the desert animals could smell water, could find the smallest puddle of moisture simply by picking up the scent of the precious hydrogen-oxygen combination. And she knew from her own experience back home that the ocean scent cleaved to the land nearby, threading through reeds, salt brush and the lush greenery inland. But only one other time had she experienced this unusual desert teaming with ocean-spray scent—the day the portal had opened, ribbons of light swirling around them and released Perry into her time. Into her life.

Now that unusual fragrance wafted into the cool air, making her nostrils flare with sudden desire, wistful hope.

Perry smiled, a genuine, opening relieved smile. "This is what I smelled that morning. What I smelled when I first got here," he said.

"Me, too," Valerie answered, and for the first time that morning a smile curved her lips.

Phil and George said nothing, only working carefully to pour out some of the precious fluid.

"That's enough," George commanded. "Let's try it again, Perry."

Perry stepped to the scales again, first with the container, without, then with again. George and Phil poured a slight bit more from the thermos-looking container, tested the weights again, and finally George pronounced it light by a few ounces.

Perry looked thoughtful, then slowly removed his hat and, squinting now, stood looking at it. Without a word, he handed it to Valerie, who couldn't see it for the sudden tears in her eyes. She held it to her chest, inhaling deeply, the scent of water and of Perry mingling permanently in her heart.

"That's it," George said. "Don't even blow your nose, Perry." He didn't give the ghost of a smile.

Phil carefully placed the heavy water in the satchel and then reached for Perry's jacket. At a momentary hesitation on Perry's part, he looked up, frowning.

Perry looked as though he wanted to say something, do something, but finally merely handed the jacket over to

Phil. He had an odd expression on his face, something between regret and relief.

Valerie, thinking she understood what caused the look, wanted to kiss him, touch him, let him know she would be with him in spirit and soul, if not in body. She was certain the regret was caused by their lack of time together, by the unfairness of fate, of destiny. And the relief was simply that, as an action-oriented man, this deadly experiment was finally about to get underway.

Phil and George gathered up the scales, scooped the wet sand from the spilled liquid into a paper bag. "It's bound to retain some of the mass," George explained at Perry's question.

Both men stood awkwardly for a moment, glancing from the rosy horizon to the barrier to Perry and then down at their watches. "About eight minutes to go, Valkyrie," Phil said.

George cleared his throat and stepped forward, brushing his hand against his jeans. He thrust it out at Perry, who took it in a single, meaningful clasp. George said, "It's been a great honor, Major Deveroux. Good luck."

Valerie wanted to scream at him for sounding as if this were the final farewell.

Phil returned Perry's jacket and stuck out his hand as George's dropped. As Perry took it, a wry smile on his face, Phil said, "You were right, you know. This is a whole lot more challenging than a video game." They shook hands solemnly, then released each other.

The two men turned and started across the empty enclosure. When they were about thirty yards away, Phil turned and called back, "Don't stay away so long next time!"

How could he be flippant when her entire life, Perry's life, hung in such precarious balance? She wanted to run after him, make him take back the lighthearted tone, make him look her squarely in the eye and acknowledge that her heart was breaking, that everything she'd ever said or done in her entire life was insignificant when compared with this moment of having to allow the only man who had ever touched her soul to leave, to step into the vast unknown, possibly even death, without her.

She realized bleakly that she was pinning everything on a single theory, a prayer really. And turning to meet Perry's agonized gaze, she saw all too clearly that he didn't believe he had that prayer.

That he believed this was goodbye. Forever.

Chapter 11

Perry didn't so much look at Valerie as study her, memorizing her. He took in the delicate line of her jaw, the pearled, perfectly straight teeth holding in her swollen lower lip, her tightly clenched, white-rimmed hands, the vein throbbing in her throat.

He felt his eyes had become one of those recorder machines they had in this time, and were etching her every feature, every nuance into some storage place, some displacement zone in his heart, for him to take out later and endlessly replay over and over.

And if there was no future, no place where he could sit quietly and remember, then hers would be the face he would see when he disappeared. She would truly and irrevocably be the last thing on his mind.

He watched her mangling his hat, turning it in her tension-tight hands, rubbing it against her face as if the soft felt were his hands, his touch, and knew she was memorizing, too.

She couldn't hide her feelings. Perhaps this, more than any other characteristic, had drawn him to her. She didn't play games, was neither coy nor sugary. She was simply herself, open, honest, her faults possibly her triumphs, her triumphs her strengths.

She was his golden girl, the rainbow's end.

And he had only seven minutes to say goodbye to her. Seven minutes to say what he'd never said to another living soul. Seven minutes to tell her everything that rested so heavily upon his heart.

He bent now, down to the satchel, knowing he would never be able to say the words and then leave her. She would have to read them, see them for herself now, or perhaps worse, after he was gone, eyes tearfully reading everything in his heart, trying to make sense of the emotions he'd written down in the letter he'd so painfully penned earlier.

His hand dipped into his jacket's inside pocket and he could feel the letter, actually had it in his hand to pull out and give to her. His fingers brushed against the small bulge made by his father's ring, his only gift to this woman of his dreams.

And he hesitated, as he'd paused when Phil had reached for his jacket. Would this mere scrap of paper, this single outpouring of all his hopes and dreams, his wishes and needs, would this be enough to offset the delicate balance of mass?

Was fate now to take another hand, forcing him to adhere to his earlier instincts, not those of this morning, but those of three nights ago, eons ago, deeming them in some higher order as right, as true? Was *not* telling her how he felt about her the best thing, after all? He didn't dare the slightest risk of hampering what slim chances he had of succeeding, of surviving this experiment. So very much hung in the balance.

He slid his hand from the envelope, aching with the need to give it to her, relieved that it would stay unsaid, unread now. If he came back, he'd give her the letter himself, tell her then. If he didn't, she wouldn't have that additional pain hovering over her the rest of her life.

If he wasn't going to come back, she needed to get on with the business of living. And much as it killed him to think about it, the business of loving someone else. Really loving that nebulous someone, not just seizing one night from a futureless void. Doing little things like passing the toast, having picnics, taking the children to school on a Monday morning, laughing, loving, growing old together. She needed those things. And giving her that letter would only be a stumbling block, a stile too heavy, too broad to cross easily.

He pulled his hand free of the jacket, closed the satchel and rose. He felt stiff and fluid all at the same time.

"You'll have to hold that backpack," Valerie said. Her voice was prim, as though she was swallowing a reprimand or a reminder. But he knew she was choking back a thousand things she also needed to say, wouldn't for his sake. She was talking just to make the few precious moments of time pass easier.

"And remember that you'll only have thirty seconds or so to dump the water. That's how long you estimated seeing yourself before. You'll have to hurry."

"I will," he said. He dreaded doing what he had to do next, but there was only one way to make things easier for either of them. He had to send her behind that barrier now, each to face this parting alone. Instead, as if his heart had managed to supplant his mind, he said, "But I want to hold you first."

Her eyes flew to his in a mixture of fear, longing and stark repudiation. Just as he'd known they would. If it had been him, he'd have done the same.

He said, "Last night you asked me to give you one night. I'm...I'm asking you this."

He knew it was unfair, he could feel it, smell the truth of just how unfair in that strangely lingering scent of water. But he could no more have resisted asking than he could have denied her last night. Than he could have denied himself that night.

A slow shudder worked through her, as if his words had broken a dam she'd constructed deep inside. With a small cry, she stepped forward and into his arms.

She didn't speak, only clung to him with a ferocity and desperation that told him far more clearly than any words what she was thinking, what she was feeling.

This is where she is supposed to be, he thought. Where he was meant to be. His stomach churned with sick relief, his loins ached to meet her, to prove again that they were meant for each other, meant to be together for all time.

Stroking her soft gold curls with his hand, too choked by his own emotions to speak, he held her and wished more strongly, more fervently than he had ever wished for anything, that he might return, might come through this safely, might have the chance to hold her forever.

But it was a barren hope, a pipe dream.

In the most stable of lives, there were no sanctions for the future, nothing that would ensure that love, life, anything would last. And in this volatile, completely irrational situation, all the pretty dreams and wishes in the world couldn't put things to rights. And, all too sadly, wouldn't put *them* together again.

"I wish I could go with you," she murmured.

His heart wrenched. Oh, how he wished that, too. He knew she was crying, could feel it in the trembling of her shoulders, in the hesitancy in her voice. He looked up swiftly, staring into that sinister swarm of color in the sky, needing to hate, seeking something to despise, ardently searching for anything to keep at bay the tears that threatened to overflow his eyes.

"I'm glad I came here," he said and clenched his jaw at her sob. "I am, Valerie. More glad than you will ever know."

When she didn't say anything, and he was certain she couldn't, he pulled her even closer, molding her to him.

Folding her into his arms, against him, trying to bring the night back to the day.

He started to continue, had to clear his throat and went on, culling from nothing, drawing only on desperation. "For this, mainly. For you. I think I've been looking for you all of my life." He chuckled raggedly. "I just never thought I'd have to come so far to find you."

He could feel her tears seeping through his shirt, staining not only his clothing, but his heart. "But I'm glad for other reasons, too. I'm glad I got a chance to see this world—what little I did see of it—in peacetime. You wouldn't believe how different everything is. And yet . . . it's the same in a lot of ways."

She quieted somewhat, and he continued, talking in a dreamy, faraway tone that he hoped would soothe, calm her, lure her to let him go, to accept his going.

"When I first got here, I thought all the men were soft. Unformed somehow. Untried, I suppose." He felt as if his hands were independent of his mind; they convulsively pulled her tight. "You were different. Something's tested you, made you strong. It's not a difference that can really be defined, but it shows in a person's eyes, in her walk. It shows in everything you do."

To his relief, she spoke, asking, "And . . . you don't think that . . . anymore?"

"No. I still believe you, and maybe many of the women of this time have been tested more stringently than your men, but I understand now that the men in my time saw things in black and white—like motion pictures—most of them, anyway, whereas the men in this time see life in other shades, too, other colors."

"You see them that way, too," she said.

He smiled, and the curvature felt alien on his lips. As if he were already slipping away, already fading into that incredible cloud.

"Wartime. That was my time. The battle, the patriotism, the purity. And the Depression. And the twenties . . .

God, what a time we all had then. But I think now that we were so very innocent." He fingered the silk of her hair, pressed it to his nostrils, to his lips. He had to close his eyes against the sharp pain of the memory of their one night together.

"I love you," she whispered.

His hand clenched a soft curl, ground it into his palm, imprinting it against his skin. He couldn't bear this. Her words tore him apart, flayed him to the quick.

He drew a harsh, ragged breath and continued as if he hadn't heard her, hadn't totally taken those three sweet and sorrow-filled words to his soul. "And I'm not s-sure that's such a bad thing."

She didn't repeat the words, and he went on, stronger now. "I've watched your amazing television programs, your pictures, and I think that what we had then—which still feels so very like now to me—was a total belief that a man has to do whatever it takes to set things right for a country...for his nation, for..."

"For his love," she finished for him.

"Yes," he said sadly. "But I can't do that here."

"You already have," she said.

"No. No, Valerie. I've gone against everything I feel is the way it should be. And while I don't regret it, not a single minute of it, I know in my soul that what we had last night wasn't supposed to be for just one night. You were right when you said that we were supposed to be together, supposed to have a future. But Valerie, if things go wrong—"

"Don't," she said, pressing even tighter against his chest. "Don't say it."

"If...I don't want you to cry for me. You have to go on with your life. Do you understand me?"

She pulled back from him slightly, her eyes, drenched with the tears she'd already shed, steeped in the shadows of his making. But overriding the sorrow was a fierce anger, a driving, hot fury that both surprised and amazed him.

She slapped his hat against his chest. "Don't you *dare* talk as if you were dying!"

He wanted to say something, anything that would chase away the anger, but the fire in her eyes stopped him, held him perfectly still.

"Okay. So I gave in to some doubts. So I cried. I've wanted to cry from the first second I saw you. *You came across fifty years!* That would make anyone awed, scared, feel a little out of the ordinary. And so I'm crying now, Perry. *I'm only human!*" She whirled away from him, furiously rubbing at her face.

He opened his mouth to speak but she whipped around, coming at him like a drill sergeant. Valkyrie in true, fierce form. *God, how he loved her.*

"But I'll tell you something, and I want you to get it straight," she barked, "You're going through that damn portal, and *you're coming back!* Do you hear me, Perry?" She grabbed hold of his arms and shook him, as if doing so would shake her words into him. *"Do you hear me? You are coming back to me, damn it."*

Tears were springing from her eyes, not merely slipping free. But she wasn't finished. She caught her breath on a heartrending sob, threw his hat to the dusty ground and laid her beautiful hands on either side of his face, making him look at her, forcing him to follow her.

"I've never, *never* loved anyone in my whole life, ever felt for anyone, like what I feel for you. Until now, I could have sworn it didn't even exist! And I'm not going to let it go. I'm not going to, do you hear me? *You're coming back!* You've got to. I need you, do you understand? I *need* you. I want to see your face first thing every single morning of the rest of my life, and kiss you good-night every night for the rest of my life. You have to come back. You *h-have* to."

She collapsed against him, crying with deep, grief-stricken, wrenching sobs, her entire body shaking, her fingers slipping from his face and digging into his shoulders, a low keening sound emanating from her throat.

Perry felt as if every single particle of his body was stretching to her, was urging him to utter the single promise he couldn't give: *I love you, too. I'll be here for you.* But she knew as well, if not more, than he, that was for fate to decide, for the future wasn't his to give or to command.

He hadn't seen Dwayne walking toward them, but was profoundly grateful when he appeared as though from thin air. The friend of his youth, now white-haired and gnarled but wise, wise with age. He bent and retrieved the much-battered hat and met Perry's eyes with rueful humor and a deep sorrow.

"Valerie . . . dear," Dwayne said, "it's time."

For a moment Valerie's gaze clung to Perry's, despair at war with longing. Then she buried her face in her hands.

Dwayne's eyes met his as he gently drew her from Perry's chest and into his own arms. Like that time before they cashiered Dwayne from the camp, Perry felt his old friend had much more to say, much more meaning in his eyes than his lips.

Valerie's sobbing figure dissolved into Dwayne's embrace. For a moment, forgetting the concrete image of his eighty-six-year-old friend, Perry knew a moment's sharp torment. And then he remembered Patty, and what Dwayne had said about the last twelve years.

As he watched Dwayne slowly turn around, his white, grizzled head bent over Valerie's golden curls, Perry thought no man should ever have to bear this much grief, this much pain.

He wanted to say he'd be back. He yearned to call out after them that he'd be back here in just a few minutes, a few seconds.

Wait for me, he wanted to scream. *Wait for me.*

But he couldn't ask such a boon. Ten minutes from this second was a dream.

So he let them walk away, watching them as they crossed the desert encampment and took their positions behind the barrier. He saw Valerie step up to the lasers and, after swiping at her face with both hands, saw her nod sharply, once, then again. He knew he was imagining it, but for a moment he was sure he could feel her eyes blazing at him across the expanse.

Come back to me.

He took hold of the satchel's strap and held on as though it were a lifeline.

"T-Minus thirty-five seconds and counting . . ." he heard Phil call.

He drew a deep breath, wondering if he should have given her the letter, wondered if he'd survive this, wondered, if he'd been able to answer her desperate plea, what he would have said. If he ever saw her again, no matter when the time or place, he would tell her. He would tell her just how much he loved her. He would sweep her into his arms, hold her and never let her go. *Never.*

"T-Minus twenty-nine seconds and counting . . ."

He tensed, his muscles already aching, stiffening as though hearing a screaming bomb falling from the blue sky. His heart seemed to pound to the rhythm of Phil's voice, bellowing the seconds he had left in this time. The seconds he had left to see Valerie.

He saw the first tendrils of rainbow ribbons threading through the sky and thought they looked alive. Hungry.

He gripped the satchel for all he was worth and sought Valerie's gaze.

Wait for me. Dear God, Valerie . . . however long it takes, wherever we may be . . . wait for me!

Chapter 12

The desert shifted and the earth colors ran and bled with the tears still falling from her eyes. Taking hold of the lasers' handles, feeling for the button blindly, Valerie had the worst, dizzying sensation of déjà vu. Less than a week ago she and her crew had stood just so, fingers poised over buttons, eyes raking the sky. But this time all eyes were on a lone figure, a man whose time had finally come.

Then her heart had pounded with anticipation, excitement, a fear that the experiment might fail and a deeper fear that it might work all too well. Now her heart scarcely felt as if it were beating at all; her breath was tangled in her aching throat, and her fingers, arms, her entire being felt numb, pummeled into twisted, unrecognizable shapes.

Less than a week, and yet her entire life had changed.

There were other differences, as well. Jack wasn't eating; he was nervously rocking from foot to foot, eyes glued on Perry. Phil wasn't talking, Pelligrew wasn't there, but she could hear his voice over the crackling radio, confirming that the mock tests against the Organ Mountains were underway. Seconds to go and everything had been recreated precisely as it had the morning of July 16, then and in this time, with the exception of two startling differences: Perry Deveroux and the few still-remaining artifacts were already on this plane, and the colorful portal in the sky already waited to snatch him away.

Less than a week...and yet all of life was different. What had seemed surreal before was now her all-consuming reality. What had seemed impossible had become real. Mirages and miracles, she had witnessed them both now. She had kissed a phantom from 1945, had fallen in love with a dream, and this was the dream's end. How could she depress the switches that would cause the alarm to ring, dawn to intrude and cast him out of her life?

She'd cried for him to come back to her, but was that even possible? When a dream ended, all that was left behind were elusive memories, snatches of emotion, threads of thoughts that were so intricately interwoven with the night that daylight eroded them, melted the gossamer wings of illusion. And when she depressed the switches—*only seconds left*— this dream would be gone. Possibly forever. And she didn't know how to go about dreaming him back again.

"T-Minus six...five...four..."

Valerie closed her eyes, unwilling to witness his disappearance, the painful uncertainty of his survival, unable to watch herself in the act of destroying the one thing she prized above all others.

"Three...two..."

On signal, command, she depressed the buttons and sobbed at her own automatic adherence to duty, to the wishes of Perry, to the hopes of everyone there that a theory, a mere half-baked theory would work.

But she couldn't hide from the truth, from the knowing, and her eyes snapped open. She had to see, had to verify for herself that Perry was all right, that shooting the lasers' beams into the portal hadn't been the single biggest mistake of her life.

A bright flash momentarily blinded her, and she cried out at the disruption of her view of Perry.

"Sorry," Phil murmured. "We needed pictures."

She didn't bother to answer, only frowned heavily, blinking away the spots before her eyes.

At Dwayne Roberts's sudden voiced sigh, she felt all others shift to look up and at the portal, but Valerie could only watch the man she loved, so alone, so brave, so soon to disappear.

As before, ribbons of color spiraled out and downward, but unlike the last time, the incredible auroras didn't sweep across the plain as if seeking likely victims, hungry for purchase. Instead the ribbons circled, shimmered, danced around Perry, bathing him in purest and most elemental yellows, violets, reds and blues.

This time the strong, fresh scent of water came, but was far more elusive. The wind that had carried the ribbons before didn't assault the barrier, but Valerie covered her mouth as she saw the force of that noiseless velocity tear at Perry's clothing, ruffle his short hair, send clouds of dust swirling, mingling in the writhing, seemingly sentient rainbow.

Yellow, green, violet and blue strips of color wrapped seemingly intelligent bands around her love, imprisoning him, holding him. Orange, indigo and red ribbons, all appearing endless and utterly fluid, danced about him, enveloping him, and suddenly he was difficult to see, hard to discern through all that beauty that no longer seemed beautiful to Valerie, but evil, hateful.

"It's shrinking!" Phil screamed, pointing upward, but Valerie didn't look. Every fiber of her being was trained on Perry, every single shred of her will pulling him back, desperately trying to link with him, to make him bend to her desire for his safety, his return.

She remembered thinking, for a sharp split second the day he'd arrived, that it had been *her will* that had brought him through time, had brought him to this place. If there was any truth to that, any justice in the universe, then her will could bring him back again.

Come back to me! she commanded silently, praying earnestly.

As had happened just a few days earlier, after thirty seconds the timing program within the computer signaled the lasers to cease their activity, and one by one the other pieces of equipment also quieted, all except the video cameras trained on Perry and the portal.

But now there was nothing there to see.

As the lasers had stopped their assault on the portal, the bands of ribbons had been reeled home, just as before, but this time they had, like fishermen of the universe, reeled in Perry, the wagon harness and the few other odds and ends of displaced time, hauling them aboard the limitless deck of the fourth dimension.

The desert floor was empty, tan once again, all evidence of Perry and the other collection of artifacts gone. Gone away.

The transfer was complete. Half of their experiment had succeeded.

But the better half had failed. The ultimate transfer hadn't been accomplished. *Perry should still be there.* Should still have been standing where he had been only moments before. Or, in the thirty-second delay, should have returned.

Perry hadn't come back. Couldn't. *He was truly gone.*

Valerie's soul shriveled and hid, and her mind felt numb with battered reality. Her theory had been incorrect. Daylight had come and stolen the dream. The illusion was over.

"NO!" Valerie screamed, lunging at the lasers. "Turn them on again! We have to find him!"

It was Bob Fenton who grabbed her, who held her back. "Nothing's set up," he said, but his words had no meaning for Valerie.

"It'll take some time to reset the computer, to realign the equipment," Phil concurred urgently.

She felt Dwayne take her from Fenton's arms, pulling her into his own, wrapping thin but strong arms around her. She found no comfort there.

He said quietly, slowly, as though compelling her to listen to him by the very surety in his voice, in his words, "He made it there, Valerie." He turned her in his arms, pressing her against his chest, stroking her hair, much as Perry had done only minutes before.

"*Listen to me!* Perry went back to 1945. I know he did. He got there safely. I don't know where he went from there, except that he did get there. I know this, Valerie."

As if his words were swords and had penetrated the terrible wall separating her from reality, Valerie shuddered at the meaning of his words. What good was his faith now? Perry had gone and hadn't returned.

He hadn't come back.

"Valerie... *he went back to 1945.* You got him there."

"There's no proof," Valerie sobbed. "All we have is that damned vision of his. There's...no...proof he's even alive!"

"There is, honey. There's proof."

She stared at him through tear-drenched eyes, not daring to hope, but clinging to the thin possibility nonetheless. "Where?" she asked. "Where... how?"

"That pack he carried...that thermos...even his damned jacket... We've got all the proof in the world."

"That's not proof," she said. "He had those when he came here."

"No, Valerie. Not all of them. Think, honey. Understand me now. He didn't have them, because I've had most of those things with *me* for forty-eight years."

"What? I don't understand," she complained. Her head was still reeling, her heart taken through that portal as surely as though it had been she and not Perry on that lonely plain.

Dwayne shook her a little. "Buck up, gal. Dry your eyes. Listen to me. I've known for forty-eight years that Perry was going to be here, now, in this time. They gave me his things. Remember? *The investigators gave me his things.*"

Valerie frowned at him, knowing this was true but not following the significance.

"Don't you get it, honey? They gave me his jacket. Even what I thought all these years was a thermos. They gave me the thermos we just brought in."

Phil let out a whooping war cry. "So he *did* make it! He made it back there."

Dwayne nodded, and the others broke into disjointed questions, answers and speculation. Valerie's heart began to pound in painful, unsteady thunder.

Finally Bob Fenton, with his ever-ready sense of order, commanded that everyone be quiet. "One question at a time, please!"

"Was the thermos empty?" George asked Dwayne. "Had he already released the deuterium oxide?"

Dwayne nodded. "The container was empty. I never did have the lid. I don't know what happened to it," Dwayne said.

"But..." Valerie protested. "How could you have known? That he was coming back, I mean?"

Dwayne met her gaze steadily, more than a hint of apology and sorrow in his eyes. "In his jacket pocket were two letters." Dwayne pulled his wallet from his pants pocket and flipped it open. He extracted two aged and yellowed, obviously oft-read and refolded letters.

His hands shook as he carefully opened the one with a single sheet. He held it out to Valerie, pointing at the signature, a scrawled, hurried example of penmanship, but what drew her eyes, what made her breath catch was the date beneath Perry's name. Today's date, forty-eight years after Perry Deveroux disappeared.

Stunned, and with trembling, almost reverent fingers, she lightly stroked the letter that was now nearly a half a century old, yet had obviously been written only an hour or so earlier today. The paper was so old and crinkled it was brittle, but she could read the words.

Take care of Valerie for me. Give her the enclosed letter after this is all over and done with. Tell her... time is relative, that one night with her was worth a lifetime with any other. There was more there, something about someone named Patty who apparently loved Dwayne, and something about how good it was to see Dwayne again after forty-eight years, but Valerie could only read and reread the lines pertaining to herself.

One night with her was worth a lifetime with any other. One night, one time.

Valerie didn't reach for the other letter. She couldn't take it now, couldn't bear to read words he'd penned only a short time ago, a message carried in Dwayne's wallet for forty-eight years.

"Why didn't you tell me?" she asked.

Dwayne shook his head. "I'm superstitious, I suppose. Maybe I watch too much television. I had the notion that if I said anything, I would be changing history somehow. And way back when, no one would have believed me anyway."

"But we would have known he was going back to 1945. I wouldn't have been so panicked, so terrified," she said. "We would have sent him back sooner."

"But don't you see, Valkyrie," Phil interjected. "The letter is dated *today*. You didn't think of the heavy water theory until this morning. It didn't arrive until about an hour ago. If we'd sent him back sooner, the letters, the thermos, the backpack wouldn't have been there for Dwayne to find."

"But where is he *now*?" she asked, her voice agonized. "It didn't work. He didn't come back *here!*"

Perry didn't feel the ribbons of color wrap around him, could only see them spiraling, creating a haze of pure reds, yellows, blues, obscuring Valerie's grief-stricken face, her tense body. He felt that dizzying, spinning sensation and knew he was again traveling the rainbow's highway through time.

He had no awareness of breathing, no sense of standing upon corporeal ground. He neither floated nor drifted, it was as if he no longer existed, yet his mind continued to think, to hope. He felt neither cold nor warm and wondered if he still gripped the satchel with the precious fluid that might allow him to return. But with no feeling, how could he reach for the thermos, how could he manage to spill the liquid free of the container?

Suddenly, as though someone was slowly pulling veils or colored curtains away from a glass enclosure, he could see he was once again on the desert floor, yet the haze of color still obstructed his view. While he had no perception of gravity, still couldn't feel the satchel in his hand, he strove to peer through the ribbons of color and see Valerie. If he could only see her, he thought, he would be okay, would survive this.

As though his will were the key to unlocking the bands of colors encircling him, the colors faded somewhat, and as if he were looking through a mist, he could see beyond the colorful prison, the rainbowed transportation.

But it wasn't Valerie he saw, it was himself. With a psychic shock, he felt ripples of déjà vu rock his mind, his heart. *He had seen this before... but in reverse.*

As if looking through a kaleidoscopic mirror, he saw his former self, the Perry Deveroux who had never even dreamed about time traveling, had never considered what the distant future would hold for him. Slouched hat, leather jacket, narrow tie loosened at his neck.

Memory slammed into him with a force not unlike that of the bullet that had torn his shoulder apart. The year 1945 again became his present. He could remember everything. All of his former life, yet with the shades of knowledge that appearing in another time had welded into his mind.

And he heard a voice call out, "T-minus twenty-nine seconds and counting..." Heard his name called, the photographer telling him, "Smile for the birdie." Saw his refusal to acknowledge. Heard his name called again and saw, as though through two pairs of eyes, two contrasting perspectives: both the front and the back of the photographer as he stepped between the two Perrys.

His former self, the Perry of nearly fifty years ago, turned, and his eyes traveled beyond the photographer's shoulders . . . meeting his own.

He felt the shock of that meeting waken his current body, lending it weight, substance. He felt this coming to life in the same way he felt he'd absorbed the initial contact with Valerie Daniels—to his very soul. How many people could honestly say that they had met their own personas, had looked deep into their own eyes and seen their most profound of selves, their future?

He saw a look of wonder cross his former self's face. An abstracted frown creased the mirror image's brow, and a puzzled, almost forlorn wistfulness settled there. He could still feel the shock, the wonder, and was now witnessing it as though he were someone else.

He remembered how he felt, how he'd thought this— himself, this thinking self—some sort of omen of his death, some portend of the future. How right he'd been, how starkly, shockingly correct.

How long he might have stood there, eye to eye with himself, with his other life, other soul, he couldn't have said, but as though from miles and miles away, he seemed to hear Valerie's voice. *Come back to me.*

He flexed his hand and felt it, knew it as his own. He saw the flare of the photographer's flashbulb and remembered how he'd been momentarily blinded. He'd forgotten that. He'd forgotten the flash of the bulb. He'd lost it in the wonder of the rainbow colors, the strange apparition inside it that looked so much, so exactly like himself.

He grabbed the satchel that had become full-weighted in his hand, thrust it open and seized the lid of the thermos-like container. He remembered Valerie's team's warning about having only seconds to spare. How many had he used already? Was he too late? Was the miracle of seeing himself, feeling himself twice, here and there, worth losing the chance at seeing Valerie again, having a future with her?

The lid stuck and he wanted to scream, but suspected there would be no sound, no voice. In near panic, he saw the photographer turn and step away, his back to both Perry Deverouxs, his thoughts on the bomb soon to explode.

And as he wrenched at the lid, finally making it twist, yanking it free, he looked up again and felt a chill stretch through every vein in his body. His other self was gone, erased, obliterated in a haze of lazily spiraling rainbows. He frantically poured the water free, watched it slowly drift on the ribbons of color, spiral down to the earth, seep into the rich brown soil and disappear. He dropped the container, the lid still in his hand, and as he reached for the satchel, he had the oddest sensation—his fingers became weightless and his body no longer felt in contact with the ground.

He needed to retrieve the letters from his jacket, needed to grab onto them, but with a shock that rocked his soul, he realized that he no longer had material form. He could see his hand but couldn't feel it. He watched, awed and more than a little afraid, as it passed through the satchel, connecting neither with his jacket or the letters inside. But he could sense them emotionally, an oddly disjointed sensation that took him back to the memory of the night before, Valerie's sweet scent in his nostrils, her silky hair teasing his chest.

And then the rainbow-colored bands rewound about his body, what must have been his body, and he couldn't see the desert any more. He heard an explosion, but his body didn't feel anything. A blinding flash of light, overriding even the colors binding him, tore at his vision. And he wondered where Valerie was, wondered if he'd ever see her again, feel her touch, and knew, with dark certainty, that love might heal all wounds, but even the greatest of loves in the world didn't have the power to move time and space.

Was he going back now, back to her time, or back to his?

And as he drifted, his soul dazed by all he'd witnessed, his heart sore with longing, his body weightless and ethereal, the scent of water clinging to him, he thought of Valerie, dreamed of her, made a reality of her in his mind. It was all he had left.

Night swooped down and inverted the desert, sweeping it up and outward, flinging it to the stars, giving the illusion of infinity. Valerie gazed at the millions and millions of twinkling lights with a dull ache. She and Dwayne had left the others back at camp and had walked as far from the site as they dared in the treacherous night-shadowed desert. They sat on a rough, sandy rise. Neither spoke for some time.

The tears were gone; she had no tears left. The day had stretched forever, like the desert night seemed infinite now.

"He never told me he loved me," she said dully. "I did. I told him. I wish he'd said it back. I wish I could have heard it from him."

"He knew that, honey," Dwayne's dry and leathery voice assured her. She didn't look at him. For some reason, she couldn't bear to. "But you've got to understand that a man like Perry, a man from our time—his and mine—doesn't throw those words around like cheap toys. We say 'em once and mean them forever. They're the words you tell your wife of thirty years, and they mean you love everything about her, from her nagging about mowing the lawn to her way of crying over some Shirley Temple movie on the late, late show. They're the words that bind you for a lifetime."

"That's what I want," Valerie said.

"That's what he wanted, too," Dwayne answered promptly. "That's exactly why he couldn't say them, honey. He didn't know where he was going, nor how long he was going to be about it. I know Perry. So do you. He's not the kind of man to tell you he loves you and then ask you to wait for him. To stare at an empty future and wonder for the rest of your days."

Valerie knew that, Perry had hinted as much before he disappeared, had all but spelled it out in that aged and yellowed letter she'd read at least twenty times already. She'd read it so many times she had it memorized, had spliced his voice over it, so she could hear the deep, rich tones in the faded writing.

What do I say to you? What can I possibly write down on this piece of paper that will give you any peace in the days to come? But maybe that's what I'm supposed to stress, that for you there really are days to come. What we shared last night, all the things we didn't say, only brought that home clearer and clearer for me.

I know it's difficult to believe in a future that has no time, no reference points. I'm having trouble with that myself. That's why I can't say the words I long to tell you the most. We are, people that is, meant to strive, to aim for, to quest for things, and all of that implies a future, demands one. The very best in us wants a tomorrow to shoot for, to curl up with on a lonely night, to take out of a drawer and look at, dazzled by the dreams and goals we've tucked away. The future is something that makes us get through the darkness, because there's hope, there's promise in the future.

I don't know what my future is. There is no way of knowing. When you turn those lasers of yours on tomorrow, I will go somewhere, to some when. You've got to believe that. And you mustn't regret it. It is still a future, though, I admit, a somewhat nebulous one.

I have so many wishes, but they all feel like ashes this morning, the remains of the rainbow fire that will soon strip me from this time. I think I would have liked it here, Valerie. I know I would have, as long as you were anywhere nearby.

Is this a test of some kind? Of courage, of commitment? I'll admit to you, I don't feel particularly brave right about now. But, as long as I'm pouring out my soul, I can tell you this: I would do it all again, jump through time, leap through forty-eight years on a rainbow, just to spend these days with you over again.

There aren't enough words in the entire world to tell you what last night meant to me. In all your television programs, in all the fancy macros you create on your computers, there couldn't be anything greater than what we've shared here. You are the single best thing that has ever happened in my life. I would trade all my unknown tomorrows for that one night with you. Perhaps I have.

There was more, much more, but those paragraphs haunted her, tormented her with his longing, with his utter despairing belief that he would never see her again.

"Why couldn't we open the portal?" she asked. God knew, after the initial disappointment of his not returning, they had all agreed to try the lasers again, to try opening the damned portal a second time. But they had met with no success. They had seen a ripple, a sudden aurora, a glimpse of the portal, the passage through time, but hadn't been able to puncture the atmosphere as they had done before, had caught no more than that gleam of the magnetic field. Like all their former tests.

"You know more about it than I do, honey," Dwayne answered. She hadn't realized that she'd spoken aloud; it didn't matter, though, it had been merely rhetorical, anyway. There was no answer.

"Where is he, Dwayne?" she asked now, knowing he didn't have an answer to that question, either, but needing some answer, any answer as long as it would make her heart come alive again, her soul come out from hiding.

Dwayne answered slowly, "I don't know where he is, honey. I don't know a thing beyond this morning."

She sighed. "That can't be all," she said. "He couldn't have simply vanished. We know that at least part of the experiment worked. He has to be somewhere. Some *when*."

Dwayne was silent for a long while, and when he started to speak, if she'd had any tears left, she would have cried. As it was, all she could do was listen in an almost listless despair.

"All these years I've known I was going to live to be at least eighty-six years old. I've known that since I was thirty-nine. I knew because of the date on that letter."

Vaguely, as if her mind needed some puzzle to work on now that her heart was dead and her soul buried in some when with Perry, she wondered what it would be like to know she had at least forty-eight more years of time on this earth. Was this the answer to his incredible faith? It hadn't been faith, then, but absolute knowledge. And then she wondered what it would be like for him, facing the rest of his days without that awareness of the time left to him.

"And I knew I'd see Perry again one day and that he'd be a young man. And when I met you, I knew he would love you. And when I read those letters over and over in the first few months, you hadn't even been born yet. All I could do was wait and see. And forty-eight years is a lot of waiting. But I don't know anything more than that. For me, for the first time in forty-eight years, the future is as much a blank as it is to every living soul."

"Like the rest of us," she said. She felt sorrow for him, and something akin to empathy, but nothing deeper. She had nothing left; she felt she was an empty shell, a container much like the one left behind by Perry Deveroux in 1945. Everything inside her, the essence of Valerie Daniels had been spilled out and abandoned this morning, and already, forty-eight years ago.

"I remember wondering if Perry was playing some kind of colossal practical joke. I even asked Oppenheimer and his boys if they thought time travel might be a side effect of the A-bomb." Dwayne paused and chuckled wheezily. "They laughed at me like I was crazy. I certainly felt like it. So I took those two letters home. Showed 'em to Patty."

Valerie felt a pang of guilt, remembering the Patty Perry had mentioned in the letter to Dwayne, knowing now she'd been Dwayne's wife but had been dead for twelve long years.

"She didn't say much then, but later that night, she read me a passage out of a Shakespeare book she had. The one about more things being on earth or in heaven than we can even dream of. I guess that's when I started to believe old Perry was really alive, but about a half century away."

Valerie sat silent, wondering how Dwayne had been able to keep the mystery to himself all those years, wondering how he had managed to keep silent when he finally met her, right where Perry had indicated she'd be, forty-eight years later.

"I read the letters again, and again. And I kept his file open and I wouldn't ever let anyone declare him officially dead, just missing. Because I knew I would see him again. And when things got too tough, when times were bad or when I was feeling blue, I'd pull those letters out and read 'em yet again.

"And I'd know, *I'd really know,* that I'd be around to be this old. Because he said he'd seen me again in this time. Talked to me."

He sighed, then chuckled. "I couldn't make heads or tails of some of the things he wrote about. But along about 1949, I heard some blather about televisions. Patty and I talked about it a long time. We upped and invested damn near every dime we had in that. And then along came microwave ovens, and dishwashers, and computers and every damned thing Perry mentioned in that letter to you.

"I'm not denying all those investments made me a fairly wealthy man. But in a way, it felt more like we were proving that we believed in Perry, believed that he'd come back. And even though we ain't got that proof now, I think we got to believe. Like kids maybe, believing in fairy tales and Peter Pan, we got to have faith."

Valerie finally spoke, though she knew her voice sounded as dull as her body felt. "I'm going to try again in the morning."

"Yes," Dwayne said. His tone indicated no doubt of her success.

"I'm going to keep trying every day. Until I find him again," she said.

"Of course you are," he said. "Like Perry said, you got spunk."

Valerie's smile felt bitter, twisted. She didn't say the obvious, that one day soon the project would be shut down, the equipment hauled away, her team assigned elsewhere. She didn't want to admit that one day, she'd have to give up, accept defeat and have to leave this desert. Do as Perry had wanted her to, go on with her life.

But Dwayne answered her as if she had spoken aloud, as if she'd been arguing with him. "You won't ever give up. Not you."

She felt his words came not from him, but from Perry, somehow transmitted through Dwayne and reaching across time, touching her, infecting her with hope, with the courage to try again.

Slowly she nodded. "If I have to, I'll keep trying until the end of time. I'll be waiting for him."

"Maybe all this happened for a reason," Dwayne said softly.

"Like what?"

"Maybe you and Perry were supposed to be together, some other time, some other place, and something went wrong. One of you got born in the wrong time. Maybe this is your second chance."

"Maybe," Valerie said. "But if that's the case, we'd better find him."

"Maybe, like the songs and movies say, it's just a matter of faith."

Valerie looked at him suspiciously. "There isn't something else you haven't told me, is there?"

Dwayne shook his head. Somewhat sadly, Valerie thought. "No, honey. I don't have my crystal ball anymore. But somewhere along the line a person's got to find that belief, that faith all on their own. I'm not talking supernatural, or even about God, I'm talking about what's inside you. What you're made of. The guts to believe in something beyond all laws of nature, beyond everything.

"I think you've got that something, honey. And I have a gut feeling that's what it's gonna take to haul Perry out of that rainbow."

"I love him so much," Valerie said, as if that were the answer.

Perhaps it was, for Dwayne said nothing, only reached out and took her cold hand in his wrinkled, gnarled grasp. And they sat there for some time, in silence, watching the stars, young hand in old one, each trying to give the other a measure of hope.

He, a man who had lived a long life knowing he would be granted only a brief glimpse of a friend he'd lost many years before, was offering her the wisdom of his time on earth, the belief in her strength. She, a woman in love, who, having lost the man she so desperately wanted, could only offer her need to find his friend, her determination to try for the rest of her life to achieve this.

Valerie looked up at the millions of prickling lights, wishing with all her might, all her strength.

I'll wait for you, she vowed. *However long it takes, I'll wait.*

Chapter 13

The slide through the rainbow was timeless, and yet, as it had before, only seemed to last seconds. Perry thought wryly that there were two essential differences to this slippage through the mysterious, viscous color ride: he wasn't a newcomer to it this time, his mind stunned and rebelling, and now, on this ride, he had a fierce determination to get back to Valerie.

The idea that this was some kind of elemental elevator darted through his mind, and he found himself toying with the notion that if it were such a transport, it should, like elevators he knew and remembered, have controls, an emergency switch somewhere.

But how does one go about searching a rainbow for the ground floor buttons? What universal porter did he ask to please stop the car and let him out? What could he do to get it to open up because he so desperately wanted off, so badly wanted to get back to Valerie?

Unless it was that simple...a matter of will. A fundamental, basic formula of mind over matter. He recalled seeming to will the haze to let him see the desert plain, the veil of color pulling aside to let him view the stunned gaze of his former self.

With all his might, he latched onto the concept, he *willed* himself free, willed himself to see Valerie again.

The deuterium oxide he'd spilled on the grassy desert in 1945 still clung to him, invading his senses. Desperately, knowing he must be frowning but not feeling the frown, not feeling anything, he conjured images of Valerie, her touch, her delicate features, her strong fingers, the way she felt in his arms, the occasional mischief in her eyes, her smile.

And he heard her laugh, a rich, tinkling chuckle, carefree and lighthearted. *Valerie,* his soul cried. Relief surged through him, and hope followed in the wide path it forged.

As if this were the magic that made the rainbow fade, he could see again, could hear, could smell the ocean spray coming from somewhere to his left, could feel the hot sand beneath his feet.

And he could see. And remember.

His heart constricted. He remembered this, recalled in sharp clarity what he'd only hazily captured before.

This was no desert; he wasn't in New Mexico.

Before him, around him, a yellow-gold sandy beach stretched inward from a softly lapping bay of purest blue water, water the color of Valerie's luminescent eyes.

And she laughed again. The laughter, like the ribbons of light, seemed to pass through him, vibrating inside him, tickling him, caressing him.

Instinctively, he turned to find the source of the laughter, the promise inherent in the light, happy sound. The happy, replete laughter of a woman who has known great sorrow but has finally achieved a crowning happiness, a full joy.

He couldn't see her, but with a shock that was easily equal to the ones he'd felt twice in 1945—once when he'd first appeared, and then again when he'd gone back—he saw himself a third time.

This self was by far the most outlandishly dressed of the three images. He—this other Perry of some unknown time and place—was wearing shorts that could easily have passed for something from Phil's wardrobe, a towel around his tanned shoulders, and his hair was longer than Perry would ever have worn it. This other self looked relaxed, even happy. A smile played on his lips and his eyes seemed lit by some inner contentment that Perry had only dreamed of, but never truly experienced.

No more prepared for this new soul-wrenching sensation of spiraling through uncharted territory, Perry felt the jolt of recognition electrify him as he once again met his own gaze.

There was shock in his other self's eyes, but other things as well: a calm certainty, a hint of wonder and a clear, strong message.

Perry's mind swam with the too-confusing images, the too many slides through this rainbowed time machine. How could he be here? How could he be where he'd never been before? *But hadn't he?* And, most confusing, how was it that this other self had apparently earned the right to Valerie's company, granting her joy, living a future, a life with her, when he was trapped in this peculiar anomaly that he'd never wanted, never dreamed would steal even his heart?

Why couldn't he see Valerie?

Then, as his other self, this thief of his own life, turned his gaze, he understood that Valerie was hidden behind a barrier of some kind. And he heard her laugh again, and this time the laughter was echoed by a child's high and light giggle and the clapping of tiny hands.

"Mommy made a rainbow, Daddy! Let me touch it, Mommy! Let me have it."

He turned wondering and jealous eyes on his usurper, this self who had managed to secure everything he most wanted.

As if in a dream, or more aptly, a nightmare, he could still feel Valerie's hands on his arms, could still hear the intensity in her sobbing voice.

Come back to me!

As though through water, the voice distorted beyond understanding, his other self spoke, not to Valerie and the child behind the barrier, but to him. And he raised his arm, the sun glinting off the ring on his hand, making a brief flash of white light that somehow didn't bend, didn't respond to the rainbow colors.

Perry thought of the lightbulb's flash, the deeper flash he'd seen in the rainbow elevator, other flashes, the sudden piercing pulse of the lasers. Was that the answer to it all, the key to the doorways of time?

But other questions overrode these speculations, drove him to consider his present predicament, his curious and untoward presence on this beach. How was it he could hear the child and Valerie so clearly, but his other self sounded distorted?

Then he thought he understood. He could hear them, mother and child, because they were in one time only, they weren't torn into separate identities, split by this odd distortion of reality. This self he was looking at was *really* himself, not some other persona, not something out of a terrible nightmare. This was him.

He wasn't lost in some alternate universe, some frightening nether world, while another him was stealing his life, usurping his love, his would-be future, his should-have-been wife and child.

This was his *future.*

Awe struck him with the force of a runaway tank. He'd begun this day facing the unknown, despair etched on every plane of his face, because there was no hope for tomorrow.

This was his answer. He had a hundred tomorrows. No guarantees beyond this point, but he had been granted, perhaps as some cosmic apology for his suffering, this beautiful, wonderful glimpse of a future that belonged to him, was his alone.

A future with Valerie.

"*. . . B-a-ck!*" he heard this other, this alternate part of himself call. Command.

Go back? Was that the message in his brown eyes? Were those the words on his lips? He would, if he knew how. If he could only know how. He struggled against the rainbow, pushing with all his might. He felt something drop, looked down and saw the lid from the deuterium oxide container roll across the sandy beach. The metallic lid caught the sun's rays and sprayed them upward in a bright flash.

Valerie laughed again, a silvery laugh, like the illusion of happiness itself. Then he saw her golden curls tease the top of that barrier that hid her from his longing gaze.

With a wrench to his gut, Perry knew that while he'd heard this laugh before, he hadn't heard it on that desert plain in New Mexico. That was one of his strongest regrets—never having heard Valerie laugh.

With a tortured cry that never escaped his lips, he felt the bands tighten around him again, and the familiar loss of sensation. Don't take me away from her, he wanted to scream, *don't take me away.*

Wait for me!

"This one has to work," Valerie said.

"Well, it had better," Phil said wryly. "The newspapers were full of U.F.O. stories last night. Seems someone took a picture of our portal and now half of Albuquerque is planning to come have a close encounter."

Valerie shot him a hard look. He grinned sheepishly and shrugged.

She turned away, knowing Phil couldn't be expected to feel the same way she did, but resenting his misplaced humor nonetheless. In less than eight minutes the sun would be fully over the horizon. The final countdown was on. She pretended to give the final check to the lasers' trajectories, but only saw Perry's face as he'd looked at her through the rainbowed, suddenly moving portal. A message, a determination had squared his jaw then, and she had imagined she could see that telltale muscle jumping there.

"I just got the word," Bob Fenton said at her elbow. She didn't turn, knowing what he was going to say, half-believing that if she didn't meet his gaze, she wouldn't have to comply. "They want the project halted. No more until some more research has been conducted. They're afraid of what might happen."

"That we might find him?"

"No, that you might lose someone else," Bob said softly. "If it's any consolation, Valerie, I didn't give the recommendation to fold up shop."

She didn't say anything, only looked at him, meeting his gaze with all the calmness she could muster.

"I didn't find you in time to give you the message, did I?" he asked softly, a slight smile curving his lips.

"Thank you," she said, equally quietly. With all her heart she had left.

When Perry had talked about the men of his time not seeing much more than black-and-white, she hadn't really been paying attention to his words, only his departure. But in Bob Fenton she could see the accuracy of Perry's words. Perhaps Fenton adhered too strictly to orders, came on as the heavy and had been stymied by a simple refusal to obey his commands, but in the last week, both before Perry's final disappearance and in the last three days, he'd offered every consideration, had rallied both his men and hers to work the data over and over again, trying to salvage the attempted rescue of Perry Deveroux. Trying to help her find the man she loved beyond reason.

He'd finally asked Dwayne for the letters found so long ago, written only days before. When he'd finished, and had had them photographed, he'd given them back to Dwayne without comment. But later, sharing a cup of coffee with the older man and Valerie, he'd abruptly said, "I couldn't have done what he did."

Valerie had known he was speaking of Perry, and knew from the suddenly flattened look on Dwayne's face that he did, too.

"What's that, son?" Dwayne had asked.

"I don't think I would have had the guts to stand out there and let that portal snatch me up again."

Dwayne said, "I don't think he had a whale of a lot of choice."

Bob shook his head. "He had choices all right. He could have just hung around and waited to see what would happen when that thing quit shrinking. He reminds me of men I met coming back from Nam. Hard-core tough. The kind of tough that comes from seeing things no man should have to see."

"War'll do that to you," Dwayne said.

Bob Fenton had turned his gaze to Valerie. "I don't think it's just that. I think maybe some of it comes from believing, *knowing,* you've met with one person on earth you could share a lifetime with, and having to say goodbye without any hope of ever doing just that."

Then Bob had stood abruptly and left the trailer, the sun glinting off his charcoal hair.

Yes, Valerie thought now, Perry had been right. Bob Fenton could see much more colors than she'd given him credit for. And now, thanks to Perry, she could, too. How many more windows than that of time had he opened for all of them?

To Dwayne, he had given the knowledge that he would live a very long life, had given him the tools, the clues to live a very satisfying life and the hope that his friend would return in a distant, hardly conceivable time. To Phil, George and Jack he had given the secure knowledge that they would continue a worthwhile career in quantum physics, that any university or government experimental lab would grant them anything to pursue their dreams. To Bob Fenton, he had given another perspective of how to run things, how to deal with people and, if his words were to be believed, a glimpse of another kind of courage.

And to her, he'd given himself. And in doing so, had given her a reason for being. Before Perry the future had been nebulous, cloudy and without form. Snared by the search for mystery, she'd never actively pursued the search for Valerie. Now she knew what she wanted with absolute clarity, with total vision.

"So we have to make this work today," she said, answering Bob Fenton, chasing all her own doubts to some nether region.

"T-Minus three minutes and counting..." George called from his position at the computer. "Phil, did you give your camera to Bob? I want snaps of today's show."

"Bob said he had it."

"Use a flash today, man. Let's see if we can't get a better angle on the color spectrum."

"Flash won't reach that far," Phil said.

"So? Let's try it anyway," George said.

"You've made the solar corrections and the rotational adjustments?" Valerie asked Jack, who nodded and pointed at his computer screen.

"All locked in," he said.

"Here," Dwayne said, handing her Perry's felt hat. "For luck."

Valerie held the hat up to her face for a moment, drinking in Perry's essence, the faint reminder of his cigarettes, his unique scent. Then she lifted the hat up in a brief salute before dropping it on her head. It was too large, but she felt safer suddenly, more certain. It was a talisman, a bit of superstitious conjuring, and it served to brighten her spirits and those of the tense people around her.

Perhaps one day, in the far, distant future, she'd be able to look at the videotapes and photographs taken during Perry's brief stay in her time, the concrete proof of his presence. For now, his hat and the dream of seeing him again was all she wanted.

Bob Fenton's hand came down on her shoulder and squeezed, though he didn't speak. One by one, her team did the same.

"One more thing," Dwayne said. "I have to admit, it completely slipped my mind before this." He fished out his wallet again, dug in a narrow slit and pulled out a gold ring.

He took Valerie's suddenly limp hand and slid the ring onto her right forefinger. "This was Perry's father's ring," he said.

But it was Perry's, Valerie thought, closing her fist around it. She'd seen it on his hand, had felt it when he grasped her hand that first moment, and later, on her bare skin.

"I brought it to him after his dad was killed. He never took it off."

"But . . . ?"

"It was in the envelope with the letters. I'm sure he wanted you to have it," Dwayne said.

"T-Minus one minute and counting . . ." George called.

Valerie stared at the ring on her finger, a ring that had traveled between times and was here again, raised her hand to touch the hat that had been left behind in this time, her heart's only real proof that he'd ever been here except for a thousand compressed memories and longings.

She had no words with which to thank Dwayne. But somehow she didn't think he needed them. Like a magician, he pulled a miracle of hope from his little black wallet. He'd slipped a circle of pure faith on her finger.

In unspoken camaraderie, in mutual determination and with a few silent wordings against failure, misread data or flubbed projections, Valerie and her crew stepped to the controls. But no matter how sympathetic, no matter how caring and dedicated, not one of them, she thought, not even Dwayne Roberts, had as much as she did riding on this. Not one of them had a heart already missing, with their entire future dependent upon a few strands of laser-induced light.

Please, she begged silently.

"T-Minus twenty-nine seconds and counting..." George called.

Valerie heard the words and felt their rightness, felt the curious ripple of déjà vu work through her system. This would be the right time.

It had to be, for this was the only time. The *only* time.

Come back to me! she called silently, forcing her soul through the handles of the lasers, compressing it to travel with the beams across the span of atmosphere, aiming it already into the magnetic field they'd discovered in the sky, willing it to find Perry. To twine around him every bit as strongly as the portal's colorful bands and bring him *back to her*.

"T-Minus five seconds and counting...four...three... two..."

And Valerie depressed the triggers and watched her soul shoot in streams of steady, pure red light, up and away, into the blue sky, leaving her feeling empty, discarded and so desperately alone.

She scarcely breathed as the lasers searched, pulsed and then seemingly paused, bending over a ripple, *the* ripple, exploring it as if the beams were flames from a blowtorch and could burn their way through.

Suddenly, miraculously, they gained entry, passed through some invisible doorway and stretched, and with them, Valerie's soul soared, flew in search of Perry, in search of the heart he'd taken with him that day.

Chapter 14

Valerie's laughter remained in his ears, the scent of water in his nostrils, and though he could feel nothing in his extremities, no sense of wind, sand or even time, he imagined he could still feel the heat of that lovely beach beneath his feet, the press of Valerie's face against his tear-soaked chest, the grip of her fingers against his arm.

Where was he going this time? Where—*when*—would he next see himself?

Or would he finally, by some miracle, be granted an unfettered view of Valerie, of his present, his future? His life?

How long he floated in that nothingness, trapped inside a living rainbow, he didn't know. He knew that forty-eight years felt like seconds, that seconds could be a full half a century. He had wanted time to think. He suspected he had it, an eternity's worth, and now, perversely, it wasn't thought he wanted, but freedom from this deathless, timeless prison.

The bands of color shimmered, shook, undulated in sudden restiveness. The ribbons became tinged with red and seemed to angrily swirl around him, as though fighting off some menace that threatened.

A strong flash of white light momentarily blinded him, and he found himself mentally grinding his teeth, girding his loins for the next nightmare, the next stop on this bizarre journey through time. But most of all, he was praying, no direct and clear-cut prayers, but complete and whole pictures of Valerie, of the way she smiled, the millions of small things she said or did that drew him to her so, that he felt as if he were already connected with her on some spiritual plane. It was as if their souls were forever united and he need only find that magical place and he would be with her forever.

He could dimly see through the hazy rainbows, the angry reds and softer blues, and knew he was once again in New Mexico, in the desert, in the early morning sunlight.

But which New Mexico? Which time—1945, trapped in a continuum that would forever take him back and forth from self to self, past to future, always and eternally missing the present?

He had thought the worst that could happen to a man was to be deprived of a sense of future, the security of planning a life, of knowing he would be there to watch it unfold, but he knew now he'd been wrong. The worst was never savoring the present, seizing it and clinging to it with every blessed fiber of being.

That's what he and Valerie had done in their one beautiful, staggeringly poignant night together. They had truly and reverently *savored* time.

He steeled himself for the gradual unveiling of the curtains of time, tried preparing himself for the sight of his own eyes, his own body, stiff with surprise, shock evident in that forever gaze.

Please let it be with Valerie. *Please...*

Then, angrily, no longer pleading, no longer able to submit to this peculiar destiny, he raged at the rainbowed bands, demanding to be released, demanding freedom.

Demanding Valerie.

Bob snapped the shutter on the camera and momentarily blinded them all with the strident flash.

"Damn it," Jack complained, blinking at the computer screen. "I can't see. I thought we had something there."

Valerie glanced from him to the sky and cried out as the lasers found their goal.

"It's back," Dwayne yelled, pointing wildly. "The portal's open again."

"Where's Perry, though?" Phil called. "He's not out there. I don't see him. *I don't see him!*"

Valerie didn't, either, and her body shrank a little, as though trying to hide itself from a disappointment too great to be borne. But she didn't take her hands from the lasers' handles, despite the fact that the computers had long since taken over. She had the irrational notion that as long as she held them, she could find Perry, could bring him back.

As before, the ribbons of light spilled out of the portal, but redder this time, as though angry at having been released.

"Give him to me," Valerie muttered, teeth clenched, feeling as though she was physically battling some jealous entity for the man she loved. The ring, *his* ring, bit into her finger, and she commanded him to come get it, to retrieve it in person.

And suddenly, without reason, without any kind of evidence before them on the empty desert floor, she knew he was there, knew he was near.

She could *feel* him, feel the sharp anger in him, a rage that matched her own, a desperation that exceeded the physical plane, felt the kind of strength that makes a mother lift a car from her injured child, the kind of determination that makes heroes of cowards, triumph of despair.

She tore her hands from the handles of the lasers. With no conscious thought other than of Perry, her whole being focused on that empty desert plain, she turned and whipped around the protective barrier. She thought someone reached for her, tried to grab her, but she shook him off violently, screaming a protest, battling at whoever it was with an almost insane need for freedom.

And she ran toward the spot under the portal, ran for everything her life was worth.

"Perry!" she called. And as though in echo, she heard one of her team members call her name.

But there was only one thought in her mind now, only one object.

"I'm here," she screamed as she ran, and though she could feel the ache in her chest, the trembling in her legs, she never slowed, never paused. She stumbled once and, sobbing, slapped the ground with her hand, regaining balance.

Perry heard Valerie call his name. He couldn't see her, but he could sense her, knew he was too close to her to let her go now. He fought the bands of colored light with everything in him. He pushed with nonexistent hands, kicked with limbs he could neither feel nor trust. He screamed out his denial of this imprisonment, exerting every ounce of his will to be free.

And suddenly, miraculously, the bands loosened and he could see her. Running full tilt, his hat blowing off her head, her glorious golden hair bouncing, swept by the force of her propulsion.

"Valerie!" he called and heard his own voice in his own ears. He lifted leaden arms, felt a tingling he'd felt before, life awakening, body restored to corporeality. He lurched forward, making his body move by sheer force of will, demanding release from the insistent ribbons of time.

"I'm here!" she cried, and almost fell, but somehow managed to right herself, her legs continuing to propel her forward, toward him.

As if her words and their combined wills worked together to exert a force too great to be contended with, or, perhaps more accurately, because the preprogrammed lasers cut off just then, the colored ribbons rolled upward and reeled back into the portal. They disappeared, seemingly reluctantly, but left Perry behind, feeling the hard-packed sand beneath his heels, the hot sun, still smelling the scent of water.

Then, running, free at last, he raised his arms, held them wide, ready at last to catch the gold at the rainbow's end.

She flew into his arms, up, off the ground, encircling his shoulders, his head, letting him grab her, pull her roughly to him, and he buried his face in her blouse, laughing, probably crying, just holding and holding on to her.

A roaring cheer went up somewhere beyond them, but Perry couldn't let her go, couldn't bear to release her.

They spoke at the same time. "I thought you were gone..."

"I was afraid I'd never find you..."

Releasing her slightly, he let her slide down until her feet touched the ground. He, of all people, knew what a boon that was. He didn't think he'd ever want to be without the solid ground beneath him again. But he knew with absolute certainty that he never wanted to be without Valerie again.

"I saw you," he said.

"I saw you, too," she sobbed, misunderstanding him. "Oh, Perry, I was so terrified."

He stroked her hair, holding her so tightly to his body that he could feel her heart beating against him, a counterpoint rhythm to his too rapidly beating heart.

"It worked, Valerie," he said. "Your theory worked."

She stilled in his arms and slowly looked up. "But it didn't," she said. "It didn't work."

Perry frowned. "But I went back to 1945. And then... and, well, I'm here."

"But you didn't come back. You've been gone for days. For *days!*" she said. Tears, either of joy or remembered pain, welled in her eyes. "I thought I'd lost you forever."

"No," Perry said, suddenly not caring about how or why he was back, only knowing that he was, that somehow, miraculously, he'd escaped and found his destiny in this time, this far-flung future.

She stilled, her hand slowly stroking his shirt. "It's still wet," she said, a note beyond joy, a quavering ring of awe in her voice. "It's still wet from the tears I cried when you left."

There was so much to tell this woman who had battled time and science for him. There was so much to talk about, to reveal about that mysterious highway through time. And there was all the time in the world to do it.

Now he had only one thing left to say. He'd waited over forty-eight years, and a few in the future, to do so.

"I love you, Valerie," he said slowly. *"I love you."*

She stood perfectly still for several seconds, then her eyes closed in an agony too sharp to be allowed.

An equally sharp fear pierced him. But when she opened her eyes and he could see, clearer than any vision he'd ever glimpsed before, the extent of her love, the depth of it, he felt that blade in his heart relax somewhat, ease.

To his amazement, to his delight, she laughed.

Her rich, tinkling laughter swept out across the desert sand, echoing in his heart, making him ache with longing, causing his arms to tighten around her in memory of that jealous fear he'd encountered somewhere down the ribbon of the future.

Her eyes, blue, tear-drenched and sparkling, met his and put to shame the vibrant colors of his rainbowed bands. "I know what that means, Perry Deveroux. I *know*. And I'm going to hold you to it. Forever."

She laughed again and, pulling away from him, threw her arms out wide. "I love you, too, Perry. Oh, I love you, too!"

Perry grabbed her back into his arms, held her as close as he possibly could, as though trying to reassure himself that she was real, that he was, and that the future really did stretch before them, full and rich as her scent, as her laughter.

He lowered his lips to hers, thankfully tasting her again, smiling, knowing he would truly be loving her all through time.

Epilogue

Perry raised his head from her breasts, which he'd been using as a pillow. His eyes met hers with a feigned hunger.

Valerie smiled, knowing perfectly well that longing was neither sharp nor, as of less than five minutes ago, unassuaged. She raised a still-tingling hand to stroke his Saturday-roughened cheek. God, how much she loved him. Not a single day had passed in the last four years without her awareness of that one, absolute truth.

"Okay, tell me honestly," he said now, the light in his brown eyes giving lie to the seriousness of his voice, "what is a man of this time supposed to do *after,* when his wife has talked him into quitting smoking?"

"Are you looking for something to do with your hands?" Valerie asked. She chuckled at his suddenly thoughtful expression.

"You may have something there," he said, reaching for her bare breasts. "Yes, that helps. But, as all those pamphlets you *subtly* scattered all over the house suggested, one of the pitfalls of quitting smoking is the failure to recognize the oral fixation.'' He flicked his tongue against an already taut nipple, making it even harder.

She gasped and instinctively arched to meet his hot mouth, amazed that after four years—especially considering how they'd spent the last hour—he could still make every touch seem like the first time.

He replaced his mouth with his thumb and forefinger, gently yet firmly rolling the turgid nipple. His eyes met hers and she could read the depth of his love for her, just as she'd been able to read it so many thousands of times in the years since he'd miraculously been brought back to her.

As if reading her thoughts, he smiled tenderly. ''Who would have guessed when you snatched me through that rainbow window that life could be so perfect in a time so far removed from everything I knew?''

In spite of the heat his hands—his very proximity—were culling from her, she had to ask him, ''*Is* it perfect, Perry?''

''You know it is,'' he said, and shifted upward to kiss her. His lips, the slow promise always inherent in his tasting of her, told her he'd spoken the truth. When he pulled away, it was with obvious reluctance. ''I'd even go back and go through another ride on that time elevator if it meant getting to do this again,'' he said, burying his face in the hollow of her neck.

Valerie grasped him to her, holding him tightly, knowing he wouldn't disappear, but unable in this moment of nostalgia to forget those days of torture, of total fear that she'd lost him forever.

He wrapped his arms around her, gripping her equally fiercely, in sympathy or, perhaps as was so common with him, in total empathy for her thoughts.

''Valerie...?'' he asked, and knowing him as she now did, she knew that lingering question in his voice no longer carried uncertainty, nor doubts about their future together. That had all ended the moment he'd enfolded her in his arms that July morning some four years earlier.

''Yes, love?'' she asked back.

"What's a sun-dog?"

She chuckled, relaxing her grip on his shoulders. Perry, as Dwayne had told her he'd be, wasn't the kind of man to waste time over words, letting the days and hours and the million things he said and did for her say it for him. He loved her with the full and rich passion of a man who intended to spend the rest of his life with her. What words could possibly say more than that?

She answered him, a smile lingering on her lips, "A sun-dog is a parhelion. A bright, often colored spot near the sun. Why?"

"This guy on the radio—" Perry still preferred the radio news programs to those on the television "—said that conditions were just right today for a sun-dog."

"I'm surprised," Valerie said, absently stroking Perry's longish hair. He'd started growing it out this past month, and she found she liked it, loved how silky and warm it was beneath her fingers. "Usually parhelions only show up when there are ice particles in the air."

"The weatherman's predicting the possibility of hail late this afternoon. Does that account for it?" Perry asked too innocently. With all the reading he'd done the last four years, he probably knew more about atmospheric conditions than she ever would, her degrees and laboratories notwithstanding.

"I suppose so," she said, pressing her lips against the scar on his shoulder. It was more noticeable with his tan, but somehow less obvious. Sometimes it was difficult for her to imagine that he'd earned this particular battle scar in 1944 in the war that should have been, but wasn't, the war to end all wars.

"Tell me what it looks like," he said. An odd note had entered his voice, a hint of repressed excitement.

"It varies. It might show up as a small halo or rainbow or even a parhelic circle."

"In English, *Doctor*," he said, raising to prop himself up
on his elbow. He smiled down at her with so much love in
his eyes that she had to swallow before translating.

"It's like a rainbow that goes around the sun, or even
around the sky horizontally... instead of the way we normally see them." She arched her hand from one side of his
head to the other to demonstrate how rainbows normally
appeared. "And then, on rare occasion, several parhelia
appear simultaneously, connected with one another by a
white arc or halo. I've only heard of this, never seen it."

"What time does Patrick wake up from his nap?" he
asked.

"Any time now," she answered.

"What if I gather up some picnic type eatables and we go
down to the cove? Do you think we could see it from
there?"

Valerie smiled. "If we can't, I've got a few prisms that we
could set out and use to make one of our own. The only
hitch is, I promised I'd get a letter out to Dwayne this afternoon."

Perry sat up abruptly, roughly drawing her to the edge of
their bed. He kissed her swiftly, no less passionately for all
its brevity. "You do that and I'll gather the supplies. We'll
reconnoiter at T-Minus twenty minutes... and counting."

Dear Dwayne,

I hope the New Mexico summer isn't beating you
down too much. Or your delightful great-
grandchildren. If you're feeling blue, hot or tired, just
remind yourself that you'll be on this lovely beach with
us in less than a week.

It's still hard for me to think of this as ours, and you
know we'll never be able to thank you enough for giving it to us. I know all that baloney about having ob-
tained it via Perry's timely clues, but it is so very
generous. What a stupendous anniversary present. (I
have to admit, I still feel shocked when I think of us

being married four years now!) And you already know how much Patrick loves it here. He has from the first moment he saw it. It was almost as if he knew it would be his someday.

The house you and Perry dreamed up is just that—dreamy. (See, I can pull a few forties words out of my hat!) With the view of the water and the airy light feel of the house, Perry seems content to give up the road and stay parked for a while. So am I. I've had enough traveling and camping in a motor home to last a dozen lifetimes, despite loving every single minute of the projects I was working on and letting Perry see all the changes forty-eight years have wrought.

But with Patrick ready for pre-school this year, we're going to use this gorgeous place to put down roots. In fact, Perry's taking steps to renew his certification for teaching. You, of course, already know what subject—American history, particularly the first half of the twentieth century.

You know, of course, that he often spoke to classes on our journeys, and the kids were crazy about him. Said they never had such a clear picture of those times before. I had to laugh when they said he made it seem just like yesterday for them. But, as you'll recall, that's what got him going on that book of his you liked so much. The sequel is coming along pretty well now, too. What do you think of the pages he sent you?

Bob Fenton continues to help us along, conjuring up necessary documents that keep Perry from getting funny looks when store clerks examine his driver's license or he has to show his birth certificate for anything. Bob really came in helpful this last week when Perry finally collected all that Army back pay. As you can imagine, it came to a fairly sizable amount. On a total side note, I have to say that Bob brings out the matchmaker in me. You don't happen to have any granddaughters running around single and who could possibly be interested in a man who came into his own on a certain desert floor in New Mexico, do you?

I don't know if Perry's ever told you or not (he said he always felt a bit odd talking to you about the whole age thing), but during the last year he's been devoting a great deal of his time at whatever hospice or retirement home we happen to be near on our travels.

He's found one here in this area, and is already spending most afternoons over there. The directors of the place are astonished—like everyone always is—how well he identifies with you old-timers. And the people in those places just love him. He takes tapes and old records, sometimes radio programs, and he sits with some of them for hours, telling them stories of things that happened to him just a few years ago, conjuring up things they'd long left behind, sometimes even forgotten.

I had a letter from Phil last week. He's still hard at it, planning to have his latest experiment take place on the space station. He'll be running this one solo. We're all holding our breath to see if he can discover a magnetic field in space.

I haven't heard from George in a while, but last I did, he was taking a year's leave of absence from Pivot Industries to go searching for Bigfoot. Don't laugh, Horatio, stranger things (as we well know) have been known to happen.

And—I hope you're sitting down—Jack is getting married next month. To a pretty physicist he met last year on a project on solar coronas. Apparently the eclipse we had last May produced some spectacular results . . . in far more than the color spectrum.

You asked in your letter if I was sorry the time projects went—as Perry would say—deep six, and I've thought about that a lot in the last couple of days. And the answer is no. I'm not really sorry. From the moment Perry came back that day, I think I was always scared that something, some new experiment, would snatch him away again.

In the last four years, when we were basically traveling from project to project, either studying some magnetic field or coming up with new ways of utilizing solar radiation, I was always a little afraid. Now that I have my own laboratory, complete with a new set of clowns, I find I don't really want to tamper with time. I don't want to stumble across some other portal that could tear up someone's life or possibly steal one of my loved ones from me.

The government called me in last month about that P-40N Warhawk that mysteriously showed up just floating in the waters off the coast of Bermuda. They wanted to know if it was the same Warhawk we had documented when Perry popped through. Since the rough usage it had been through had obliterated a couple of the serial numbers, I said I couldn't be sure, and that was that. But it did give me a funny feeling. And a good one. It made me realize that somewhere, sometime, I would have found Perry again had he not come back through that morning. That faith sustains me always.

Still, I'm continuing that never-ending search for things we can't explain, things outside the realm of conventional physical laws, that quest for what lies at the end of the rainbow. And with that in mind, today, because the weatherman's said conditions are right, and because Perry and Patrick are restless, I'm taking a handful of giant crystal prisms to the fort that you and Perry built on the beach for Patrick. And I'm going to make my two loves a rainbow.

Perry's already waving at me to hurry, that miraculous satchel of his stuffed full of things to eat, stuff, he never fails to remind me, that does not taste good in a microwave.

Ever since we talked about creating a natural rainbow on the beach, he's been in the wildest mood, something between elated and nostalgic. Perhaps some of it infected me, as well, and hence this quick letter.

So, with eternal love, I bid you farewell, for now. The light is right, the future is ours and we're off to find a rainbow.

Love,
Valerie

*   *   *   *   *

For all those readers who've been looking for something a little bit different, a little bit spooky, let Silhouette Books take you on a journey to the dark side of love with

SILHOUETTE Shadows™

If you like your romance mixed with a hint of danger, a taste of something eerie and wild, you'll love Shadows. This new line will send a shiver down your spine and make your heart beat faster. It's full of romance and more—and some of your favorite authors will be featured right from the start. Look for our four launch titles wherever books are sold, because you won't want to miss a single one.

THE LAST CAVALIER—Heather Graham Pozzessere
WHO IS DEBORAH?—Elise Title
STRANGER IN THE MIST—Lee Karr
SWAMP SECRETS—Carla Cassidy

After that, look for two books every month, and prepare to tremble with fear—and passion.

SILHOUETTE SHADOWS, coming your way in March.

Silhouette®

SHAD1

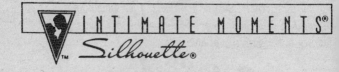

INTIMATE MOMENTS®

Silhouette®

CONTINUES...

Come back to Conard County, Wyoming, where you'll meet men and women whose lives are as dramatic as the landscape around them. Join author Rachel Lee for the third book in her fabulous series, MISS EMMALINE AND THE ARCHANGEL (IM #482). Meet Emmaline Conard, "Miss Emma," a woman who was cruelly tormented years ago and now is being victimized again. But this time sheriff's investigator Gage Dalton—the man they call hell's own archangel—is there to protect her. But who will protect Gage from his feelings for Emma? Look for their story in March, only from Silhouette Intimate Moments.

SPRING FANCY

Three bachelors, footloose
and fancy-free... until now!

Spring into romance with three
fabulous fancies by three of
Silhouette's hottest authors:

ANNETTE BROADRICK
LASS SMALL
KASEY MICHAELS

When spring fancy strikes, no man is immune!

Look for this exciting new short-story collection
in March at your favorite retail outlet.

Only from

Silhouette®

SF93

where passion lives.

AMERICAN HERO

It seems readers can't get enough of these men—and we don't blame them! When Silhouette Intimate Moments' best authors go all-out to create irresistible men, it's no wonder women everywhere are falling in love. And look what—and who!—we have in store for you early in 1993.

January brings NO RETREAT (IM #469), by Marilyn Pappano. Here's a military man who brings a whole new meaning to macho!

In February, look for IN A STRANGER'S EYES (IM #475), by Doreen Roberts. Who is he—and why does she feel she knows him?

In March, it's FIREBRAND (IM #481), by Paula Detmer Riggs. The flames of passion have never burned this hot before!

And in April, look for COLD, COLD HEART (IM #487), by Ann Williams. It takes a mother in distress and a missing child to thaw this guy, but once he melts...!

AMERICAN HEROES. YOU WON'T WANT TO MISS A SINGLE ONE—ONLY FROM

IMHER03R

What a year for romance!

Silhouette has five fabulous romance collections coming your way in 1993. Written by popular Silhouette authors, each story is a sensuous tale of love and life—as only Silhouette can give you!

SPRING FANCY

Three bachelors are footloose and fancy-free...until now.
(March)

Heartwarming stories that celebrate the joy of motherhood.
(May)

SILHOUETTE SUMMER Sizzlers

Put some sizzle into your summer reading with three of Silhouette's hottest authors.
(June)

SILHOUETTE Shadows

Take a walk on the dark side of love—with tales just perfect for those misty autumn nights.
(October)

Silhouette CHRISTMAS Stories

Share in the joy of yuletide romance with four award-winning Silhouette authors.
(November)

A romance for all seasons—it's always time for romance with Silhouette!

**Silhouette Books
is proud to present
our best authors,
their best books...
and the best in
your reading pleasure!**

Throughout 1993, look for exciting books
by these top names in contemporary
romance:

CATHERINE COULTER—
Aftershocks in February

FERN MICHAELS—
Whisper My Name in March

DIANA PALMER—
Heather's Song in March

ELIZABETH LOWELL—
Love Song for a Raven in April

SANDRA BROWN
(previously published under
the pseudonym Erin St. Claire)—
Led Astray in April

LINDA HOWARD—
All That Glitters in May

When it comes to passion,
we wrote the book.

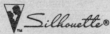 *Silhouette*®

BOBT1R